MURDER

IN THE
RUE URSULINES

THE CHANSE MACLEOD MYSTERIES
by Greg Herren

Murder in the Rue St. Ann
Murder in the Rue Dauphine
Murder in the Rue Chartres

MURDER

IN THE

RUE URSULINES

A CHANSE MACLEOD MYSTERY

GREG HERREN

alyson books
NEW YORK

Manufactured in the United States of America

This trade paperback original is published by Alyson Books
245 West 17th Street, New York, NY 10011
Distribution in the United Kingdom by Turnaround Publisher Services Ltd.
Unit 3, Olympia Trading Estate, Coburg Road, Wood Green
London N22 6TZ England

First Edition: October 2008

08 09 10 11 12 13 14 15 16 a 10 9 8 7 6 5 4 3 2 1

ISBN-10: 1-59350-095-5
ISBN-13: 978-1-59350-095-5

Library of Congress Cataloging-in-Publication data are on file.

Cover design by Victor Mingovits
Interior design by Jane Raese

This is dedicated to Michael Ledet,
with fond memories of the screen porch

"We are two monsters,
but with this difference between us.
Out of the passion and torment of my existence
I have created a thing that I can unveil,
a sculpture, almost heroic, that I
can unveil, which is true.
But you?"

—from *Sweet Bird of Youth* by Tennessee Williams

MURDER

IN THE

RUE URSULINES

CHAPTER ONE

"CHANSE MACLEOD TO SEE LOREN MCKEITHEN," I said to the pretty woman at the reception table. She looked to be in her late thirties, and of mixed racial heritage, her skin the color of a delicately mixed café au lait, her hair copper-colored. She gave me a wide smile. There was a wedding ring on her left hand, and a diamond tennis bracelet on her right wrist. Her nails were done in a French manicure. On her forehead was a smudged cross made of gray ash. I was tempted to ask what she'd given up for Lent, but decided against it.

"Have a seat, and I'll let him know you're here." She gave me a smile, picking up her phone. "It shouldn't be more than a few minutes."

I nodded and took a seat in an overstuffed leather chair, picking up an issue of *Crescent City* magazine and idly paging through it. I was tired, probably way too tired to be taking on a new job. The aspirin I'd taken hadn't kicked in yet, either. Every muscle in my body ached. I'd planned on spending my entire Ash Wednesday in bed, or lazing around my apartment, recovering from the overindulgence of the last five days. But Loren was a good guy, and threw me some work every now and then. So, I'd roused myself out of my post-Mardi Gras stupor and come to his office.

Besides, it never hurts to have a prominent attorney in your debt. You never know when you're going to need one.

"Mr. McKeithen is waiting for you in his office," the receptionist said, nodding her head to the left. "Just down that hallway, the last door on the right." She set her phone back down into its cradle and turned to her computer screen.

I thanked her and walked down the hallway. Loren was sitting behind his desk, leaning back in his chair, a phone cradled between his shoulder and ear. He waved me in, motioning for me to shut the door. "All right, well, my eleven o'clock is here, so let me review the paperwork and I will call you first thing in the morning . . . okay. You, too." He slid the phone back into its receiver, and walked around his desk to shake my hand.

Loren was short, about five-seven and thickly built, his stomach protruding over the waistband of his slacks. His shiny skin was the color of toffee, his face round, and his cheeks chubby. His gray silk suit screamed expensive at the top of its lungs. His tie was black with golden fleur-de-lis scattered over it. Like the receptionist, he had the ashy smudge of a cross on his forehead. "How have you been?" he asked, giving me a broad smile.

"Good." I took the seat he offered me, and declined coffee or anything else to drink. He went back around his desk and sat down. "I can't complain." I laughed. "Well, I can always complain about something, but overall, things are good. And you?"

"The usual." He shook his head. "You look good, Chanse. You're taking care of yourself, that's great." He looked down and pondered the expanse of his stomach. "One of these days I need to get my fat ass back into the gym." He patted it and rolled his eyes. "I'm giving up liquor for Lent."

"That's good," I replied, and couldn't resist adding, "I think."

"Well, we'll see how it goes." He barked out a short laugh. "But you're supposed to give up something you'll miss, right? What are you giving up?"

I grinned at him. "Catholicism." It was my standard answer.

He rewarded me with another laugh, and chattered on, the usual small talk about Mardi Gras and the usual complaints about the slow recovery of the city and the requisite bitching about the uselessness of the federal government. Loren was a self-described "yellow dog Democrat." I knew he was very active politically, and often went up to Baton Rouge to lobby for gay rights at the capital. I waited for him to get to the point, nodding or politely responding when it was called for. Finally, he looked at me over the top of his glasses. "Chanse, is your time your own right now?"

I crossed my legs, keeping my face impassive. "In three weeks, I have to take a business trip, and then I'll be out of town for several weeks. For now, though, I am free and clear."

"Excellent." He beamed at me again. He cleared his throat. "I represent someone who has some work for you, but you have to be completely at their disposal. It shouldn't take more than three or four days, if that, and they're willing to pay you five thousand dollars a day for your time, plus a substantial bonus when the work is done."

I whistled. That was a lot of money. My usual rate was five hundred a day, plus expenses. Fifteen or twenty thousand dollars was an awful lot of money for three or four days work. Always beware the lawyer dangling a large sum of cash in front of your nose. "I won't do anything illegal, Loren." That wasn't an absolute; I'd danced over that line several times in my career—but it's not wise to advertise a willingness to bend the law up front. Apparently, these clients, whoever they were, had money to burn—so maybe they'd be willing to pay a little more to bend my sense of ethics.

Loren laughed. "I'm not about to lose my license, Chanse. Everything will be legal and aboveboard, I can assure you." He slid a file folder across the desk to me. "Are you interested?"

"It depends on what the job entails." I leaned back in the chair.

"Would you be willing to sign a confidentiality agreement?"

"I don't make a habit of breaking my clients' confidences," I shot back, getting annoyed. "I wouldn't be in business long if I did."

"All right, that's fair enough." He leaned back in his chair. "I'm going to tell you more than I should without your signing the confidentiality agreement, all right? My clients are Jillian Long and Freddy Bliss. You have heard of them, haven't you?"

I whistled. "Last I checked, I wasn't living in a cave, Loren." I laughed. "Of course I've heard of them." And now, of course, the confidentiality agreement made sense.

Jillian Long and Freddy Bliss were two of the biggest movie stars on the planet. Everything they did, everywhere they went, everything they wore and said was reported breathlessly by the news media. They'd even gotten one of those nauseatingly cutesy names, like Brangelina and Bennifer; they were known collectively as Frillian. They'd been married for three years, and had bought a huge mansion in the French Quarter on the first anniversary of the levee failure—a fact they played up in the huge press conference they held to announce their move, and the reason behind it. Freddy, had co-founded a nonprofit organization called Project Rebuild, dedicated to rebuilding the Lower Ninth Ward.

After the press conference, Frillian had become the major topic of discussion in town. *I saw them riding their bikes in the Marigny . . . I ran into Jillian at the CC's on Royal Street, she just drinks regular coffee . . . have you seen them yet?* Overall, most residents felt it was a great thing that they were lending their celebrity and fame to bring worldwide attention to the continuing plight of New Orleans. But, like everything else, after a few weeks, the local hubbub had died down, and no one really paid much attention to them locally, despite the fact their every move was still national news.

Naturally, they'd want anyone who worked for them in any way, shape, or form to sign a confidentiality agreement.

"If I take the job, I'll be more than happy to sign a confidentiality agreement. But you know as well as I do that won't survive a subpoena, if it ever came to that."

Loren gave me a faint smile. Of course he'd thought of that, the smile told me. "You will be paid by me, so you are acting as my agent, and are bound by client privilege."

I nodded. "All right. What do they want me to do, Loren?"

He stood up. "Why don't we let them tell you themselves? They're waiting in one of the conference rooms."

Jillian Long was a great beauty, with long, thick, beautiful red hair, porcelain skin, and the hugest, most amazing gray eyes—hauntingly beautiful eyes impossible not to notice and admire. But she was more than just another beautiful

actress—her talent as an actress surpassed even her flaw-
less beauty. She'd won an Oscar for one of her first films, *In-
decent,* playing a low income mother who'd murdered her
no-good boyfriend when she found out he'd been molesting
her four-year-old son. She'd been major news ever since.

I'd lost track of her marriages, divorces, and lovers—it
really wasn't any of my business. But it was hard not to be
aware of her personal life when headlines scream at you in
line at the grocery store. When she'd hooked up with Freddy
Bliss, a major new male star twenty-odd years younger than
she was, it was as though entertainment journalists had died
and gone straight to heaven—especially since Freddy had
left his wife to be with Jillian. Freddy's wife, Glynis Parrish,
had been on the cover of every magazine telling her story of
"heartbreak" and moving forward. I think she may have
even written a book, but I could be wrong. I don't really pay
that much attention to that kind of thing.

But one thing I liked about them was that "Frillian"
seemed dedicated to using their fame for charities and to
help underprivileged people, not only in this country but
around the world. Jillian had long earned a well-deserved
reputation as an activist—and traveled the world on good
will missions for the United Nations. Even before they met,
Freddy was doing the same—but for inner-city neighbor-
hoods and schools. Individually, they'd accomplished a lot.
Together, they were accomplishing more. I'd been one of the
people who'd been pleased when New Orleans recovery became one of their issues. The country had moved on from
the disaster as though it had never happened—and they
were working to make sure New Orleans wasn't forgotten.

Even though I knew they were just two normal people,
like me or anyone else, I felt more than a little nervous about
meeting them in person.

When Loren led me into the conference room that opened just off his office, the first thing that struck me about them was that they were both rather, well, small. Granted, I'm six-feet-four and weigh 230 pounds, so I'm usually one of the bigger people around. But when Freddy Bliss rose from his chair and stepped toward me, flashing that big toothy smile that lit up movie screens and inspired the kind of passions in teenaged girls that frightened their parents, my first thought was, *but he's so short. That can't be.* I felt like a huge clumsy ogre as my hand closed around his. His grip, though, was firm and the big smile seemed genuine. His brown hair was artfully unkempt, and he hadn't shaved in a few days. The smile—and the light in the big brown eyes—were infectious and I found myself smiling back at him. He was wearing an LSU football jersey—the white home one with the gold and purple stripes at the shoulders—and loose-fitting, worn jeans over dirty-looking white sneakers. "Freddy Bliss," he said, as he shook my hand firmly three times before letting go. I detected a slight trace of a Midwestern accent in his voice, something I'd never noticed on screen. "I understand you played ball for LSU, Mr. MacLeod."

I felt like I was grinning like an idiot, but couldn't seem to stop. "Yes, sir, I did. I played four years, lettered three. And it's Chanse."

"Freddy's become a big fan." I turned and watched as Jillian Long rose from her chair in a steady languid motion, her face going from impassive mask to friendly warmth. Jillian Long was always picked for those "most beautiful women in the world" lists, but I'd always assumed her great beauty was assisted by makeup, lighting, and camera work. However, in person, with little or no makeup, she was even more beautiful than on film. Her skin was pale white, but had a strange shimmer and sheen to it that reminded me of mother of pearl. Her long, thick, reddish hair hung loosely past her shoulders, contrasting with her black cashmere sweater. Her thick lips were a pale pink, and I could see tiny blue veins in her neck.

Her large gray eyes looked as though they had a thin sheen of ice over them. She was shorter than Freddy, perhaps not even five feet tall. She was also wearing dirty white sneakers and worn-looking jeans. She was wearing very little makeup, and her voice was deep and throaty, which seemed strange given her slender frame. There were slight wrinkles around her eyes and mouth, but she showed none of the telltale signs of having corrective work done. She looked very delicate, but her small hand gripped mine tightly.

"Every Saturday during football season, we live and die with the Tigers. I'm Jillian Long. It's a pleasure to meet you, Chanse."

"The pleasure's mine." I somehow managed to pry the stupid grin off my face, and assumed what I hoped was a confident, professional smile.

"But you're so young." She frowned, and turned to Loren. "You didn't mention he was—" she waved one of the delicate hands in a graceful, fluttery move, "—so young."

"I'm thirty-one," I replied. What did my age have to do with anything? "And my record speaks for itself."

Her eyes widened for just a moment, the pupils expanding and retracting as the hand she'd waved went to her throat. She swallowed and nodded. "Yes, of course. My apologies." Her face relaxed into a charming smile. "I was just startled—I was expecting someone older. Do forgive me."

"Not a problem," I said, my face filling with blood.

I may have been only thirty-one years old, but I felt much

older. I've killed two men in the course of my career—both times in self-defense, but it had taken a toll on me emotionally. My partner Paul's death, the hurricane . . . in my thirty-one years I'd already seen a lifetime's worth of tragedy and death and destruction. *Calm down, Chanse, take some deep breaths, you're overreacting,* I said to myself.

"Let's be seated. Does anyone need anything?" Loren asked, moving over to the end of the table where they'd been seated. He sat down at the head of the table. Freddy and Jillian went back to their seats, and I sat directly across the table from them, with Loren to my left. The chair was expensive, made of black leather, and so comfortable it seemed to wrap itself around my body.

"Are you willing to sign the confidentiality agreement?" Freddy asked, taking Jillian's hand.

"It's really very important to us." She opened her eyes wider. She turned first to Freddy, then Loren, and finally looked me directly in the eyes. Her eyes were amazing, mesmerizing. The gray was flecked with gold, and they did seem to be sheathed in ice. It was impossible to gauge them, to get a sense of what she was thinking. "This is an incredibly sensitive matter. This cannot get into the press under any circumstances."

A part of me wanted to say yes—which surprised me. "I'm sorry." I swallowed, forcing down the unusual desire to please. "But you're not willing to tell me anything until I sign it—and I'm not willing to sign something without knowing why I'm signing it. Or letting my own lawyer look at it first." I smiled. "But in these four walls, it's just us. Anything you tell me—well, all you'd have to do would be to deny it, right? And Loren can go along with you. My word against yours—and who am I?" I didn't expect her to buy it, and I wasn't disappointed.

"You'd be surprised," Jillian said. Her voice was tired. "Everyone has their price, Chanse. And you'd be surprised what they'll print—and what they're willing to pay for it." She closed her eyes. She fluttered her hand again. "You have no idea what it's like."

"No, you're right, I don't. I can't even imagine what it's like, and I don't expect you to trust me right off the bat, either. So, we're kind of at an impasse. I can't help you unless . . ." I pushed my chair back, and paused.

It worked.

"I'm getting threatening e-mails," Freddy cut me off. Jillian spun her head quickly to stare at him, while Loren started to clear his throat. He held up his hand as Loren started to speak. "We want you to find out who it is."

I stared at him for a moment, confused. Threatening e-mails? Why on earth did that need to be kept a secret? They had websites, surely, Myspace pages, you name it—there were any number of ways to send e-mails to them. And then I got it. "You mean on your private account? You think it's someone you know, don't you? Someone close to you. And that would be a scandal."

Loren broke in. "Regardless of who it is, it would be tabloid fodder." He started drumming his pen on the table.

"There are—" Jillian bit her lip, closed her eyes, and squeezed Freddy's hand. "There are things about both of us we would like to keep private, if at all possible." She swallowed again. "In order to help you figure out—and stop—whoever it is, we're going to have to tell you things." She opened her eyes and looked at me. "Things that you cannot, under any circumstances, tell anyone else. That's why you need to sign that confidentiality agreement, Chanse. We're willing to pay you well." Her voice became plaintive, pleading. With a jolt, I realized I'd heard her use that tone of voice before. In a movie, whose name I couldn't remember.

She was, after all, a very good actress.

"Are these threatening e-mails . . ." I hesitated. "Is there a hint of blackmail involved in this?" I'd dealt with blackmailers before. One was even homicidal. "Because you need to understand that it never stops with payment. If this person truly *knows* something that could be damaging to you . . ."

Freddy said, "They're just making threats, whoever it is." He gave me a reassuring smile—the same one he'd given Cameron Diaz in *Love Unbound,* when he was trying to get into her pants, despite his wife. "There's nothing *criminal* in either of our pasts. Sure, there are things we'd prefer the general public not know about us—" He stopped himself. "I probably shouldn't say anything more."

"Let me see that." I gestured to Loren, who passed the folder over to me. I opened it and looked at the paper. I read it carefully. I didn't really need to have a lawyer look it over. It simply stated that as a requirement for doing work for them, I was signing this and promising never to reveal to an outsider the nature of the work, or anything I might discover about them or anyone involved with their lives, without their permission. If I violated the agreement, I would have to repay any moneys paid to me by them, and possible damages, to be determined by private, confidential, and most importantly, independent, outside arbitration. "You realize, of course, that if I am ever subpoenaed, this is just a piece of paper?"

"I'm not worried about any subpoenas," Loren replied. "I can have a clause added that this agreement is invalid if you are called to testify in court, which is a moot point, as it will never happen." He looked over at them. "Do you have any objection to that?"

Jillian opened her mouth, but Freddy spoke. "No. Do whatever's necessary."

Loren took the document from me and excused himself.

"You were going to say something," I said, looking at Jillian.

"No." She shook her head, drumming her fingertips on the table.

An uncomfortable silence descended.

The smart thing to do, I figured, was to refuse to sign the thing and not take the job. They were actors, and good ones. They'd convinced millions of viewers they were any number of different people. They played roles for a living. How would I ever be able to ascertain the truth of anything they told me? But I was also curious; I wanted to know what the hell was going on with them. I watched their faces, but got no clues. *What was in those e-mails that had them so rattled?* There was more here than met the eye, but I wasn't going to find out until I signed that agreement.

My curiosity was getting the best of me.

On the other hand, they weren't exactly normal people either. Most people don't have every aspect of their life offered up to the general public for discussion and conversation.

Loren walked back in, and handed the revised agreement to me. A check for twenty thousand dollars, drawn on the firm's account was paper clipped to it. I read it over quickly. It was straightforward. I hesitated for just a moment, then took a pen from my jacket pocket and signed it.

Jillian let out a huge sigh of relief. "Oh, thank you." She got up and walked over to the sideboard, pouring herself a glass of ice water.

Loren rose. "I'll go make a copy of this for you, Chanse, and give you three some privacy."

Once the door shut behind him, Jillian took her seat

again. "As we said, over the last couple of weeks, Freddy has been getting some bizarre e-mails." She reached into a bag and pulled out a file folder, which she slid across the table to me. "Vaguely threatening."

"One of them does include a death threat," Freddy said as I opened the file folder. "Not *I'm going to kill you* but *I could just kill you.* A technicality, sure, but it's enough to worry us." They exchanged another look.

I read the first one.

Freddy Freddy Freddy:

You just think you're hot shit, don't you? A professional do-gooder, right? What would everyone think if they knew the truth about you? You don't deserve to live.

It was unsigned.

"That's my private e-mail account," Freddy went on. "No one has it, except family, friends, and you know, our staff. It's not even registered through the server as being mine, you know? Our assistant, Doreen, set us both up with a private account under her name." He waved a hand. "I'm sure somehow someone could have found out—I'm not the best with this computer stuff—but . . ."

"Who do you think would do this?"

"Where to start?" Jillian gave a tired laugh. "There's my latest crazy ex-husband, Freddy's ex-wife, my own mother . . ." She waved her hand again. "Everyone either one of us has ever been involved with has their own axe to grind, their grubby hands out for more money. We're targets, Chanse, always targets. Remember that. Even when we are doing good work for charities—you'd be amazed at the things people say. I've been called every name in the book . . . but I am getting off the subject." She wiped her eyes and smiled at me. "I do that, sorry. But I'm convinced it's one of those three . . . I'm just not sure what their game is yet. But they don't want to kill Freddy, I don't believe that for a minute. Why would anyone want to stop our work here?"

"Let's start with your ex-husband," I said, mentally adding the words *at least, your most recent ex-husband.* I thought for a moment. "You were married to Dale Monteith, right?" Dale Monteith was a character actor who somehow had managed, through hard work and talent, to become a star of sorts. "I'm assuming the breakup wasn't a happy one?"

"Well, forget everything you've seen in the tabloids." Freddy replied. "The public story is that when we were making *The Odyssey*, we fell madly in love and left our spouses to be with each other."

"Dale and I had not been husband and wife for two years before Freddy and I met," Jillian continued. "I was going through a very rocky period when Dale and I met, is the only defense I can offer—we were fine for a year, and then I realized—" she rubbed her eyes. "I realized that Dale just wasn't serious enough for me. He wasn't interested in anything other than all that Hollywood bullshit, you know? I moved out of his house a year after we were married. Yes, we never bothered to file for divorce until I met Freddy, but we also had barely spoken in those two years. When I moved out, he knew it was for good. So, no, Dale has no reason to be resentful of Freddy—no matter what the tabloids say." She gave me a horrible smile. "And the publicity was good for Dale's career. He wasn't getting work until he got to play cuckolded husband for the entertainment of the masses."

"Likewise," Freddy said, "my ex-wife Glynis and I were having problems for a while before I met Jillian." Glynis Parrish had been a television star when she'd married the sexiest man alive. After the breakup, she'd been everywhere: every talk show, every magazine cover, weeping quietly over her great heartbreak and humiliation. "Glynis played the jilted wife to perfection, as you must be aware. Hey, the marriage was over, and she was milking the publicity to make herself sympathetic to the audience, you know? So, I let her play it out—she got some movie roles out of it—and what did we care if people hated us?" He smiled at Jillian. "It all blows over after a little while—and people still came to see *our* movies."

"But these e-mails started coming two weeks ago," Jillian went on. "And just two weeks ago, Glynis blew into town to make a movie."

I hadn't heard about that. "She's making a movie here?"

Freddy laughed. "She plays a woman who comes to New Orleans to rebuild her life after her husband leaves her for another woman." He rolled his eyes. "Original concept, huh?"

"Okay." I shook my head. "Kind of interesting that she came into town around the same time the e-mails started."

"My mother is here too." Jillian spat the words out, placing particular loathing on the word *mother*. "And I wouldn't put anything past that *bitch*."

Interesting. "Have some problems with your mother?" Jillian's mother, Shirley Harris, had been a musical comedy star for years, moving between Broadway and film effortlessly. Until a bout of ill health had recently sidelined her, she'd been a huge draw in Las Vegas.

"How much time do you have?" Jillian laughed bitterly. "Look, my mother and I don't have a relationship. I tried for years to have one with her. She doesn't understand boundaries, she doesn't understand anything other than what she needs. I don't want anything to do with her. She knows this, but keeps pushing." She sighed. "Wherever I go, there she is. Maybe if someone would give her a job, she'd forget all about me." A pained look crossed her face. "My mother was always desperate for the limelight . . . and now that her star has faded, the only way she can get any attention is by talking about me." Her lips narrowed. "It's really pathetic, if you think about it."

"Where is your mother staying?" Somehow, I doubted that Shirley Harris would stoop to this level of harassment, but one of her employees might.

She shrugged. "I don't know, but she's here. I can sense her evil."

Okay, probably best not to push that one. "And your staff?"

"Doreen Benson is our assistant," Freddy said, passing me another folder. "Inside this folder are cell phone numbers for Dale and Glynis, as well as the resumes for Doreen, our nanny Cindy, and Jay Robinette, who's the head of our security detail—along with our cell phone numbers. Our *private* numbers." He glanced at his watch. "Those numbers, needless to say, aren't for public knowledge. Cindy, Doreen, and Jay have been instructed to cooperate with you fully—anything you might need. If you need to meet with us at the house, just call us, and we'll let Jay know to let you in. You know where the house is?" When I nodded, he laughed. "Everyone knows where our house is, right? But as for the rest—" he shrugged. "If any of them are doing this, I doubt they'd want to talk to you."

"All right." I picked up both folders to put into my shoulder bag. "I'll be in touch as soon as I know anything concrete, or if I need something."

"Thank you," Jillian said. "Please—get to the bottom of

this quickly." She reached over and touched my hand. "And please—be discreet."

"I'll do what I can."

I watched them exit the conference room, and sat there for a moment. I opened the folder with the e-mails, and leafed through them. They were all insulting, some making derogatory remarks about Freddy's genitalia—which naturally made me think of Glynis Parrish . . . until I remembered that a photographer had snapped pictures of Freddy sunbathing nude in the south of France a year or two earlier. Everyone in the world had seen him naked. Even I had—I hadn't been able to resist clicking through the gallery of images when they'd been posted on a gossip website. There was no question that Freddy was a beautiful man—my best friend Paige had said when they'd moved here, "You know, I'll see every movie he makes, because he always shows his ass. And he has such a nice one . . ." We had both laughed.

With a sigh, I shoved the e-mails back in the folder.

Loren came back into the conference room. He shook my hand. "Thanks for doing this, Chanse."

"No problem," I replied, and walked back out to the elevators. Frillian were long gone, and as I waited for the elevator, I wondered again if I'd made a huge mistake.

They were movie stars. They were paid lots of money to play roles, to become different people, to be convincing. It was their *job*. So, I would have to take everything they told me with a grain of salt, and be careful not to simply trust them. The feud between Jillian and her mother was well-documented in the tabloids—but then again, she'd also told me not to believe everything I read about them. So, what was true and what wasn't true? They both claimed their former spouses held no grudges against them, that everything between them was fine. They'd been very careful, though, to point out that someone started sending the e-mails right around the time Glynis came to New Orleans to make her movie.

The hardest part of this case would be to curb my natural curiosity. I didn't need to know *why* the e-mails were being sent. I was being paid to find out who was sending them— and that's what I was going to do. I'd file a report, destroy all copies of the files to maintain confidentiality, and then I could just walk away from all of this.

I climbed into the elevator, and hit the lobby button.

No, I wasn't going to be able to take them at face value. And though I was trying not to let my curiosity run wild, I couldn't help myself from thinking about it on the way down to the lobby.

There was something more going on here than either of them wanted to admit.

I was going to have to be very, very careful.

CHAPTER TWO

A NINE-YEAR-OLD probably knows more about computers than I do.

Don't get me wrong, I can use mine. I know how to turn it on, I know how to open a program—I can even load software. I know how to hook my digital camera into it to download pictures. I can download music for my iPod. I can log onto the Internet to do research I used to have to do on the telephone, by mail, or in person—which is an incredible time-saver. But beyond that, it's like trying to read Vietnamese. I don't understand why it crashes, nor do I know what to do to make it stop crashing. I don't know how to wipe a hard drive (although discovering by accident is one of my biggest fears) or how to retrieve a file that's been erased. I don't know how to hack into someone else's computer, or into a website—and have no desire to know. I barely know how to work with the spam filter on my e-mail account.

Tracing an e-mail back to the computer it came from is completely beyond my limited computer skills. From time to time, I think I should learn how to be more effective with the computer—and it's not like I don't have the time when I'm not working. Yet somehow I can never bring myself to take a course, or even spend the extra time to go through the tutorials that come with the software.

Fortunately, I have a great computer nerd to turn to.

It was my best friend, Paige Tourneur, who found him for me. I had just spent a small fortune getting some repair work done on my computer, and it still didn't work right—even though they'd kept it for three weeks. Every time it froze up on me, I had to resist the urge to put my fist through the screen, or pack it up and shove it up the ass of the guy at the computer hospital. That night, Paige had come by in a fine foul mood with a bottle of wine. After relaxing over a couple of joints and when the bottle was half empty, she was finally ready to let me know what had gotten her goat that day. It was one of her favorites: the incompetence and total failure of the Louisiana public school system. After listening to her rage about how we as a society were failing our youth for quite a while, giving my obligatory nods and agreeing noises (which is all she requires while on a tirade), I asked what triggered this latest and well deserved disgust with the school system.

"I talked to this kid today, and he was the sweetest guy, Chanse, and we failed him." She took another hit off the joint. "Take this kid," she said, flourishing the joint, "a poor kid from the Irish Channel. His mother was a manager at a McDonald's and trying to raise a family of three kids on those wages, if you can imagine that. Not a goddamned pot to piss in. His father was a total deadbeat, a drug-addled loser who killed someone in an argument over drugs and was sent up to Angola before any of the kids were even in school. Like those kids are going to have any kind of chance, right? And we wonder why they turn to crime. And one of the kids is this incredibly bright kid, with an aptitude for computers, but no one notices or sees or cares at his school because they're too busy trying to keep all the rest of the kids from killing each other—rather than teaching them anything. So, he teaches himself all about computers, how to use them, how to build them, how the software and hardware works, all of that, you know? It's almost like he's a genius with computers, right? So, he starts using his self-taught skills to hack into computers, change grades for money . . . and no one catches him, and then he moves on to other things . . . stealing credit card numbers, people's personal information . . . and when he's seventeen, he gets caught. His mother can't afford a lawyer, so he gets a public defender—and you know what those are worth in Orleans Parish. He cops a plea, goes away for three years, gets out after eighteen months, and who's going to hire him? He got his GED while in jail, and learned even more about computers there. Bright, sharp, and the sweetest guy you can imagine, and he's barely eking out an existence because no one cared, or noticed, his abilities and nurtured him from an early age." She sighed. "It's just awful . . . the way we waste the youth in this town."

"He's really good with computers?" I asked, glaring at mine from across the room.

"Brilliant—he's absolutely brilliant." She shook her head. "Such a fucking waste—because you know he's eventually going to have to go back to criminal shit if he wants to eat."

"Do you have his name and number?" I hooked a thumb at my computer. "That stupid fucking thing is still all fucked up. And I'd rather pay this kid to fix it than those know-nothing assholes at the repair shop."

Fixing my computer was the first job I'd given Jephtha Carriere. He came over, and did a few things on it. Fifteen minutes later it was working better than it had when I'd first bought it. He tried explaining what the problem had been, but it made no sense to me. I wrote him a check, and then asked, "Could you design a hack-proof system for a computer network?"

"There's no such thing as hack-proof," he'd scoffed, shaking his head. "As long as someone wants to get in, they will. Anything I design might work for now, but someone would crack my system soon enough." He gave me a sunny smile. "You know, for most hackers, it's not so much about the information they can access or crashing a system—that's what people don't understand. It's the challenge . . . to see if you can outsmart the original programmer. The harder it is, the harder they'll try. And when you pull it off, it's a rush better than any drug."

"Are you willing to give it a try?" I asked. Paige had been right. He was incredibly bright and likeable. I also liked that he hadn't assured me he could do something he didn't think possible. "The pay would be really good, and it could be a regular gig—updating the system, making it even more secure. I'll tell you what—why don't you see if you can hack into the system, and give me an analysis of what needs to be done. Like I said, the pay would be really good. And I might need you to do some things for me from time to time—like fix my computer, or things I don't have the skills to do."

"I don't want to do anything illegal," he replied. "I don't want to go back to jail."

"I wouldn't ask you to do anything illegal. I could lose my license."

"Yeah, sure." He'd shrugged. "How good is the pay?"

I told him, and his eyes widened. "Are you serious?" When I nodded, he said, "I'll get right on it." Two days later, he e-mailed a detailed analysis of the weaknesses in the system—and it went right over my head. But one thing I did understand was *I was able to hack into the computer network in less than ten minutes. The only reason I can see that no one has so far is because it hasn't occurred to anyone.*

I took the report to my boss at Crown Oil, Barbara Castlemaine, and she immediately authorized me to hire him. He started work that very day.

A week later, we did a test run on his system.

Not a single computer programmer or expert at Crown Oil could break into it.

He's been working for me ever since.

Over the years, I'd become fond of Jephtha. His jail experience had the effect it should have—he was firmly on the straight and narrow path now. He had no desire to ever go back.

Jephtha lived with his current girlfriend in a single shotgun on Constantinople Street in the Irish Channel. His girlfriends were one of Jephtha's freely admitted problems. The Bourbon Street strip clubs—and the huge-breasted, bleached blondes who danced there, were his biggest weakness. He'd dated a string of them—falling madly in love each time, swearing she was "the one"—until she walked out on him or stole from him. Since he'd started working for me, I started doing background checks on every last one of them—not that it made a bit of difference to him. When Jephtha was in love, he didn't want to hear anything bad about the object of his affection—because she was a goddess of perfection in his eyes.

His current girlfriend's stage name at the Catbox Club was Tiffani. Her real name was Abby Grosjean, and she was worth all of her predecessors combined. Abby was from Plaquemines Parish, the oldest daughter of a shrimper. She'd left home when she was nineteen, when her father took a second wife she didn't like, and headed for New Orleans. Her only work experience was waiting tables in a small diner. She did that for a while after she got into town, tired of it quickly, and made a decision to, as she put it, "put my body to work for me instead of the other way around. God gave me big boobs, he must have wanted me to use 'em, right?" She bleached her dark hair white-blonde and applied for work as a dancer at the Catbox Club. "I was on the drill team in high school," she'd told me after she'd moved in with Jephtha. "I just use the same moves we learned at drill camp and voila, I became a stripper." I liked her because she was honest and a hard worker, and unlike her predecessors, she actually cared about Jephtha. She did her best to make sure he ate decent and regular meals, and tried to keep the house as tidy as she could. She was taking a couple of classes at the University of New Orleans, majoring in pre-law, no less.

The house on Constantinople had belonged to his grandmother. She'd died while he was in prison and left it to him. It was a typical New Orleans shotgun house—so-called because if you stood in the front door and fired a shotgun, the bullet would go all the way through the house and out the back door without hitting a wall. Typical of the style, the house was long and narrow. It was badly in need of paint. The yard was also a mess—Jephtha rarely remembered to mow the small patch of lawn, and the roses his grandmother had planted grew wild and out of control. The house also listed slightly to the right. Jephtha's beat-up old Oldsmobile, with its cracked windshield, leprous-looking paint job, and a screwdriver holding the driver's window shut sat out in front. Some of the shutters on the windows hung loose—Abby was always nagging at him to do something about them because of the way they banged against the house in the wind. "It's like talking to a wall," she'd once told me after haranguing him to no avail.

I parked behind his car, wondering again why no one

ever had it towed as abandoned. I opened the gate and winced as it screeched. Inside the house, the dogs started barking. The front door opened before I even made it up the groaning steps onto the porch.

"Hey," Abby said. She was wearing what looked like a Catholic school uniform—at a school with very lax moral standards. There was no bra under her white shirt, which she'd tied to show her midriff, and I could see the nipples outlined through its tightness. Her feet were bare, showing dark pink polish on her toenails and the scorpion tattoo on her inner calf. She looked like she was about thirteen—except for the massive breasts—and her face was clear of makeup. She never wore makeup unless she was going to work, and she'd tied the bleached hair back in a ponytail that made her look even younger than she usually did. She was smoking an unfiltered Camel. She flicked ash and stood aside. "Go on in—he's at the computer, where else would he be?" A hint of annoyance crept into her voice.

"Everything okay, Abby?"

She shrugged. "I just get tired of nagging him to mow the damned lawn. I might as well just give up and do it myself." She took another drag, and winked at me. "Go on in, Chanse. I just made some sweet tea—it's in the fridge. Help yourself."

I leaned down and kissed her on the cheek. "Thanks."

"I just put a strawberry cobbler in the oven. It'll be ready in about an hour. You want some?"

I winked and patted my stomach. "Not on my diet."

She made a farting noise with her lips. "You and Jephtha both could use a little more meat on your bones, you ask me."

I laughed and walked inside. Despite Abby's best efforts, the house on the inside always looked unkempt. It was probably the dog hair coating the 1950s-style furniture. I greeted

Rhett and Greta, the huge matching black labs, with the head rubs and back scratching that sent them in paroxysms of dog ecstasy, and headed back to the "computer lab," as Jeptha called it.

The computer lab always looked like a bomb had gone off recently. Sometimes I thought my need for order in my house bordered on the neurotic—my therapist claimed it was a "control issue"—"subconsciously, you have a need for control, and since you cannot control the future or what's going to happen to you, you exercise that need for control by controlling your home environment." He'd even said that was part of the reason I worked out regularly—to gain "control" over my body. While going to the therapist was helping me, there were times I thought he was full of shit.

But even my therapist would understand why walking into Jephtha's computer lab made me cringe inwardly. There was a thick layer of dust on everything—he refused to let Abby clean in there. Piles of newspapers and paper covered every available surface. Empty plastic soda bottles were scattered all over the floor. Jephtha was partial to every conceivable kind of snack that came in a bag—potato chips, pretzels, and corn chips. If Abby didn't cook, he would probably live on chips. He always kept the curtains closed, and the only light he ever turned on was the one on the desk by whatever computer he was working on.

Predictably, I sneezed. He looked up from the computer screen and grinned at me. There was an open bottle of Coke next to his keyboard, and in one hand he held a bag of Funions. As I watched, he tilted the bag over his mouth and shook the crumbs out in a shower—some of them missing his mouth and dusting his cheeks. I don't think I've ever seen him when he wasn't eating or snacking on something, but somehow he never gained a pound. He was taller than me—

about six-feet-six with maybe 150 pounds on his long-limbed frame. He wore his light brown hair long and was always pushing it out of his pale face. His face was long and thin, and he was wearing his glasses. "Hey, Chanse, buddy," he said, spitting out Funion crumbs as he wiped his hands on his Che Guevara T-shirt. "You got something for me, man?"

I reached into my backpack and pulled out the folder of e-mails. "I need you to trace the computer these came from." I handed it to him.

He didn't even look at them, just slid the folder on top of the stack closest to his computer. He waved a hand. "Piece of cake—so easy it's hardly even worth my time. I keep telling you—let me teach you how to do it yourself, save you a trip over here and some money, too."

I shook my head. "Nah, I'd rather pay you to do it."

"Well, you know my rule. I have to charge for at least an hour's worth of work." He said it apologetically. He always seemed to regret charging me for the work he did for me, no matter how much I insisted it was more than worth it to me.

"That's fine." Jephtha's hourly rate was ridiculously low. "I don't want you to have to go back to a life of crime."

"No worries on that score, trust me." He waved his hand dismissively. "Like I said, it won't take more than ten minutes, tops." He grinned at me. "But you got to check this out, man." He enjoyed writing programs, but his real love was designing computer games. He confided in me once that should one of his games ever catch on and become a success, he wanted to start a foundation to help kids like him.

"I don't want some other kid to wind up in jail the way I did," he said simply, "just because there wasn't anyone around to help out." That was the kind of person Jephtha was. There was no doubt in my mind that one day he'd finally design the game that would make him millions. I suspected the only reason he hadn't so far was his macabre sense of humor. His games were usually inspired by something that irritated him. He used the computer games to vent his spleen. Some of them were so brilliantly funny—if slightly disturbing—that they just might catch on in the increasingly violent world of computer gaming.

I looked at the computer screen and recognized *Tourist Season,* his latest game. In it, the player walked through the streets of the French Quarter with an automatic weapon. You got points for killing tourists doing things they shouldn't. But if the tourist was just walking along doing nothing wrong, you lost points for shooting them. You also lost points for killing locals. It certainly cracked me up. The more horrible the tourist, the more points you got. For example, if you shot a tourist taking a piss on the street, it was worth two thousand points. Shooting the couple having sex in public was worth five thousand points. Blowing away the jerk throwing trash in the street was only a thousand points.

The game was paused. An obvious tourist, in one of those ridiculous Hawaiian shirts and khaki shorts, was pissing in front of the Cabildo. "I've been working on this some more. Pull up a chair, man." He started the game again, blowing the man to bits, and then reset the game. "You want to play while I trace this? It won't take ten minutes, I'm telling you." He grinned at me. "You know you want to kill some tourists."

It was a hard offer to resist. I moved a pile of newspapers, magazines, and crumpled empty bags of chips on top of a pile already on the floor. I pulled the chair over next to his. He rolled his chair over to another computer, and started typing away at the keyboard. I looked at the computer screen in front of me and clicked on the mouse to start the game. I took aim and shot at a woman running across Burgundy Street pushing a baby in a stroller in front of her as a car slammed on its brakes. As the woman's head exploded, I said, "Um, this game is kind of sick, Jephtha."

"Yeah, well," he replied grimly, looking over at the screen in front of me, "that very thing happened to me yesterday when I was taking Abby to work. Some stupid pregnant woman with a baby ran right out in front of my car. Why would anyone do something so stupid? I mean, what if my brakes were bad? And there wasn't a car behind me. She couldn't wait twenty seconds for me to go by?" He glowered. "Just because you can breed doesn't mean you should." He pursed his lips at me. "At least in the game she's not pregnant. And besides, you don't kill the baby. If you do, you lose points." He shook his head. "I'm not *that* sick." He gave me an innocent grin.

"Well, no video game company would allow that. People would get pissed."

"And it would make the national news. The family values assholes would get up in arms—even though women who risk their kids' lives like that—that's who they should be pissed at—and every teenaged boy in the country would want to play it, and I'd make a bazillion dollars." He reached for the folder he'd set down on the desk beside the computer screen. He opened it and removed one of the e-mail printouts, then handed the folder back to me. "All I need is the information on one of these." He peered at the paper, and laughed. "Chanse, this is not even a challenge, you know? When you going to give me something hard to do?" He sighed. "It's like taking candy from a baby. You want lunch or something? Abby's making a strawberry cobbler . . . her cobblers are fucking awesome, man. It's like going to heaven." He raised his eyebrows and licked his lips.

My stomach growled, but Jephtha had treated me to lunch once before. He'd made me an "Elvis special," a fried peanut butter and banana sandwich. It had sat in my stomach for the rest of the day like a lead weight. "No, I'm meeting someone for lunch in about an hour," I lied, glancing at my watch. "You'll be done by then?"

"I told you, I'll have this IP address in like two seconds . . . there it is." His eyes gleamed. "Okay, give me another few minutes and I'll know whose computer this is . . . well shit fire." He sneered at his computer screen. "This e-mail address is one of those dummy ones, you know, the kind where you don't have to give any personal information?" His fingers flew over the keyboard. He shrugged. "Okay, so this is going to take a few more minutes. I'll have to trace the computer—if they registered it." He glanced over at me. "Don't look at my screen, okay? I'm going to have to do something you won't approve of. Just keep playing *Tourist Season.*"

"I don't want to know what you're doing." I turned back to the screen in front of me. A man and a woman were copulating in a doorway. I aimed, fired, and they both exploded. Five thousand points! In spite of myself, I grinned in satisfaction. *Everyone in New Orleans is going to want to play this game,* I thought to myself. "You know, you're probably right about this game." I said as I took aim at another drunken tourist, this one staggering out in the road carrying a forty-eight ounce daiquiri cup and wearing a feather boa. BLAM! Another twenty-five hundred points. "It's kind of addicting." I fired at a car with MICHIGAN plates crawling along at about five miles an hour while everyone in the car gawked at the buildings going by. It exploded, body parts flying everywhere, giving me another ten thousand points. I couldn't help myself. I laughed out loud.

It was *fun.* "The New Orleans Tourism Board would probably pay you not to put this on the market," I added, aiming at a couple of girls in sorority sweatshirts puking in a gutter.

I missed, and shot a woman walking her dog on the other side of the street. I lost ten thousand points. Locals were worth a lot more than tourists.

"There." Jephtha leaned back in his chair with a triumphant grin. One of his printers began to hum. Pages began coming out into the drop tray. "I told you it would be a piece of cake. I'm printing out the bill of sale right now. But—" he held up a long and bony index finger, "this is the person who *bought* and registered the computer. It doesn't mean they still have it." He picked up a page and whistled. "Glynis Parrish? As in Glynis Parrish, the movie star?"

With real regret, I turned away from *Tourist Season* and took the paper from him. Sure enough, there it was in black and white. A MacBook Pro, purchased at an Apple store in Beverly Hills. I definitely didn't want to know how he got this. I stood up and smiled at Jephtha. "E-mail me an invoice, and I'll get a check to you this week."

"Aren't you going to tell me if it's *the* Glynis Parrish or not?" He stuck out his lower lip in a pout that made him look about ten years old.

I laughed and winked at him. "What you don't know won't hurt you." I slipped the bill of sale into the folder with the rest of the e-mails, and tucked it under my arm. I called out a goodbye to Abby, and headed out the front door.

My cell phone rang just as I was getting into my car. I grinned. It was my best friend, Paige. "What's going on, Paige?"

"Hey, you have dinner plans? Ryan has his kids tonight, and I thought he should have some quality time with them," she said. She'd been dating Ryan Tujague for a few months now. Usually she blew off a guy after a couple of dates, so this could be serious. I was happy for her. She'd had a rather checkered past when it came to men.

I replied without missing a beat. "It's really insulting that you only call me when your boyfriend blows you off, you know." Paige and I met in college, and have been close ever since. Her favorite thing to do is give me shit—and over the years, she's gotten really good at it. I don't mind, because I know it's how she shows affection. So I give her shit right back. People listening to us talk would probably think we couldn't stand each other. Her sense of humor is a little warped, so we make a good pair. There's nothing quite like watching a bad movie with her over a few joints and a bottle of wine. She worked as a reporter for the *Times-Picayune,* and had even been nominated for a couple of Pulitzer prizes. One of the paper's biggest stars, she was remarkably humble about it. When people complimented her on something she'd written, she'd just dismiss it with a simple, "Just doing my job, but thanks."

She's also been a valuable resource for me with her access to the paper's morgue. Through her job, she met a lot of people in town—and for some reason, people liked to tell her things.

Since the storm, though, she'd expressed a lot of dissatisfaction with her job, and was threatening to quit every other day. I doubted she ever really would—she loved being a reporter. I couldn't imagine her doing anything else, to be honest with you. She loved New Orleans as much as I did, even though what she saw in the city while doing her job often broke her heart.

"But alas, my social calendar is open—which is really a rather sad commentary on me, isn't it? So instead of telling you to go fuck yourself, which is I what I should do, I'll be more than happy to let you treat me to Port of Call." I looked at my watch. It was just past one. "Say around six?"

"Great. I could really use a Port of Call burger." She let out a sigh. "I am having the shittiest day; you have no idea. I am about ready to kill someone—I'll tell you all about it at dinner." She moaned. "And I don't mean Ryan." She hung up.

I found the list of phone numbers Frillian had given me. I dialed Glynis Parrish's number. I stopped before pushing the "send" button.

They'd only hired me to find out who was sending the e-mails. They'd said nothing about confronting the person. Technically, my work was done. All I had to do was call Loren, let him know that the e-mails had been sent from Glynis's computer, and the job was over. Five thousand dollars for taking a meeting and spending about twenty minutes playing *Tourist Season* was really a pretty decent payday. I'd have to return the rest of the retainer they'd given me, but I could just drop a check to Loren in the mail.

But this had been way too easy, and that didn't sit right with me.

I couldn't get rid of the feeling there was more going on here than just these e-mails.

Just because Glynis's computer had been used to send the e-mails didn't mean that *she* had sent them. And they'd hired me to find out who had.

I might as well get her side of the story before turning everything over to Frillian. They had said everything was fine between them and Glynis. It hadn't quite rung true to me.

I hope I don't live to regret this, I thought to myself.

I hit the send button on my cell phone and it started dialing.

Maybe some day I'll learn.

CHAPTER THREE

As I MANEUVERED my car into a parking spot on Burgundy Street in the Quarter, I couldn't help but think, *Paul would have been so thrilled to meet Glynis Parrish.* When he was alive, we used to watch her television comedy series together every Thursday night. It was one of our favorite shows—even the episodes that weren't quite up to its usual standard of excellence were better than every other show on the air. She'd played a young woman just out of college who'd gotten a job at a sports magazine (obviously based on *Sports Illustrated)* and found herself in ridiculous situations almost every week.

The show had run almost seven years before Glynis pulled the plug, deciding to try to make it on the big screen. It was odd that she'd gotten a role in a movie being filmed in New Orleans after her ex-husband and his new wife had been so public about moving here. It could, of course, just be a coincidence. After all, before the failure of the levees, New Orleans had been actively courting film and television series. With our economy in such a shambles since the disaster, the return of "Hollywood South" had been a triumph for the city. I turned the car off and took a deep breath.

Paul.

It had been four years since he was killed, and while the passage of time had helped some, I wasn't completely over it yet. I sometimes wondered if I ever would get over it. My therapist thought I was making progress, but I wasn't quite so sure. Since his death, I'd dated a couple of guys, trying to move on with my life, but one after another, the relationships fizzled out. My therapist suggested that they failed because I kept myself emotionally unavailable to anyone new. It sounded like pseudo-psycho bullshit to me, and whenever he brought that up, it never failed to piss me off. I'd made myself emotionally available to my last boyfriend, hadn't I? And look how that had turned out. I'd started dating Allen, the guy who owned Bodytech, my gym, after the hurricane. It had gone well for a few months, but he'd eventually gotten back together with his ex. Things had been awkward at the gym for a while, but we'd somehow managed to get past it. My therapist thought that was a positive thing. I just figured it was easier to do than find a new gym.

As I locked my car, I took a deep breath and closed my eyes, willing the sadness away by focusing on the job at hand. *Maybe someday I'll be able to remember without getting sad,* I thought, as I firmly closed and locked that door in my mind.

Ah, progress.

I started walking towards the corner at Ursulines. The house Glynis was renting was between Burgundy and Dauphine, in the lower Quarter. This part of the Quarter was mostly residential and quiet. You'd never know that the madness of Bourbon Street was just a short walk away. I didn't expect Glynis to confess to sending the e-mails—that would be too much to hope for—and I decided to approach the entire subject in a non-threatening way. Frillian had claimed there was no animosity there, but I wanted to see how Glynis reacted to my questions. I wasn't even sure how my clients wanted this whole thing handled, but I needed to find out who else had access to Glynis's computer. As I rounded the corner, I decided the best way to play this was to be on *her* side, to act as if I believed she hadn't sent them.

The house she was renting was nice, but looked like nothing spectacular from the street. It was a one-story Creole cottage, painted a deep purple, with yellow shutters. There was no front yard; the house, like most in the French Quarter, was right on the sidewalk. It was a four-bay, with two sets of french doors and two sets of double-hung windows between them, their yellow shutters closed. Two large pots of trailing flowers hung on chains from the roof overhang.

I climbed up the short flight of stairs to the set of doors on the right—where the doorbell was—and stood a moment before ringing. Glynis had answered my call, and when I'd identified myself, she'd interrupted me, "Yes, yes, Freddy told me you might call. You might as well come over and let's get this over with." She hadn't sounded pleased, but I could hardly blame her.

I took a deep breath and knocked. I heard footsteps moving toward the front door.

It swung open and I found myself looking down at a small, rotund woman with reddish-blonde hair. She was wearing a gray T-shirt with the *Make levees not war* slogan on the front, and a pair of black jeans. Her pale round face was covered with freckles, and she smiled, revealing slightly crooked teeth. Her greenish-gray eyes lit up, taking her from slightly plain to pretty. "Yes?"

"I'm Chanse MacLeod," I replied. "Here to see Ms. Parrish?"

"Yes, yes, we're expecting you." She held out a small hand for me to shake. Her hand was soft, warm, and a little damp. "I'm Rosemary Martin, Glynis's personal assistant. Won't you come in?" She stood aside to let me pass, and I walked into the sparsely furnished front room. A couple of wingback chairs faced a fireplace on the far wall, with a table in between them. There was a faded Oriental rug on the floor, and the walls were bare except for some Audubon reproductions. She closed the french doors and turned the key in the lock. "I've never met a private investigator before," she said, looking me up and down, still smiling. "Your work must be terribly exciting." She giggled—a surprisingly girlish sound for a woman I judged to be in her early to mid-thirties. Her voice also sounded younger than I would have expected, almost like that of a thirteen-year-old. She stared at me expectantly.

"Not really," I replied, giving her a little smile in return. "It's not like it is on television.Usually, it's quite boring."

"I don't believe you," she replied, the smile never wavering for a moment. "I used to want to be a private eye when I was young." She laughed. "If you can imagine that. I wanted to be one of Charlie's Angels." She shrugged, a tiny movement. "Glynis is in her study. Come this way."

I followed her down a hallway that ran the length of the house, and she knocked lightly on the second door before opening it. "Glynis? Mr. MacLeod is here."

I walked into a beautiful room painted a dark emerald green. The fixtures were all brass, and the hardwood floors gleamed. A brass chandelier cast light into every corner of the room. The furniture looked expensive, but comfortable and lived in. Glynis Parrish was seated on a green and gold brocade sofa, the day's newspaper spread out all around her on the cushions and the floor in front of her. She folded the section she'd been reading and let it drop to the floor. On the coffee table in front of the sofa stood a golden statue of a winged woman holding a globe—an Emmy award. Right next to it was a closed MacBook Pro laptop computer. She rose, and held out her right hand. "It's nice to meet you, Mr. MacLeod," she said, giving me a warm smile.

"Call me Chanse," I said, shaking her small hand.

She, like Freddy and Jillian, was diminutive. She couldn't have been taller than five feet, and her figure was equally small, and almost girlish. She was wearing a very tight, low-cut tank top that emphasized her large breasts and deep cleavage. Her waist was small, her hips flaring slightly in her tight low-rise jeans. She was barefoot, her toenails painted red. Her dark brown hair was pulled back in a pony-tail, and she was wearing just a hint of blush. Her eyes were slanted, almost cat-like, and they glittered green in the light from the chandelier.

She applied no pressure to the handshake, her hand limp and dry in my much bigger paw. There were dark circles under her eyes, and she looked tired. Her chin was dotted with small red pimples, and after I released her hand, she self-consciously ran her hand over her chin. Her nails looked ragged and chewed. "Please, have a seat. And call me Glynis." Her green eyes flashed at me. She plopped back down on the couch. She folded her legs underneath her. She saw me looking at her Emmy and smiled. "You can pick it up, if you'd like. Everyone always wants to." She shrugged. "Go ahead."

What the hell, I thought, bending down and hefting it in my right hand, grasping the winged woman around the waist. It was surprisingly heavy. On a gold band around the base were engraved the words *Outstanding Achievement by a Lead Actress in a Comedy Series: Glynis Parrish in SPORTSDESK.* I set it back down. "Thank you."

"Like I said, everyone wants to do that. The great aura of

an award, I suppose. But then again, I take it with me every-where." The corners of her mouth lifted a little bit, her eye-brows arching up in self-mockery. "I was nominated seven times, but only won once." She shrugged. "After winning, it didn't seem quite as important as it did all the times I lost. Please, have a seat."

I sat down in a green wingback chair, sinking several inches down into it. She gave me a smile. "I don't really know why Freddy wanted me to meet you, or why he needs a private eye, but I can never say no to him."

"Did you need anything else, Glynis?" Rosemary asked from the doorway.

"May I offer you something to drink, Chanse? I have prac-tically everything," Glynis asked me in a pleasant tone. "The bar is quite well-stocked."

"I'm fine, thank you."

"I'll call you, Rosemary, if we need anything," she said, dismissing her assistant without even looking at her. I heard the door shut behind me, and the sound of footsteps reced-ing to the back of the house. She closed her eyes for a mo-ment, her face expressionless, then opened them and smiled again. "I'm not having a good day, I must apologize to you in advance." She sighed. "What can I help you with, Chanse? What's going on with Freddy?"

I cleared my throat. "Well, Freddy and Jillian—" it took a conscious effort not to say *Frillian*—"have hired me to look into something, and I'm hoping you can help me out." I made my voice sound as sincere as I could. Granted, I wasn't in her league as an actor, but I could play a part too.

"What's this all about?" she asked, rubbing her eyes. "I have to admit, when Freddy called and was so mysterious about my talking to a private eye, I agreed to see you more about satisfying my own curiosity than anything else . . ."

She shook her head, the ponytail flying. "We've been divorced for years now. And while we get along better than can be expected under the circumstances, I don't mind admitting that I'm sick to death of talking about Freddy and his new wife." Her voice dripped with scorn as she said the last three words. "I'm tired of being defined as the sad little wife he left for the glamorous superstar."

I put the file folder containing the printouts on the coffee table. "Someone has been sending Freddy threatening e-mails."

She looked me directly in the eyes. "And Freddy thinks I may have sent them?" She threw her head back and laughed the way she had on her show. "Oh, the arrogance! Some things never change. I guess he thinks I'm just sitting around pining away for him." The catlike eyes rolled. "Trust me, Mr. MacLeod—Chanse—most days I don't give Freddy and his wife a first thought, let alone a second. That was a hundred years ago, it seems. We've all moved on—even though the tabloids love the idea that I'm pining away. I can assure you that is most definitely not the case." She scratched her chin again. "In fact, I'm seeing someone else now—I won't say who, because we're not ready to go public with our relationship. I'm sure you can understand why. I'm tired of being tabloid fodder. Was I upset when he left me for someone else? Of course I was! Who wouldn't be? But I *have* moved on."

Considering her reluctance to refer to Jillian by name, I found that a little hard to believe. I cleared my throat and plunged forward. "Well, unfortunately, I've traced the e-mails to the computer they were sent from." I leaned forward and removed the receipt from the folder and handed it to her. "They were sent from a Mac you bought." I gestured at the laptop. "Is that your only computer?"

"But that's impossible." She took the receipt and looked at it, then set it back down on top of the folder. Her eyes widened, her forehead creased. She shook her head. "I mean, that's a copy of my receipt, but I can assure you I haven't been e-mailing Freddy threats—or e-mailing him about anything, frankly. If I want to talk to him, I call him." She made a helpless gesture. "I mean, yes, I have a website and I have e-mail, but I don't usually use the computer for much of anything." She shrugged again. "Most of the e-mail comes from my website, and someone in my publicist's office takes care of all of that for me, answering it, sending out au- tographed pictures, things like that." She picked up the folder and opened it. She pulled out one of the printouts and squinted at it. "This isn't my e-mail account." She put the folder back down with distaste.

I hadn't expected her to admit to sending the e-mails, so I went ahead with my game plan. "I didn't think so, honestly. Who all has access to your computer?"

"Well, it's always here in the house—I never take it on set with me. So, anyone who comes into the house could access it—but why would anyone do such a thing? That doesn't make any sense. I mean, why my computer?" Her eyebrows came together and her face reddened a bit. "That's simply intolerable."

"Someone could be trying to make trouble for you," I replied, injecting sympathy into my voice. "Who regularly comes into the house?"

"Well, Rosemary, obviously. She's here every day, and sometimes stays over." She rubbed her eyes, and leaned for- ward. "My housekeeper, Darlene, comes in three times a week and is here all day—usually when I'm on the set. She does the grocery shopping and makes meals as well as cleaning. My trainer, Brett Colby, comes by here when I'm not working. I have a massage therapist—Charity—who comes in twice a week. And of course, my director and cast mates stop by every once in a while." She shrugged. "I'm not much for entertaining, frankly, but I guess any one of them could get on my computer without my knowing it. But why would they send . . ." she stopped, picking up the folder again and opening it. She paged through the e-mails. "These e-mails are absolutely vile." She tossed the folder back down on the table, her face showing her distaste. She narrowed her eyes. "I most certainly didn't write or send them. If they came from my computer, someone else had to have sent them." She stood up. "ROSEMARY!" she bellowed, making me jump. She smiled at me. "Sorry."

The door opened and Rosemary stepped into the room. "Yes. Did you need something?"

Glynis stood up in a fluid motion. "Rosemary, you haven't been using my computer for anything, have you?"

"Of course not!" Rosemary's face reddened.

"If you're lying to me—"

"No, no, no!" Rosemary cowered, stepping back into the doorway.

I stared at her. She acted like she was *afraid* of Glynis. I looked over at Glynis. Her hands were on her hips and she was breathing hard, her face red. Her eyes narrowed as she took a few steps forward. Rosemary visibly shrank. Glynis's voice continued to rise as she spoke. "Have you seen anyone—Darlene, Brett, Charity, *anyone*—using my computer?"

"No!"

"I'm going to need to speak to each of them." I interrupted.

Glynis's head whipped back around to me. Her entire face relaxed into a smile. "Of course. I want this matter cleared up just as much as Freddy does, I'm sure." Without looking at her, she commanded, "Rosemary, get their phone numbers together for Chanse." She sank back down on her sofa. She waved her right hand in a fluttery motion. "I'm getting a headache. Rosemary, after you get Chanse the numbers, would you mind showing him out?" It was an effective dismissal. I thanked her for her time and followed Rosemary into the hallway. Rosemary shut the door behind us. "Go wait in the front room, and I'll join you shortly," she whispered, and hurried off down the hall.

I walked back to the front room and sat down in one of the chairs. I opened the folder and started paging through the e-mails. The next step, I figured, was to make a calendar of the dates and times the e-mails were sent—and compare that with the household schedule. Granted, that was assuming Glynis hadn't sent them herself. I closed my eyes and went over the entire interview again.

Was she telling me the truth?

I opened my eyes as Rosemary came back into the room. She handed me a piece of paper with the names and numbers of the rest of Glynis's staff printed clearly on it. I smiled at her. "She seems like a rather difficult woman to work for."

"Oh, no, she's just having a bad day." Rosemary smiled at me. "She gets these horrible migraines—suffers terribly from them. Today is one of her bad days. Most of the time, she's an absolute doll—very kind and thoughtful. One of the best employers I've ever had."

I stood up. "How long have you been with her?"

"Since she came to New Orleans." Rosemary pushed an errant lock of hair back from her forehead.

"So, about two weeks?"

Her eyes widened. "Two weeks? Oh, no, she's been here for about two months now. I was hired about a week or so before then—her former assistant had quit to have a baby—

and I put the house together for her, found the housekeeper and everyone else." She looked down. "It's really an honor to work for her. I've been a fan for years." She bridled a bit. "She says she wants me to come back to California with her when the movie wraps."

"Wow." I smiled at her. "Are you going to go?"

"I've always wanted to live in California," she said wistfully. "And it's a wonderful opportunity for me." She took the piece of paper back from me and pulled a pen out of her pocket. "Let me give you my cell number. You can call me anytime. I'm at your disposal." She wrote it down. "I'll let everyone know you're going to be getting in touch with them, and that it's okay for them to talk to you."

"I appreciate that." I folded the paper and slid it into the folder. I walked over to the front door.

"It was nice meeting you," she said, offering me her hand again. "And remember, call me if you need anything, okay?"

All the way back to my apartment, I replayed the whole interview in my head. Rosemary seemed okay, but I didn't quite buy the "she's a great employer" routine. It seemed a little rehearsed—and the way Glynis had acted toward her made it seem like bullshit. Granted, maybe Glynis *was* having a bad day—she'd said she was—but something my landlady told me once about another woman in her social circle kept coming back to me.

Barbara Castlemaine moved in the stratosphere of New Orleans society—and had been one of my first clients. I'd handled something for her with discretion, and we'd become friends over the years. It had been at a party she'd given at her Garden District mansion, and after I 'd been talking to this perfectly charming woman for nearly an hour, Barbara had peeled me away from her and in a low voice warned me away from her. "She's a horrible woman," she'd insisted over my protests. "You can always tell what kind of a person someone is by how they treat the help—and she treats hers like garbage."

Glynis had certainly treated Rosemary that way. I wondered if she was that way with her other employees.

I called Loren to check in with him, see how he wanted me to proceed—or if he wanted me to. I got his voice-mail and left a rather detailed message about my progress so far—tracing the computer and so forth. I closed with, "Unless I hear otherwise, I'm going to proceed with checking out the people who had access to Glynis Parrish's computer."

I left messages for Glynis's posse, then sat down at my desk and turned on my own computer. I opened a spread-sheet, and started logging in the dates and times the e-mails had been sent. It didn't take long for the pattern to start to emerge. All of them had been sent in the early afternoons—and always on Mondays, Wednesdays, and Fridays.

I started reading them again. Glynis had been right about one thing—the e-mails were all vile. They all alluded in some way to something Freddy had done—how his public persona was not who he really was. *You act like such a do-gooder,* one taunted, *but those of us who know what you're really like know better. You might be able to fool the world with your St. Freddy act, but I know the real Freddy. How do you sleep at night?*

What on earth did that mean?

I logged onto the Internet and did a search for Freddy Bliss—and was promptly rewarded with over a hundred thousand hits. I moaned. It would take me forever to wade my way through all of them—and Glynis and Jillian probably had just as many on-line mentions. I sighed, and started clicking on links. A lot of them I was able to dismiss out of hand—movie reviews, fan sites, etc. What I was interested in was gossip. But even that wasn't much help. Outside of his pre-Glynis romances with any number of actresses, Freddy appeared to have lived a fairly blameless life. There were no drunk driving citations, no crazy or errant behaviors in public. He was in his early thirties—close to me in age, actually—and had been born and raised in Newton, Kansas. He'd gone to a small university, Emporia State, for a couple of years, taking courses in theater, before he dropped out and headed out to Los Angeles to try to make it as a movie star. He'd guested on some TV shows, but his big break came in a small role in a film called *Separate Vacations,* about a married couple who always took separate vacations. He played a beach bum who seduced the wife, and had all but stolen the movie. After that, he signed with a major agency and moved on to starring roles. His marriage to the reigning television queen of sitcoms had been a big story—although they hadn't been called Frynis or Gleddy. Despite being called a "golden couple" by the gossips, they hadn't been big enough to become a one-word entity. That story, though, had been eclipsed by the affair with Jillian—and the messy divorce that followed.

I stood up and stretched. It was just past five, and I wanted to take a quick shower before heading down to meet Paige for dinner. My neck was sore from hunching over the computer screen. I tried calling the people on the list again, but once again didn't get anyone. I made a mental note to check in with Rosemary again after dinner, to see if she had in fact called them all for me.

At five forty-five, I pulled into a parking spot just past St. Philip Street on Burgundy. It was about a six-block walk to Port of Call from there, but my standard rule of parking in the French Quarter is to always grab the first parking spot I saw—there may not be another one in the entire neighborhood. And there's nothing I hate more than driving around trying to find one. Besides, I always enjoy strolling through the Quarter—and Paige would be late as she always was. I decided to walk up Ursulines past Glynis's house—it was on the way. I got out and walked down to the corner at Ursulines, and turned right. It was already dark, and the street lamps were casting their glow over the sidewalk. There wasn't another soul to be seen anywhere. I looked over across the street. The gas lights on the front of Glynis's house were flickering. There was no sign of light behind the closed shutters. I glanced at my watch—five fifty-two. I shrugged and started walking down the street.

I was about halfway down the block when Glynis's front door opened. Out of the corner of my eye I saw a man step out and slam it loudly. I stopped walking and looked over to watch. He came down the front steps in a hurry, almost stumbling on the bottom step and having to grab the metal rail to keep from falling onto the sidewalk. He was wearing a loose-fitting pair of jeans, and a hooded purple sweatshirt with LSU emblazoned on the front in bright gold. The jeans hung down low enough for me to see his lower abdomen and the waistband of his underwear. The hood was pulled up over his head, hiding his hair. It was also pulled down low in the front, covering the top of his face. Something flashed in my brain—*I know that guy*—as I watched him, trying to remember who it was and where I knew him from. There was something about the build, the way he carried himself, that struck a familiar chord.

New Orleans is a small town, and that happens a lot. Everyone looks familiar, but when I see them out of a familiar context, at first I blank on who they are and where I know them from. I once had a long conversation with a guy in a bar, never once giving away that I had no idea who he was or where I knew him from. Two days later, when I went into Café Envie, one of my regular Quarter hangouts, there he was, working behind the counter—and thankfully, wearing a nametag.

This guy across the street didn't seem to notice me, and I was just starting to think I was mistaken when he reached the bottom of the steps and turned to walk towards the river. In that moment, he was directly under a street lamp, and I did a double take.

It was Freddy Bliss.

I opened my mouth to shout hello before crossing the street, but before I could form the word in my throat, he started walking up the street at a very fast pace, breaking into a run when he got to the corner at Dauphine. I stared after him until I lost him in the darkness.

I glanced back at the house. It was silent, no sign of life there other than the gas lights. *That's odd,* I thought, *what the hell was Freddy doing there?* A cold chill went down my spine as I remembered my call to Loren. Surely Loren had passed the information along . . . had Freddy gone over to confront her?

You might be fooling the world with your do-gooder act, but I know what you really are.

I shuddered in the chill evening air.

I laughed to myself a little bit, trying to shake the feeling. I crossed the street and stared at the front of the house for a moment. I debated whether I should knock or not.

The house was completely silent.

A dog barked, and I jumped.

Get a grip, Chanse. Besides, it's really none of your business, is it now, what Freddy was doing there?

I shrugged, put it out of my head, and headed to Port of Call.

CHAPTER FOUR

PORT OF CALL is on the edge of the French Quarter on the corner of Dauphine and Esplanade streets.

I was on Dauphine about halfway down the block between Barracks and Esplanade when I was assaulted by one of my favorite smells in New Orleans: burgers, being cooked over an open flame. I stopped for a moment, standing there on the sidewalk, my eyes partly closed, savoring the smell. My knees got weak, my stomach growled, and my mouth filled with saliva. There's nothing I love more than hamburgers—and if they're cooked over an open flame or charcoal, so much the better.

Every publication and website having to do with New Orleans always ranks Port of Call as one of the best places in the city to get a burger. They also have great drinks.

I was hoping there wouldn't be a wait—the majority of tourists who'd come in for Mardi Gras were probably already on their way home, nursing their hangovers and swearing off liquor permanently. I crossed my fingers as I reached the corner, *please, no line, please no line.* I hadn't realized how hungry I was until I got a whiff of the grill, and now I was starving. As I walked around the corner, I breathed a sigh of relief—not only was there not a line; but, miracle of miracles, Paige was sitting on the steps leading to the door, puffing on a cigarette.

Paige is an unrepentant smoker; I'd finally managed to quit, although the desire for a butt never really went away. Louisiana had finally passed a law about smoking in restaurants, something to do with how much of the place's income derived from food vs. liquor . . . after which Paige swore she would never eat anywhere that wasn't legally considered a bar rather than a restaurant.

Her protest didn't last long. It was harder to swear off Port of Call than it was to quit smoking.

She stood up when she saw me come around the corner, and flicked her cigarette into the street with a practiced snap of her fingers. She was wearing a rather nice knee-length black skirt, a red silk blouse, and black high-heeled shoes. If given her preference, she would dress more like a gypsy, but her new editor at the *Times-Picayune,* whom she referred to as "that bitch Coralie" had imposed a dress code on the reporters . . . which was also driving her crazy.

"More professional, my fat white ass," she'd snarled when she told me about it. "Does that stupid bitch really think it makes me a goddamned better writer if I dress the way she wants me to? God, I hate her." Paige's shoulder-length red hair with blonde streaks looked tangled, and her lipstick had rubbed off on her cigarette butt. The most striking thing about Paige was her eyes—they were mismatched: one green, one blue. "Christ, what's wrong?" She asked as she presented her cheek for me to kiss. "I got here before you? I am surely slipping in my old age."

I showed her my watch. "You're even early."

She ran a hand through her hair. "Oh, dear lord. It surely must be the end times." She laughed and shrugged. "Well, these days I can't get out of the office fast enough. That bitch

Coralie was definitely in rare form today." Paige's longtime editor, Joe LeSeuer, had retired after the hurricane and left New Orleans. "Maybe the book will sell for a million dollars and I can tell her where she can shove her fucking dress code." Ever since we graduated from college, Paige had been puttering around with a romance novel called *The Belle of New Orleans*, set during the War of 1812. A few months after the flood, she'd taken all of her accrued vacation, grabbed her laptop, and rented a cabin in the Tennessee mountains for eight weeks, determined to finally finish the thing.

Oddly enough, though, once she got up there she started writing a new book called *Head Above Water*, an autobiographical novel about her experiences during the hurricane and the weeks thereafter. "Once I started it, I couldn't stop writing it," she'd confided to me when she returned to the city, "It was like it took on a life of its own." I'd tried reading it, but it was too painful for me. Everything the city had been through—and was still going through—was still too fresh, raw, and painful for me to relive it all through Paige's writing. She was damned good—too good. She'd rewritten and revised it several times, and now it was in the hands of several high-powered literary agents in New York, all of whom were interested in it. It had become a kind of mantra for her: *When the book sells for a million dollars, I am telling Coralie where she can put her dress code and I am walking out the door.*

She rolled her eyes. "Get this—she wants me to try to be more 'warm and fuzzy' in my pieces. Warm and fucking fuzzy!"

"What did you say?" Much as I hated to admit it, I found the endless power struggle between the two women highly amusing.

"I told her I worked for a newspaper the last time I checked, not fucking Hallmark." She sighed. "Get this—she put out a jar. Every time someone uses bad language"—she made air quotes around the words—"you have to put a quarter in the jar, and she's going to use the money to go toward the office Christmas party." She gave me an evil smile. "I got up, put a twenty in there, and gave her the finger."

"She's going to fire you one of these days."

"I can only hope."

We entered the dimly lit restaurant and took a table in a quiet corner. It wasn't crowded, and our waitress looked somewhat tired as she took our drink orders. She looked as if she hadn't slept in days, and most likely, had been working double shifts throughout Carnival. We went ahead and ordered our burgers as well. After the waitress moved away from us, Paige gave me a wicked glance. "Thanks for having dinner with me." She sighed. "After the day I've had, I needed to be around someone with a brain."

I couldn't resist. "Good thing Ryan's with the kids, then—since he obviously doesn't have one."

"Because someone with a brain obviously wouldn't date me. Right. I get it." She rolled her eyes. "When do you leave for Texas? That's coming up, isn't it?" The waitress placed our iced teas in front of us and scooted away.

"Not for a few more weeks." I hesitated and bit my lip. I always talked about my cases with Paige—and she often used her resources at the paper to get information to help me out.

"That bitch Coralie started harping on me getting an interview with Frillian again." Paige didn't seem to notice my hesitation, wrapped up as she was in her own anger. She took a sip of her tea, grimaced, and added a pack of artificial sweetener to it. "Like it's that goddamned easy, like I haven't tried everything I can think of! She's so stupid, I guess she probably thinks I can just drop by their place sometime and they'd be thrilled to see me." She sighed. "I swear to God, she must have gotten her journalism degree online or from a mail order catalogue. If I'd only known she was going to turn into such a power hungry bitch, I'd have taken the damned job myself when they offered it to me."

Paige had often theorized that part of the reason Coralie seemed to pick her out for "special" treatment was because management had offered her the job first. Paige had turned it down. She smacked her forehead. "Stupid, stupid, stupid. But then no one had the slightest idea she'd turn into such a fucking Nazi."

This was just great. I cursed the goddamned confidentiality agreement—even though I knew I could trust her. She'd be furious when she found out I was working for them and didn't tell her. I made a mental note to ask them the next time I saw them to give her the interview. The worst thing they could do was say no, right? And I owed Paige many favors. "I don't see what the big deal is," I said. I had wondered how I could get her to talk to me about Frillian without telling her I was working for them. What a stroke of luck that bitch Coralie had opened the lines of communication for me. "I mean, yeah, I get it, they're movie stars, but so what. Nobody even talks about them anymore, you know? They're just part of the city now."

"Try telling that to that bitch Coralie," Paige groused, squeezing her lemon into the tall glass of tea. "And besides, you know damned well that celebrities are about the only thing people want to hear about on the news anymore. Every time Britney Spears farts, it makes *CNN Headline News.* If you ask me, it's all a big government-controlled conspiracy. Who cares if we're in a stupid war or the economy is going into the toilet, as long as we know that Paris Hilton flashed her cooch getting out of her Ferrari? Or that some other useless waste of oxygen they've decided we should care about went into rehab again, or is having a baby, or getting a divorce? So once again, she's got a wild hair about an exclusive interview, and of course I'm the one stuck trying to get the damned story. If I ever see Joe again, I'm going to kill him for retiring and sticking me with that bitch."

"It was rather inconsiderate of him."

"To say the least." She sighed again. "I called Sandy Carter today, again, and she promised to see what she could do."

"Sandy Carter?"

"Oh for God's sake, Chanse. Do you ever listen to *anything* I say to you?" She gave me a look. "Sandy Carter is the one working with Freddy Bliss on Project Rebuild—you know, the one who does all the work while he runs around raising money and getting publicity. You've *met* her, you big idiot."

"Oh, yes." I'd met Sandy Carter the first time before the storm, when she'd been running for an at-large seat on the city council. Her campaign had been all about cleaning up the corruption at city hall—which meant her campaign was doomed to failure from the beginning. A lot of snide remarks had circulated in the media back in the fall of 2005 about corruption in Louisiana, about how the federal government shouldn't give us money because our politicians would just steal it all. Of course, in the years since, the vast majority of the politicians who'd spread that story had all been caught in some kind of ethics or corruption scandal—because of course, there was NO corruption in any other state or the federal government. The only difference between New Orleans politics and that of the rest of the country is that we *expect* our politicians to be corrupt. We may be jaded, but I think it's better than being naïve.

And I'd been right with Sandy Carter—she'd been defeated resoundingly, since no one trusts a politician who claims not to be corrupt. I'd liked her when I met her, and had voted for her. She was a short woman with short hair she'd let go white and a booming laugh that filled a room. She was full of energy, and once she'd married off her youngest daughter, she'd thrown herself into making changes in the city.

She was always raising money for this group or that group, talked frankly about everything, and had no qualms about calling, for example, the esteemed U.S. senator from Metairie a "complete jerk and moron not fit to work as a trash collector" in an op-ed piece when Mr. Family Values's long-term patronage of a prostitute was exposed.

After the flood, she'd helped organize a group of women to campaign for levee board reform; to hold the Army Corps of Engineers accountable for the city's destruction; and had testified in front of Congress in one of the interminable and endless hearings on what had happened. I'd met her a few times since then—my landlady and employer, Barbara Castlemaine, was one of her dearest friends—and I liked her more each time.

"Do you think she'll come through for you?" I asked

"Well, if anyone can, it's Sandy." Paige smiled at our waitress as she placed our plates in front of us, and then refilled our tea glasses. "She says that Freddy and Jillian are really committed to the city, and if I can promise that the focus of the interview will be on Project Rebuild, they'll probably agree to it." She snorted. "It actually kind of pissed me off—

like I'd ask them anything about their personal lives! I could give a rat's ass why Freddy left his ex-wife . . . she's in town, you know."

I took a bite of my burger and sighed in delight. "Who's in town?" I asked after I swallowed, even though I already knew. When Paige was on a roll, it was best to let her have her head.

"Freddy's ex-wife, Glynis Parrish. The TV star?" She rolled her eyes. "Honestly, Chanse, are you sure you're gay? It's pretty sad when a straight woman knows more about movie stars then a gay man. I bet I could stop any other gay man on the street and he could tell you everything there is to know about Glynis and Freddy's divorce."

I laughed. "Well, I wouldn't take the bet."

"Anyway, Glynis is in town making a movie—how weird is that?" She shook her head. "I'm waiting for that bitch Coralie to ask me to interview her next . . . although come to think of it, she probably will want me to interview Glynis to go along with the piece about Frillian. I'm sure she could give a rat's ass about Project Rebuild, the bitch." She rubbed her eyes. "WHY on God's green earth they gave her the city editor job I will never understand. She must have slept with someone." She swallowed a mouthful of potato. "Anyway . . . yeah. But you're probably sick to death of me bitching about the paper."

"I never get tired of listening to you bitch." I gave her a winning smile.

"And guess who else is in town?" Paige rolled her eyes. "Jillian's mother, Shirley Harris." She peered at me. "You do know who she is, don't you?"

"Yeah. She did a bunch of musicals in the fifties and six-ties, right?"

Paige started laughing. "Well, you got the gay musical

gene at the very least." She shook her head. "She actually called the paper, *wanting* to be interviewed . . ."

"I bet Coralie was all over that." So Jillian had been right on that score.

"Yeah, right—that's what I thought too." Paige moaned. "And they put her through to *me*—which reminds me, I need to kill the dumb bitch at the switchboard—so I put her on hold, called Coralie, and said, 'Hey, I got a star on the line who wants to be interviewed, should I set it up?' and I literally thought she was going to have to change her panties— and then I told her who it was."

"She wasn't interested?"

"I should say not." Paige sat up straight, and did a dead-on imitation of Coralie. "Oh, no, Paige, we couldn't possibly do an interview with Shirley Harris. Don't you know *anything?* Jillian and her mother are not on speaking terms. If we do an interview with her, we'd *never* get Jillian to talk to us, and that's the fish we want to fry."

"She called Jillian a fish?"

"And you wonder why I want to quit?" Paige sighed. "I felt sorry for Shirley, to tell you the truth. I mean, I could tell she'd been drinking—she was slurring her words, you know—and to have to go back to her and tell her that we weren't interested . . . poor thing." She rubbed her eyes. "I couldn't do it. So I agreed to meet her. Tomorrow, at her hotel."

"Where is she staying?" I hoped my interest seemed friendly rather than curious.

"She's registered at the Ritz-Carlton under—get this—the name 'Sally Bowles.'"

The name seemed familiar. "Sally Bowles?"

She groaned. "Liza played her in *Cabaret*. I swear, you're going to lose your gay card if you keep this up."

"You think Coralie will run the piece once you write it?"

She snorted. "Yeah, right. Good one." She pushed her plate away with a groan. "I'm going to need an hour on the elliptical machine to get rid of this meal tomorrow. Something else to look forward to." She exhaled and leaned back in her chair. "So, what's going on with you? How was your Carnival? Sorry I missed you yesterday in the Quarter—I dragged Ryan down to the Fruit Loop, but we couldn't find you." She laughed. "Ryan was pretty popular with the gay boys."

"He's a good-looking guy." Ryan was the older brother of our friend Blaine Tujague. He and Paige had gone on a date once before, when he was freshly divorced, and Paige had had one of the most miserable experiences of her long and storied history of dating tragedies, although I forget the details. I wasn't exactly sure how she'd managed to hook up with Ryan again—there was some vague story about running into him at a party and they'd hit it off the second time around. She even liked his kids, which was saying a lot, as kids usually made her uncomfortable. They'd been dating for several months now, which was a record for Paige. She never said much about Ryan's ex-wife, and I delicately never brought her up. I had met the ex-wife once, before the divorce, at a party Blaine and his partner had thrown in their house across the park from my house —and had disliked her immediately. "What did you guys wear for costumes?"

"I went as Eleanor of Aquitaine, and Ryan went as my court jester." She gave me a sly wink. "Just black and white tights, black and white boots, and we used body paint on his torso."

I whistled. "No wonder he was so popular."

"Well, we're never doing that again. It took forever to put on, and it was even more of a pain to take it off." She laughed. "And there was no way I was letting him ruin my sheets."

I held up my hand. "Sorry. Way too much information."

"Give me a break." She rolled her eyes. "After all the times I've had to listen to your adventures, you're going all squeamish on me now?" She raised an eyebrow. "And I've never really given you the gory details." She pursed her lips. "A lady never tells." She burst into laughter, which I joined in.

"So, are you and Ryan getting serious now? Wedding bells around the corner. I can see you now, all covered in white polyester, with a crown of white lilies.."

She tossed her napkin at me. "Oh, for God's sake, shut the fuck up."

"Hitting a little close to home?"

She shrugged. "We're just having a good time, taking things slow. I don't have a lot of experience with relationships, and he's a good guy. I don't want to rush things. If it's meant to be, it'll evolve. But I do like him, Chanse. I like him a lot. It kind of scares me."

"Yeah, I know what you mean." I reached over and took her hand. "There should be a manual or something."

She burst out laughing. "You won't even read your cell phone manual."

"Bitch." We both laughed.

"So, did you have fun over Carnival?"

"Yeah, I really did. It's nice—" I cut myself off. I was about to say *it's nice to have fun again,* but I was afraid I would jinx things. Stupid, that was the kind of thing my mother used to always say when I was a kid. I'd have to remember to bring that up with my therapist. I took a deep breath. "It's nice to have fun again." There, I'd said it. Let the universe do its worst.

"Yeah." She scratched her nose. "I know what you mean." She looked around the half-empty dining room. "You know, I can barely remember what it was like *before* anymore. Isn't that weird?"

"No, not really." I thought for a moment. "It seems like, oh, I don't know . . . sometimes when I think back about Paul and me—this is going to sound crazy, I know, so don't roll your eyes at me—it seems almost like it was a dream, like it all happened to someone else, or that it happened a million years ago."

"Kind of like the flood marked the end of an era." She nodded. "I know. Sometimes I think that way too. My therapist—" she stopped herself and blushed.

"You're seeing a therapist?" I hadn't known that, and it kind of surprised me that she hadn't told me.

"Oh, yeah. I started when I came back from my trip with the book done." She nodded her head, her messy hair bouncing. "I knew I couldn't handle it all on my own, and it wasn't like I could dump everything on my friends, because they had their own shit to deal with. So I started seeing someone. It's helped some, and she's given me some really good things to think about, things I need to work on." She started playing with her tea glass. "You're still seeing yours, right? How's that going?"

"Listen to us," I said, avoiding that one, "comparing notes on our therapists."

"Yeah, well." She shrugged and glanced at her watch.

"Need to be somewhere?"

"Ryan's coming over after he takes his kids home." She smothered a grin. "And don't get all smart-ass on me either, bub."

"Maybe we could all have dinner sometime."

"That would be cool." She smiled at me. "I do like him,

Chanse. Hard to believe he's the same tool I went out with all those years ago—but maybe he was just in a bad place from the divorce. I don't know."

"I'm glad." And I was. For a long while, I'd never quite understood why Paige had so much trouble with men; if I were straight, I'd be crazy about her, and I couldn't grasp why so many men seemed to be unable to see everything she had to offer. She was funny, caring, and smart. She'd had a rough time growing up, with an alcoholic mother who had a revolving door to her bedroom. She didn't speak to her mother anymore—hadn't in years, although I knew her mother tried. I was at her apartment once when her mom had called and left a long, whining message on her answering machine.

Paige, who'd been in the middle of pouring a glass of wine, had paused, her face tight and drained of color, until the message ended . . . and then went on as though nothing had happened. She refused to discuss her mother, and the only reason I knew anything at all about their relationship was because Paige had collapsed in a paroxysm of alcohol, grief, and guilt one night shortly after I'd returned from the evacuation.

And after that, I completely understood her problems with men.

It was also why I was glad to hear she was seeing a therapist.

"And you're going to find the right guy someday." She smiled at me and stopped me from giving the waitress my credit card, fumbling in her purse and handing over hers instead. "I want to treat, okay?" After the waitress had gone away, she went on, "You know you will, right?"

"Yeah." I grinned back at her. "I know. Someday my prince will come, right? And next time, let's hope I don't screw it up the way I did with Paul." I hesitated. Paige and Paul had been very close, but her smile didn't falter. "But sometimes I wonder if what Paul and I had was all that."

She signed the charge slip and stood up. "You and Paul were good together, Chanse, and he loved you so very very much." She slipped her arm through mine. "I used to envy you and Paul—and you used to piss me off because I was so afraid you'd screw it up."

I froze for a moment and took a deep breath.

"I'm sorry. I didn't mean that the way it sounded." She squeezed my arm.

"It's okay." I forced a smile, even though my heart was pounding fast. *Think about something else, think about something happy, think about the beach and the warm breeze and the gentle waves coming up to the shore. What happened to Paul wasn't your fault. You just never had the chance to work things out, and she didn't mean anything by it, and she's right, you did almost blow it with him, not just once but many many times.* "Seriously. I'm okay."

We walked out of the restaurant, and I gave her a big hug on the sidewalk. "Call me tomorrow," she instructed. "I know you're anxiously awaiting the next Coralie update."

I laughed and made sure she was in her car, and that it started, before I waved and started walking down Dauphine Street to my car. I was kind of glad I had to walk six blocks—it was a start, working off the meal.

I was also happy that I'd managed to avoid going down into the dark place. The therapy was working, after all. In the past, I wasn't even able to think of Paul without starting on the downward spiral that left me aching and feeling empty. Now, I could remember him without that happening—although it still wasn't easy. But I was healing from everything—Paul's death, the hurricane, and the evacuation.

My life was going along just fine—actually, it was better than fine. So what if I was alone? When the time was right and I was ready, someone would come along. I could try to get Paige the interview she needed to get that bitch Coralie off her back. Maybe I'd invite Paige and Ryan over for dinner. I could make dinner for us at—

I started laughing at myself. Listen to me, planning an evening with the happy couple! I started whistling. It was a beautiful night, the air just warm enough to be pleasant. The sky was full of clouds, glowing pink from the reflection of all the neon on Bourbon Street. I saw a tabby cat run across the street, and that made me smile a little bit too. I'd go home and smoke some pot, get nice and stoned, set the coffeemaker before I went to bed, and get a good night's sleep. Surely there'd be some bad reality television show that I could watch and laugh at. I'd just chill out for the evening, maybe even open a bottle of wine and have a glass or two. The bells of St. Louis Cathedral began chiming the call to evening Mass, and it felt good to be alive. I stopped walking for a moment, and listened to the bells. It was quiet in the lower Quarter, except for the occasional car driving past on Esplanade. *This would be the perfect time for a cigarette,* I thought, before banishing the thought from my mind. It had been too hard to quit. I wasn't about to start again.

I'd just reached the corner of Barracks when my cell phone rang. I grinned, pulling it out of my jacket pocket, assuming it was Paige.

The caller ID read LOREN MCKEITHEN.

I got a sick feeling in the pit of my stomach.

"MacLeod," I said, wondering what this could be about.

"Chanse, it's Loren. How quickly can you get over to Freddy and Jillian's?" His voice was tense, and warning bells went off in my head.

"I'm not far. Probably about ten minutes, max," I replied. "What's going on?" This couldn't be about the e-mails—that wasn't really all that urgent. I felt goose bumps come out on my arms.

"Get here. Now. It's important." He hung up.

That didn't sound good.

"So much for things going so well," I said out loud. Something had happened—only I couldn't imagine for the life of me what that could be.

I started walking faster.

And I couldn't help but hear my mother's voice saying, *Don't ever tempt fate by talking about how good things are. That's just asking for trouble. Fate will be more than happy to let you know who the real boss is.*

I hated that she was right.

CHAPTER FIVE

I STARTED SWEATING as I walked hurriedly up Esplanade Avenue. A cool breeze was blowing from the direction of the river, but with the air so damp and warm and heavy, a thick blanket of gauze was dropping down over the entire Quarter, making it feel haunted. The streetlamps acquired a halo effect, surrounding their white light with a rainbow circle of color. The streets were silent other than the clip-clopping of a mule's hooves in the distance and every once in awhile, a wisp of voice would break through the silent fog, a broken fragment of a sentence swallowed again into the quiet. As I crossed Bourbon Street, the headlights of a yellow Toyota caught me by surprise and I jumped onto the opposite corner, my heart pounding from the close call. *That would have been five hundred points in Jephtha's game,* I thought to myself, shaking my head. I took some deep breaths to calm myself, and started walking again.

Loren hadn't had to tell me Frillian's address. The location of their house wasn't a closely guarded secret. Everyone in New Orleans had known within moments of their decision to buy a house here which properties they were looking at— and the smoke signals were already floating before the ink was dry on the bill of sale. To outsiders, the idea of any sort of privacy in the French Quarter may have seemed insane—but ironically, if privacy was your main concern in choosing a home, the Quarter was actually the place to go. Many of the homes were hidden from the street by massive brick fences with broken glass embedded in the top, or coils of razor wire to deter those with criminal intent. Even those houses whose front wall brushed the sidewalks were closed off once the shutters were shut and latched.

And Frillian's home was one of the most secluded houses in the lower Quarter. It was L-shaped. One narrow side of the L touched the sidewalk. The shutters were always closed on that side. It was brick, and a seven-foot brick wall that leaned towards the street extended from that edge of the house all the way to the wall of the next house. The previous owner had opted for razor wire rather than broken bottles for the top of the fence. Almost in the very middle of the fence was a solid black iron door, with a mail drop slot at about waist level.

A few yards further down was a black iron garage door. On the other side of the brick fence, tall bamboo lined the inner side, so that a passerby could just catch a glimpse of the upper floor of the house, where it sat on the very back of the lot. Nothing inside the fence was visible from the sidewalk. A riot of bougainvillea spilled purple flowers and green leaves over the top between the gate and the garage door. Black hitching posts with horse heads lined the gutter. Next to the gate, a gas lamp flickered through the fog.

As I approached the door, I glanced up and, inside the bougainvillea, saw a tiny security camera pointing a small, glowing red light at me. I resisted the urge to wave at the camera. There was a bell to the right of the door, and I was reaching to press it when the door swung open silently.

"Come on. Get inside before someone sees you." A man about my height, dressed completely in black, grabbed my left arm and pulled me inside. I weigh 230 pounds and stand six-feet-four in bare feet, so this was no mean feat. He slammed the door behind him and I got a good look at him when he turned back to me. He was actually a few inches taller than me, and he had the solid, thick body of a power lifter. He had to weigh at least three hundred solid pounds. His biceps strained at the sleeves of his tight, short-sleeved black cotton shirt. He was also wearing pleated black pants. He looked to be in his forties; his head was completely shaved. His eyes were dark brown, and his face was creased with lines radiating out from his eyes and the corners of his mouth. "Sorry to be so rough." He gave me a sheepish grin. "But you wouldn't believe what the paparazzi will pull to try to get in here." He stuck out a huge hand. "Jay Robinette, head of security."

His grip was strong, and I got the sense he wasn't even using a tenth of his strength to squeeze my hand. I was grateful for that, but when you're built like that, you don't need to show off how strong you are. "Chanse MacLeod. Nice to meet you, Jay."

"Nice to meet you, too, Chanse. Everyone's waiting for you in the carriage house. That's where their offices are."

Inside the brick wall, it was like stepping into a park. The garage door opened onto a cobblestone carport. There was a black town car parked next to a bright red Mustang convertible. The rest of the courtyard was green grass with a fountain in the center. The house, a long, two-story building with a gallery on the second floor, actually ran along the left side of the lot, beginning at the sidewalk. Across the courtyard was a two-story carriage house. Thick rosebushes lined the brick walk that led to the front door of the carriage house. I followed Robinette along the brick path, glancing over at the main house. Two children, one dark, the other Asian, were watching me from one of the upstairs windows. I waved at them. They stepped back, allowing the curtains to close. One of Frillian's causes was adopting third world orphans, I recalled. Robinette knocked once on the carriage house door, opened it, and stood aside to let me pass.

"Chanse!" Loren crossed to me and shook my hand. There were beads of sweat on his forehead. He'd taken off his suit jacket, showing patches of sweat on his wrinkled shirt. He'd loosened his tie at the neck, and he reeked of stale cigarette smoke. "Thanks for getting here so quickly."

I looked around. "No problem. I was already in the Quarter." The entire bottom floor of the carriage house was just one big open room, with a small kitchenette at one end. The walls were covered with work by James Michalopoulos, a local artist who specialized in paintings of New Orleans architecture in bright colors, but with the perspective slightly off. I'd always wanted one of his paintings, but they were way out of my price range.

A DVD player mounted on the wall was playing classical music; Mozart, I thought. Just above it was a large flat-screen plasma television. A ceiling fan turned lazily overhead. Bookcases lined one wall, and at the far end of the room, two desks were pushed against the wall. One was neat, the other had papers and folders scattered all over the top of it. Freddy and Jillian were seated beside each other on a long wine-red sofa. Jillian was smoking a cigarette, the smoke curling gently around her head, but her hand was shaking. Those glacial eyes were unreadable, but she gave me a slight smile and nodded her head at me.

Freddy's eyes were red, and he kept swallowing over and over again, licking his lips. His hair was disheveled, sticking up in every direction, and he still hadn't shaved. He looked like hell.

I turned back to Loren. "What's going on?"

"Glynis Parrish is dead." Jillian crushed her cigarette out. "Murdered. Clubbed to death in her house."

I couldn't have heard that right. "What?" I turned to Loren, the numbness of shock spreading from my brain down my spine. "How—"

Loren wiped at his forehead with a handkerchief and shoved it back into his pants pocket, only to start sweating again. "Her assistant came back to the house and found her about an hour ago."

"She called us. And we called Loren," Jillian said, sucking on the end of her cigarette.

"She called here? Why would she do that?" I looked over at Freddy. His eyes were watery, and he was biting his lower lip. "You did tell her to call the police, right?"

"Of course I did," Jillian snapped. "She was hysterical, not thinking clearly. Of course, I asked if she was certain Glynis was dead, but she said she checked for a pulse, and there wasn't one. I told her to hang up and call 9-1-1." She shook her head.

I can certainly attest to the horrible shock of discovering a dead body. It's happened to me more times than I would prefer. "Did she say anything else?"

"Apparently, Glynis was hit over the head with her Emmy." Jillian's voice shook a little bit. She glanced at Freddy.

"That Emmy meant everything to her," Freddy said in a monotone.

My God, I picked up that stupid thing, I thought, a ball of acid starting to form in my stomach.

Loren patted at his forehead again. "Of course, the police are going to check the phone records—and how is it going to look when they see Rosemary called here before she called them?"

"It's going to look bad, is how it's going to look." Jillian stubbed her cigarette out. "Can't you just hear the news jockeys? *Why did Glynis Parrish's assistant call Frillian before she called the police? What are they trying to hide?*"

I couldn't believe my ears. A woman was dead and she was worrying about what the papers would say? "Um, I'm sorry, but—"

"You think I'm a cold bitch, don't you?" Jillian lit another cigarette, her shaking hand barely able to click the lighter on. "This is a terrible tragedy, make no mistake about it, Chanse. I didn't want her dead, and I certainly didn't want this to happen. But going to pieces about it right now is the worst thing Freddy and I can do."

Freddy opened his mouth and then shut it again.

Jillian blew smoke towards the ceiling fan. "This is going to sound incredibly callous, Chanse, and I want to make it clear that on a personal level, I'm horrified. I just frankly feel kind of numb right now. Poor, sweet Glynis." She swallowed. "This is a horrible, horrible thing to have happened. I feel terrible because I knew and liked her. Her family and friends and fans are going to be devastated. But this is going to be a nightmare—not just because we lost someone we were close to—but because this is going to be prime scandal material." She patted Freddy's leg with her free hand, which was still trembling. She seemed like she was barely holding it together.

"This is going to be a feeding frenzy for the media. This could have a serious impact on our work with Project Rebuild—if people think we're involved somehow . . . and the press is going to have a field day with this. It's going to be news all over the world." She stubbed the cigarette out angrily. "And that stupid assistant calling here—what was she *thinking?* One would almost be tempted to think that she was deliberately trying to cause trouble for us . . ." She waved her hand. "But I suppose there's no sense being angry with her, the poor thing. It must have been quite a shock to come home to find Glynis murdered like that . . ." She shuddered and her eyes filled with tears. She wiped at them angrily with her free hand. "DAMN it."

"It is going to look bad—" I started to say, but she interrupted me.

"*Assistant calls Frillian before police.*" She made air quote marks, letting tears slip from her huge eyes. "*That's* going to be the headline, you know. They're going to drag out all the nonsense about the divorce again. People will speculate that we did it—it doesn't matter that neither one of us could have done it." She sighed. "And those damned e-mails she was sending us . . . well, *you* read them. It's going to look like we killed her to shut her up, keep her from spilling some big secret about us." Again she grabbed Freddy's hand, squeezing it tightly, "There isn't anything, of course. I want to keep those e-mails out of the newspapers."

"But—" I was confused. I remembered her saying at Loren's office, *there are things about us we don't want anyone to know.* "I don't think that's going to be possible, Jillian. The police will check out her computer, And they'll find them—so it would be better to be upfront about it—otherwise, the police will think you're trying to hide something." I shrugged. "It seems to me that unless the e-mails are evidence, there's no reason for anyone outside of the investigation to ever know about them." She seemed a bit paranoid.

She glanced at Freddy, and turned back to me again. She bit her lower lip. "There has to be a way." She let go of Freddy's hand. "Okay, we weren't completely honest with you this morning. We suspected Glynis was sending the e-mails, but we didn't want to tell you that, because we wanted you to have an open mind, not focus on her in case we were wrong. My mother? She isn't smart enough to send e-mails, frankly." She gave a bitter laugh. "My mother isn't sober long enough to learn how to work a computer. And now we know Glynis sent them, anyway. What we want you to do now is find out who killed Glynis."

I shook my head. "That's best left to the police, Jillian. They're better equipped to handle this kind of thing, and I'm not going to have access to the evidence."

"The police are going to be under pressure from the media—and every blogger in the world. Everyone is going to be focused on us." She made a face. "We want to release a statement through our publicist saying that we've hired you to help the police look for Glynis's killer."

I couldn't believe her self-absorption. I wasn't a reporter, but it seemed to me like the real story was Glynis's murder—not Frillian."With all due respect, Jillian, I'm not sure how I feel about being used as a public relations ploy." I was tempted to remind her of how O. J., after his farce of a trial, had claimed he was going to devote the rest of his life to finding the real killers of his ex-wife and Ronald Goldman. The comparisons were going to be made, in my opinion, and no one would take my hiring seriously. "If you really want me to find Glynis's killer, I'll do what I can—but like I said, the police have all kinds of access . . ."

"It's not a publicity ploy." Her voice was firm. I recognized the tone—she'd used it when she'd played Mary Queen of Scots. "With no offense intended, I'm not sure I trust the police. In these kinds of cases, they always seem to botch things up. And I certainly don't trust the New Orleans district attorney's office. This is going to be very high profile, Chanse—it would be even if we weren't involved." She wiped at her face. "Glynis was a celebrity too—and she was a pretty nice person, to boot. I liked her. She and Freddy were still close. I want her killer found, Chanse. This case has to be solved. Glynis deserves that."

I could understand her concern. As long as Glynis Parrish's killer was free, her murder would haunt Freddy and Jillian—and their careers. No one would ever forget it. It would be headlines for months, maybe years. Then there would be books, documentaries, maybe even movies. Everyone would have an opinion, and Jillian was right. The blogosphere would go crazy debating who killed Glynis. Glynis's entire life and career would be put under a microscope. Personal information she would have never shared willingly with the public would undoubtedly leak out of the police department and the district attorney's office—things that could prove embarrassing to Frillian. E-mails, phone records.

Everyone who had anything to say or write about the situation would make a nice sum of cash selling information and stories to the tabloids. The stigma would follow them around for the rest of their lives—the question was, would their careers hold up under the dark cloud?

The thought of the feeding frenzy that was about to explode made my blood run cold.

And the murder of a movie star was a public relations nightmare for the rebuilding of New Orleans.

The city's rising crime rate had made national news. One

broadcaster had even called living here "like being in the Old West." What nobody ever mentioned was that crime had been a huge problem *before* the flood. When the filthy water receded and the rebuilding began, we'd all kind of hoped that with the help of our federal government, the problems that existed before would be solved. Instead, the government had washed its hands of New Orleans, and the body count started to rise again. The question was, would the media fixate on Frillian, or the crime rate of New Orleans? Or would it be both?

And how would this affect the rebuilding of the city's film industry?

Film had become a big business in New Orleans over the last ten years. A concerted campaign had been launched by the city and the state to lure filmmakers and television producers to the city; it was called "Hollywood South." The city, recognizing that it simply couldn't depend so heavily on tourism, had bent over backwards to make the Hollywood types welcome here. After all, the movie industry was recession proof; tourism wasn't. When the flood had effectively destroyed the tourist industry, with the media doing its part to discourage tourists from returning, the city's economy remained in ruins. So getting the film industry back was vital to the recovery effort—and the unsolved murder of a movie star was sure to cripple those prospects. It would be a disaster that could finish off Hollywood South once and for all.

I felt sick to my stomach, and wondered if my friends Venus Casanova and Blaine Tujague would be assigned to the case. They had one of the best records in the department for closing cases. But the political pressure would be intense. Obviously, the mayor and the City Council would be pressuring the police department to wrap it up quickly.

"All right," I said slowly, trying to ignore the warning

bells going off in my head. *Stay calm and focused, Don't get stressed out. You need to do this for the city.* "You said earlier that neither one of you could have done it. Why is that?"

Jillian glanced at Freddy. "We were together all day."

I stared at Freddy. That feeling in the pit of my stomach got worse. I closed my eyes for a moment and pictured myself walking down Ursulines again. The door slamming, the guy in the sweatshirt and jeans. "That's not possible," I said, keeping my voice level and expressionless. "Freddy, I saw you by yourself earlier this evening."

Freddy seemed to snap out of his shock. "What? What are you talking about? That's just not possible."

"What are you saying?" Jillian's tone dripped ice.

"I was meeting a friend for dinner at Port of Call. I parked on Burgundy, and was walking up Ursulines around five-forty or thereabouts when I saw you coming out of Glynis's house." I folded my arms. "You were wearing a pair of jeans and an LSU sweatshirt."

Freddy and Jillian looked at each other, their faces pale.

Freddy said, "How would you know where Glynis's house is?"

"I interviewed her there earlier today."

"You're absolutely certain?" Loren said grimly. "You're sure?"

I thought back, and nodded. "Yeah. I'm sure." The room was silent.

"So you're saying you saw Freddy coming out of Glynis's house during the time she might have been murdered?"

A headache was starting to form behind my right eye.

"That's not possible." Freddy shook his head. "I was here all afternoon. Jillian and I spent the afternoon with the children, and, around five, we came over here to the carriage house, to review scripts. We've been here ever since."

"When did you get here, Loren?"

"After they called me—around seven, wasn't it?" He looked over at them.

Her face tight, Jillian nodded.

"Are you sure, Chanse?" Loren asked again. "Are you absolutely certain it was Freddy you saw? Think, Chanse. Are you positive it was Freddy you saw?"

I opened my mouth, and shut it again. My burger was churning in my stomach, and I felt like I was going to throw up any minute. *Also, I was beginning to doubt myself.* Loren was a damned good attorney, and that's the role he was playing—he was cross-examining me. I closed my eyes and thought back. "Yes, I'm certain." But now I wasn't quite as certain as I had been.

"How far away were you?" Loren asked.

It was like being on a witness stand—which is something I've never enjoyed. A good lawyer can make you doubt yourself, twist your words to make it seem as if you were saying something other than what you meant. I swallowed and estimated the distance. "About twenty yards, maybe. I was under a street light, and when he walked under the streetlight just down from the house, I saw his face clearly. It wasn't foggy yet, and yes, it was dark already, but I got a pretty damned good look at his face. And my eyes are good—I just had an examination a few weeks ago. They're twenty-twenty."

"Are you sure it wasn't just someone who looked like Freddy?"

"How many people look like a movie star?" I replied, raising my eyebrows. "Like Freddy Bliss?"

Freddy shook his head. "I'm telling you, it wasn't me. It couldn't have been." His voice was shaky.

I stared at him. There was no point in arguing with him—he wasn't going to change his story.

And he was an actor. He fooled people for a living.

Who would believe me over Freddy Bliss? And Jillian Long?

After all, I was just a gay private eye no one had ever heard of . . .

Loren went on. "You may have seen *someone—*" he emphasized the word, "come out of the victim's—Glynis's—house right around the time she may have been murdered."

And I was in her house a few hours earlier. I handled the murder weapon.

I was starting to feel really sick to my stomach. "I saw Freddy," I insisted.

"You were mistaken." Jillian said, her voice rising. "You couldn't have seen Freddy. He was here with me." She crossed her arms.

"I know what I saw," I replied.

"God *fucking* damn it!" Jillian exploded, lighting yet another cigarette. "I'm not going to argue with you." She shook her head. "I know you're wrong."

I opened my mouth to make a sharp retort, but Loren cut me off.

"Jillian, if Chanse thinks he saw Freddy coming out of Glynis's home, you're not going to talk him out of it—and you shouldn't even try. He's a witness in a murder case." His tone was gently rebuking, implying that there could be legal ramifications. But I also noticed and bristled inwardly at the use of the word *thinks*.

"Fine, fine." Jillian turned to Freddy, and stroked the side of his face. She turned back to look at me. "You know, the great irony of all this is that in death, Glynis is going to get what she always wanted—to be a huge star. She'll be a much bigger star in death than she was when she was alive." She sighed. "It's so wrong." She covered her face with her hands and began to cry.

I'd seen her do that in *Life in a Northern Town*. She got an Oscar nomination for that movie.

"Get him out of here," She said between sobs. "I don't ever want to see his face again."

I resisted the urge to roll my eyes. It was quite a performance.

"Come on, Chanse, I'll walk you out." Loren opened the door.

Once we were outside the brick wall, standing on the sidewalk, Loren lit a cigarette of his own. "Christ, what a fucking mess this is turning into." He exhaled, leaning back against the brick wall. "Well, I'm sure their million-dollar-a-year attorneys will soon be flying in and bumping me off this case. It can't come soon enough." He looked at me. "I recommend when you get home you unplug your landline."

"Why would I want to do that?"

"They're releasing that statement in time for the ten o'clock news locally, and its going to break nationwide at the same time." He shook his head. "When they talk to the police, they're going to have to tell them about the e-mails and hiring you." He made a face. "Leaks happen, Chanse. That's going to get out—everyone in the world is going to be calling you once that story breaks. I don't know if the news about Glynis has broken yet. Every reporter in the country is going to want 'your story' after that statement is released, and they're going to be relentless, Chanse. And when they find out you're a material witness?" He shook his head. "Do you have any idea what this is going to do to your life?"

I still felt like throwing up. "I can handle it."

"Then do me a favor. Just hide out and get a lawyer. You know the cops are going to want to talk to you. For tonight, just hide the fuck out. For God's sake, get yourself a good lawyer before you talk to them."

"A lawyer? What the hell do I need a lawyer for?" I could feel my mind starting to slide down that dark path again, and I took some deep breaths. *Imagine you're on a beach, with the waves gently rolling to shore, and the sun is baking your skin while you lie on a towel.*

Loren stepped closer to me and lowered his voice. "Chanse, you're walking on dangerous ground right now. This is going to be bigger than the fucking O. J. Simpson, Robert Blake, and Phil Spector cases fucking combined! Hell, I don't know if I can handle this shit myself. Jillian wasn't kidding when she said there was going to be a media circus. When she and Freddy got together, her 'stealing' him from Glynis was major news. Glynis was even on the cover of *Vanity Fair,* as the 'wronged wife.' Now, someone's killed her. You may or may not have seen Freddy Bliss coming out of her house around the time she was killed. You also worked for Freddy and Jillian—and you know all about the e-mails. Hell, you were the one who found out where they came from. Yeah, you fucking need a lawyer. You needed a lawyer about an hour ago—and do not under any circumstances talk to the police without your lawyer. And I know Casanova and Tujague are your friends—but you can't even trust them. Do you understand me?"

"I—" I stared at him. I really hadn't put that much thought into it. The concept that *I* would be a news story had never occurred to me. I'd killed two people, and both times it was maybe three paragraphs buried deep inside the pages of the newspaper. With a sinking feeling, I remembered Kato Kaelin.

Could my life bear that kind of scrutiny?

"People are going to offer you money for your story," he went on. "That's got Jillian and Freddy scared as hell. Sure, you signed a confidentiality agreement, and I hired you . . . the e-mail thing was bad enough, but you're now a material witness in a major murder case."

"I know what I saw." I stuck my hands in my jacket pockets. "I saw Freddy, no matter what Jillian might say. They're lying, Loren."

"We shouldn't even be having this conversation," he replied. "I'm violating all kinds of ethics here. I'm talking to you now as a friend, not as a lawyer. Please listen to me, okay?" He ground his cigarette out with his shoe. "Depending on what evidence is in that house, those e-mails look bad for Freddy. A reputable eyewitness saw him leaving the scene of the crime around the time it may have happened. If Freddy wasn't a major star, the police would haul him based on that alone." He sighed. "I'm a good lawyer, but if they arrest him, they're going to have to bring in a real heavy hitter. That lawyer is going to have to discredit you and your testimony, Chanse. I don't doubt you can handle yourself with the police . . ." His voice trailed off. "I'm really not trying to scare you, Chanse . . . but think about it. You got a big check from Freddy and Jillian today. You were in Glynis's house earlier today. You were in the vicinity of the house around the time she was killed. What do you think a lawyer would make of that in court?" He folded his arms. "Maybe you confronted her and there was an altercation . . . you see where I'm going with this?"

My fingerprints were on the murder weapon, unless the killer wiped it clean.

"She was alive when I left the house." I said, trying to keep my voice steady. "Her assistant can testify to that."

"Do yourself a favor." He reached into his wallet and handed me a business card. "Give this guy a call. I'll phone him and let him know you're calling." He nodded and shut the door behind him.

I looked at the card.

STORM BRADLEY, ATTORNEY AT LAW.

I put it in my wallet. Feeling a little nauseous, I headed back to my car.

CHAPTER SIX

If you solve this case, you'll be famous, I thought as I walked back to my car. I felt a little numb—and nervous. My heart was racing, and I recognized what could be the signs of an onset of an anxiety attack. My palms were damp, and I could feel wetness under my arms. My breathing was fast, so I tried to focus on slowing it down. Esplanade Avenue was deserted, no signs of life anywhere. Not even a car passing through an intersection in the distance.

Glynis was dead; and according to Loren, I was all but arrested and charged for it. But there had to be an upside to this thing, right?

I let my imagination go. This could be the opportunity of a lifetime—solving one of the highest-profile murder cases in history. Whoever tracked down the killer would make headlines, would wind up being interviewed by the likes of Anderson Cooper and Larry King—and why *shouldn't* that be me? Visions of fame and money danced through my head as I walked through the thickening fog.

I could get a book deal, and it would surely be made into a movie or a mini-series—at the very least an episode of *City Confidential* or *American Justice*. The trial would air live on Court TV.

Dream on, Chanse.

There was a piece of it that was real, though. Sure, Loren was right—I was mixed up in the middle of the whole thing. But the best way to clear everything up really would be to prove that Freddy hadn't killed his ex-wife—and neither had I.

I was disturbed by the weak identification I was going to have to make to the police. It bothered me that Loren had so easily shaken my identification of the guy coming out of the house. I'd been completely sure it was Freddy at the time—it was only later that doubt crept in. And that doubt had been planted by Loren.

It's pretty much taken for granted that eyewitnesses make mistakes. Defense attorneys frequently hammer that point home to juries. We see what we expect to see. Our memories are filtered by our experiences and prejudices. I'd seen someone dressed similarly to the way Freddy had been at our meeting earlier that day, and with the same kind of build, coming down the front steps of his ex-wife's house. It was entirely possible that all of those factors had added up in my mind to recognition.

Had it really been Freddy?

If Freddy was indicted and went to trial, his attorneys would dig into my past.

Can your life bear that kind of scrutiny?

I remembered how other witnesses in major murder trials had been treated by the press. I didn't want to be another Kato Kaelin. They would dig up everything they possibly could on me, and make it public knowledge. They'd track down my parents in Cottonwood Wells, my brother Rory, my sister Daphne in Houston—and I could be relatively certain Daphne wouldn't appreciate the intrusion. I could give a rat's ass about my parents—I hadn't talked to them in years.

I imagined the look on my father's face when some reporter asked him about his gay son, and it made me smile. The thought of how humiliated he'd be when everyone in that miserable little town found out that his big football star son was a big old homo was a very amusing one indeed. But Daphne—and my brother Rory—how would they feel about having their own lives intruded on? I hadn't talked to Rory in years, either. I'd cut him off when I'd cut off Mom and Dad.

The thought of having all the stuff about Paul dredged up also worried me. Not because it made me look bad—it might, it might not. My therapist was always telling me that the situation wasn't as bad as I made it out to be . . . but there was his family to think about. How would the Maxwells, who'd taken me in as part of their family, and maintained that tie after Paul died, feel about having their beloved son's memory tarnished and trashed on the national news?

He'd been kidnapped by an obsessed stalker, someone who'd struck him a terrible blow to the skull in order to take him from his apartment. Maybe with prompt and immediate medical attention, he would have had a chance. Instead, he'd been handcuffed to a bed, not fed or given anything to drink, and he'd begun the slow and agonizing process of dying. By the time we found him, he'd lapsed into the coma from which he'd never wake. After a few days, his family made the agonizing decision to turn off the machines that breathed for him, and he'd died. For the next year, I'd thought of my life as being clearly divided by that terrible day at Touro Hospital—*before* and *after.* In my misery and grief, I'd tried to move forward with my life.

But I felt guilty about Paul's death; guilty because while I was looking for him I'd allowed myself to get distracted away from my primary objective—finding him—because of other things that were going on, side trails I'd followed that eventually proved to have nothing to do with him. I kept thinking, *If only I were a better detective, I could have found him sooner, I could have found him when there was still a chance for him to make a recovery and he would still be with me.* Instead, he'd died, and that guilt haunted me.

But maybe none of that would come up.

Maybe it wouldn't come to that.

Maybe, like my therapist said, I was just imagining the worst again.

But I was in a bad spot, and the best way out was to solve the case.

But how? I wouldn't be able to interview witnesses, get access to evidence, or even conduct any semblance of a normal investigation. The police wouldn't want me interfering in their investigation.

As for the fame, truth be told, it was a nice fantasy. When I was young, I used to fantasize about being rich. I always, when I was a kid, thought the reason our lives were so miserable was because we were poor, because we lived in a trailer park, because we didn't get to wear nice clothes and have nice things like so many of the other kids in Cotttonwood Wells. Daphne, Rory, and I weren't the only poor kids in town—but it seemed to me like we were. Other kids didn't have mothers who wore faded old sweats and reeked of gin or vodka at the Kroger. Other kids didn't have clothes that didn't quite fit right, didn't wear their clothes till they wore through in places, and didn't have to eat bologna sandwiches for lunch every day.

When I started playing football and became someone more than the big kid from the trailer park, when I started getting invited to the parties the rich kids threw, I never felt like I belonged there, no matter how badly I wanted to. I wanted to be rich and famous and come back to Cottonwood

Wells and make all those rich kids who made me feel like trailer trash grovel before my wealth and power. But as I got older, I was more concerned with getting out of Cottonwood Wells then avenging myself on the rich kids

At LSU, I had a taste of fame as a three-year letterman on a damned good football team. Other students recognized me when I walked to class, and in restaurants and bars, so did the more rabid football fans. But I knew damned well that if I wasn't on the football team, Beta Kappa would have never given me a bid to join their fraternity. I was never comfortable with the status I had as a football player..

So forget the fantasy. I didn't want to be famous. I didn't even care about being rich anymore. All I cared about was being comfortable, not having to worry about paying my bills—and I'd already achieved that.

But if Glynis Parrish's killer was never brought to justice, my credibility would be gone forever. I would be known as "that guy who blew the case because he couldn't make a positive identification of Freddy Bliss—who paid him money." I'd be even more notorious than Mark Fuhrman.

Could Barbara Castlemaine, my boss at Crown Oil, afford the bad publicity of keeping me on under those circumstances?

I could lose everything.

That reality was the final trigger. As I slid behind the wheel of my car, the anxiety attack started for real.

You're going to lose everything you've worked for your entire life. Your life is fucked now. You don't have a choice. You're going to have to hope that either the police solve the case or you solve it for them. If the killer is never found, it isn't just Frillian's heads it will hang over—it will hang over yours. You will always be known as the guy who fucked up the Glynis Parrish murder. No one will hire you. People will whisper about you when you walk by. You'll lose your job with Barbara, and then what the fuck are you going to do?

The thoughts swam through my mind as my heart raced and my breath came in gasps.

Think happy thoughts, Chanse. Go to that beach in your head. Green waves lapping against the white sand. The sun is shining and a soft breeze is blowing. You're lying on a towel, soaking up the sun's rays, everything is peaceful, everything is fine.

My heart rate slowed.

The dark spots in front of my eyes disappeared.

I'd beaten it again.

I sat there, behind the wheel, focusing on breathing in and out slowly and carefully. I started the car, turning the defroster on high, and watched as the fog on the windshield started to clear from the bottom up. I glanced at my watch. It was barely nine o'clock. They were about to send out their press release.

Even if they didn't say a word about me, it was only a matter of time before my name would be uncovered as a witness.

My life was going to change completely—it would never be the same again.

You should have gotten out of this when you had the chance.

In less than twenty-four hours, my life was going to be completely different. I pounded on the steering wheel in frustration.

It wasn't the first time this had happened to me. No matter how many times it happens, though, you never get used to it. You go through life always expecting things to be the same, or the changes to be small and gradual. You never think about all the horrible things that could happen to take the wind out of your sails and knock you off your feet. The first time my life had changed due to circumstances beyond my control was when Paul died. The second time was Hurricane Katrina, obviously. The evacuation, the destruction, the long time away, the return to a city that at the time seemed—and sometimes still seemed—broken beyond repair; the way of life that all of us who lived in New Orleans had known and loved and somehow taken for granted was gone forever. Again, I began dividing my life into *before* and *after.*

But this wasn't the same. My therapist was helping me deal with my feelings of guilt over Paul's death, and I was coping with it a lot better. The two ordeals, barely a year apart, had forced me to reevaluate my life and myself—who I was, the kind of person I was and the kind of person I wanted to be for the rest of my life. My therapist helped a lot—I was doing a lot better than I had been, and I'd been a better boyfriend to Allen than I had been to Paul. I no longer felt as though I needed to be punished, and the truth was, I had started to realize that I had always felt that I needed to be punished, and this went back to my childhood. A sense that I didn't deserve good things to happen to me, and anything good that came into my life was just a tease, a tantalizing glimpse of what happiness could be—something to be yanked away from me just as I was beginning to enjoy myself and my life again.

I'd really had no choice in either of those situations—Paul wasn't kidnapped and murdered to punish me; it had happened because he had made soft-core porn wrestling videos and had attracted the notice of someone who belonged in a mental hospital. And the hurricane? Well, I have no control or say over the forces of nature, and it would have been the height of self-absorption to think that an entire city had been destroyed to punish me for any sins I may have committed in my life.

This was different. This time I had a choice, some control over what was going to happen. I realized this as I sat there in my car waiting for the windshield to clear. I could be proactive and take charge of the situation. Frillian was going to do what was best for them. They didn't care what impact all of this might have on me, my career, and my life. Why should they? They were trying to protect their own careers, the life they'd built together, the work they were doing to rebuild New Orleans.

I needed to do the same thing. I had a good life. I'd rebuilt it after the hurricane. I'd taken control. I'd gone to a therapist to work through all of my own issues. I was doing better emotionally. My career was going well. My personal life might not be the greatest, but I was working on it.

It was a very bad situation for me. But I could take this bad situation and turn it into an opportunity. It would come at a price, of course.

Everything does. It's a question of being willing to pay that price.

I could feel the anxiety rising again, and I cleared my mind again.

Can your life bear that kind of scrutiny?

"Stop it," I said out loud. "Just don't go there, Chanse."

After I graduated from LSU and went to work as a cop in New Orleans, I scrimped and saved every cent I could, worked every overtime hour I could get my hands on, so that I could leave the force and go out on my own as a private eye. I was a good cop, but I hated being accountable to superiors with their own agendas and ambitions. My career with the force had no blemishes—those two years could certainly bear scrutiny.

My first client as an investigator was my landlady, who was so grateful for the job I did for her that she'd reduced my rent to $100 a month and gotten me the gig with her company, Crown Oil. There are undoubtedly many negative things people could say about Barbara Castlemaine, and most of them were true. But it was also true that she never forgot when someone did her a good turn, and she was incredibly loyal. I knew I could count on her not to turn her back on me. There was also Paige—and Venus and Blaine. They'd stand by me. The Maxwells would, too.

Was there anything I'd done in my work that wouldn't bear scrutiny? Well, I had killed two men—that could easily be twisted into making me look bad. But they were both murderers, and in either case the district attorney's office had closed the file without pressing charges. They'd determined I'd acted in self-defense, and the matters were closed. Still, an enterprising reporter or a lawyer trying to make me look bad could make something of that.

The windshield finally cleared enough for me to see through, so I pulled out into the street and headed home.

While I was stopped at the light at Canal Street, I relived that moment on the Rue Ursulines over and over in my head. Loren had done a pretty good job of shaking my confidence in my memory, but I was pretty certain I'd seen Freddy Bliss. It was definitely Freddy I'd seen. Yes, eyewitnesses were notoriously unreliable, but I was trained to observe and notice things. I didn't just think it was Freddy, it *was* Freddy Bliss under the streetlight. As I sat there, listening to Rihanna sing about her umbrella, I wished any number of things— that I hadn't parked where I had; that I'd walked another block up Burgundy before turning the corner; that I hadn't returned Loren's call that morning. The credibility issue was going to be crucial: who would be believed, me or Frillian?

They were going to alibi each other, and I *knew* that was a lie. I generally don't like it when my clients lie to me, but their first concern wasn't so much the murder investigation but preserving their careers. *Of course* they would alibi each other, and they were actors; they'd be convincing. And me? Who was I but a nobody private eye in New Orleans—a gay one, at that—who'd shot and killed two people?

"Have you ever killed anyone, Mr. MacLeod?" I asked aloud as I waited for the light to change. "Oh, you've killed two men. Did you ever stand trial? No? Oh, you've killed twice in self-defense? What a dangerous line of work you're in, Mr. MacLeod."

I shivered.

How much scrutiny would my life bear?

"So, stop thinking about it. Don't worry about it. There's nothing you can do to change anything at this point anyway." The light changed as I scolded myself. I hit the gas pedal and flew across Canal Street. I remembered something else my mother used to say: *There's no sense in worrying about things you can't control. That's just borrowing trouble, and life gives you enough without having to borrow extra.*

I turned into my driveway. While I waited for the electronic gate to open, I felt the panic starting up again. I parked in the lot alongside the house and got control of my breathing again.

"I've had a hell of a day," I said out loud, grabbing my stash box from under the couch. I loaded my pipe, and took a long drag, letting the marijuana start clouding my brain. I reached for the remote control and turned on the television. It was past ten. The statement from Frillian was going out over the wire services as I sat there. Remembering Loren's warning, I got up and unplugged my land line. I sat back down and looked up at the framed print of Paul over my

mantelpiece. It was a black and white view of him from behind, seated in a chair. I thought about calling his mother,
Fee. She'd been like a mother to me ever since Paul died.
Originally from County Cork, she had Paul's sparkling green
eyes and an Irish brogue I could listen to all day long.

But what could I tell her?

*"Sorry to bother you, Fee, but I seem to be in a bit of trou-
ble. I got mixed up with some movie stars and now one of
them is dead, and you're probably going to be hearing all
kinds of crazy shit about me in the media. Yeah, I know. Just
don't believe what you hear, okay?"*

Fee wasn't the kind of person to put up with self-pity
though. She'd just give me a long distance bitch slap and tell
me to put my chin up.

I took another hit and started laughing. She'd be right,
too.

I went into the kitchen and poured myself a glass of wine.

"One hell of a day," I toasted Paul's picture, and took another hit of the pot.

I sat down at the computer and logged on to the Internet.
As soon as the home page loaded, a headline screamed at
me: GLYNIS PARRISH MURDERED. "Damn, that was quick."
I thought, clicking on the link.

Emmy Award–winning actress Glynis Parrish, 34, best
known for her long-running role on the hit series
SPORTSDESK, was found brutally murdered in New Orleans. Parrish was in New Orleans making a movie. Her
body was found by her personal assistant, Rosemary
Martin, earlier this evening.

Parrish became a star playing the role of Gwen New-
berry on the long-running television series, SPORTS-
DESK. After the show went off the air, she turned her

attention to films, appearing in several critically ac-
claimed and commercially successful films, including
MARRY ME, a romantic comedy co-starring Ben Stiller.
She was divorced from the actor Freddy Bliss after his
very public affair with Oscar winner Jillian Long became
headline news around the world while they were filming
THE ODYSSEY.

A statement from the New Orleans Police Department
stated that Parrish was killed by a single blow to the
head, and the police are following several leads. The police are also looking for a possible witness. This witness
allegedly claims to have seen a man leaving the Parrish
home around the time the murder took place.

What? I stared at the computer screen. How the hell did
that already leak out? The only people who knew about my
being a witness were Loren and Frillian . . .
They'd leaked it to the press.
But why would they do such a thing? That made no sense
at all. If anything, they'd want to hide that information.
What kind of game were they playing? I read on:

Freddy Bliss's publicist released the following statement:
'Freddy and Jillian are deeply saddened by this senseless
tragedy. Their hearts go out to her family, friends, and
her fans, and they pledge to do everything they can to
help bring her killer to justice. They are offering a ten
thousand dollar reward for any information that leads to
the arrest and conviction of her killer.

I whistled. That was a nice move. I wondered if it was
their idea. Jillian was a very smart woman—and her people
were going into major damage control. Of course, it was

going to piss off the police. Rewards always brought the cranks out—and ten thousand dollars was a nice sum. Every lunatic in New Orleans who wanted ten grand was going to be calling the hotline number mentioned in the article—and in a high-profile case like this, every single lead was going to have to be checked out. They couldn't take the chance that a lead, no matter how unlikely, might turn out to be the right one in the end.

I could hear Venus swearing right now, and couldn't help myself. I grinned.

The New Orleans police department had not exactly had the best reputation before the flood—and the conduct of some larcenous officers during the flood had further damaged their reputation. A huge number of them had deserted their posts and evacuated. The department hadn't yet recovered from those blows—and the constant focus of the national media on the rising crime rate here was even more damaging. They were having a tough time recruiting, and the city was on shaky financial footing to begin with. The reward hotline was going to bury them in work, chasing down leads on the chance it might actually be something. Everyone at city hall would be applying whatever pressure they could on the department—and interfering in the investigation.

And that didn't even take the media into consideration.

I could sympathize with the cops, but at the same time this was a lucky stroke for me.

They wouldn't welcome my own investigation, and I'd have to walk very carefully—but if I kept my head down, it was possible I could move faster then they could. I didn't have to deal with the city politics—and hopefully not with the media either.

I sipped my wine and looked at the clock in the lower right hand corner of my computer screen. It was just after ten; probably too late to call anyone. I checked the voicemail on my business line. No messages; no one had called me back from Glynis's list of staff.

I took another hit off my pipe and leaned back in my chair. *Okay, Chanse, think about it. Who had access to Glynis's house? Obviously, her staff did. Rosemary Martin would be the primary suspect, if you hadn't seen Freddy coming out of the house. But what motive would Rosemary have for killing her boss?*

I got a new spiral notebook out from a drawer where I kept fresh supplies and opened it to the first page. *Okay, assume for a moment that Freddy didn't kill Glynis. Pretend you didn't see what you did this evening. Who would want Glynis dead?*

I sighed. I didn't know enough. It always seemed to come back to Freddy and Jillian.

I grabbed the e-mail folder and started leafing through it. Whoever sent the e-mails knew something about Freddy— something they obviously didn't want to become public knowledge. But the one person who knew Freddy better than Jillian could only be his ex-wife.

But whatever she might have known hadn't concerned him enough to keep his fly zipped when he met Jillian—and if it hadn't come up during the divorce, why would she wait three years to start threatening him?

Unless it was something she'd only recently found out— some big secret he'd managed to keep from her the four years they were married.

Something Freddy was willing to kill to keep secret—willing to risk the scandal of a murder trial to hide.

In all the articles I'd read about Freddy earlier that day, I hadn't seen anything about his family or his life before he became famous. The background was all sketchy—I read from some of the pieces I'd printed out. He was born and raised in Newton, Kansas—no mention of family or siblings. He'd gone to Emporia State for two years before dropping out and heading to Hollywood. He'd become a star in less than two years after arriving in Southern California—and his life was pretty well-documented from that point on.

So, it had to be something from his past—from Kansas.

The combination of pot, wine, and Mardi Gras exhaustion was making me sleepy. I yawned and did a search on Glynis Parrish. Again, there were hundreds of thousands of mentions of her on the web. I found a bio of her on a movie-star site and read through it quickly. She'd been born on Long Island, the oldest of three daughters. Her mother had been a bit of a stage mom, trying to get her oldest daughter into show business. Glynis had started doing commercials as an early teen, got some bit parts in movies and television shows, and then had guested on an episode of *Law and Order,* which brought her to the attention of the casting director for *Sportsdesk*. Once the show aired its first episode, it had been an instant hit and she'd become a big star, the "it" girl of that television season.

The rest was Hollywood history.

I clicked through the gossip sites, and found no pieces about her personal life before she started dating Freddy. She'd gone to openings and awards shows with her mother as her date. Of course, after she started dating the sexy superstar, there were plenty of pieces on them. *Glynis's Desperate Desire to Have a Child*—and other invasive things. Then, of course, came the heartbreak of Freddy leaving her for Jillian, the divorce, and her courage in rebuilding her life.

I frowned. They made it seem like she was the first woman whose husband had cheated on her.

Since the divorce, she'd dated some other actors, but nothing serious.

I'm seeing someone now, we aren't ready for it to go public . . .

I made a note. Rosemary Martin would probably know the identity of the latest man in her life.

It was pretty standard when someone was killed to look at the people closest to them. It was always loved ones who seemed to kill the objects of their affection. If a child disappeared and turned up dead, it always seemed to be one or both of the parents. It was enough to make you not want to fall in love, get close to anyone—it certainly increased the likelihood someone would kill you someday.

So, it stood to reason that after Freddy, the man in her life was the most likely suspect. It was just a matter of finding him. Why wasn't she "ready to go public"? Was he married?

That opened up a whole new line of thought—but my brain was getting fuddled.

I stood up and stretched with a jawbreaking yawn. I was bone tired. The day had been an emotional roller-coaster, and I'd been tired when Loren's call had awakened me. My bed was calling to me. I reached down and unplugged the landline, remembering Loren's admonition. My cell phone number was unpublished—granted, it wouldn't be hard for some enterprising reporter to dig up the number, so I set it to vibrate and left it sitting on my desk. I took Storm Bradley's card out of my wallet and set it on the keyboard. I'd call him first thing in the morning.

CHAPTER SEVEN

I'D KNOWN Venus Casanova for almost ten years.

She was a striking woman, not beautiful, but with the kind of arresting looks that not only catch your attention but hold it. Her skin was dark and ageless—she looked like she could be anywhere from thirty to somewhere in her fifties. She had strong features and prominent cheekbones from native American blood somewhere in the distant past. She always wore her hair cropped close to the scalp, and was one of the few women I knew who could get away with it. She was about six-one or two, and her body was muscular and defined. Like me, she'd gone to LSU on an athletic scholarship (hers was for basketball, and she'd played on the national team) and had kept her body in shape since then. She was the first black woman to make detective grade in the New Orleans police department—a combination guaranteed to make her unpopular.

Whispers that she was a lesbian had abounded in the department when I'd been on the force, but no matter what her sexual preference (she was actually straight), Venus was a damned good cop. She was honest—a rare quality in the New Orleans police department—and committed to her job. She was proud of her rise in the department, and frequently spoke to high school students about the importance of education and working hard. I didn't know her well until the flood, but I'd always respected her. She'd always dealt with me honestly and fairly, even when I intruded into one of her cases. When Paul had been kidnapped, she'd kept me in the loop of the investigation, which I appreciated.

After the flood, Venus and I had become closer. She'd lived in New Orleans East in the house she raised her two daughters in, and had lost everything. I knew her partner on the force, Blaine Tujague, much better than I knew her. She'd moved into the carriage house behind Blaine's house on Coliseum Square until she had been able to find an overpriced apartment in the Quarter—which she regularly griped about. For months after we all came back, Paige and I had met her and Blaine every night for drinks, at the Avenue Pub on St. Charles Avenue, and I'd grown to like her. She had an odd sense of humor, and was bluntly honest.

She'd considered taking her insurance settlement and retiring from the force, moving to Memphis to be closer to her daughters and their kids, but had decided to stay and be a part of the recovery. She could have taken the tests that would have improved her rank, but Venus wasn't an administrator. "I'd rather stay where I am," she always said, "where I can do some good for the people of this city. That's why I became a cop, not to have to deal with all the bullshit that comes with a damned desk job."

Her face was impassive when she walked into the interrogation room, shutting the door behind her. She nodded to me, and then inclined her head toward Storm Bradley, my attorney. "You think you need a lawyer?" She raised one of her eyebrows.

I'd called Storm after waking up and taking a shower. As soon I said who I was, he'd cut me off and insisted, to use his phrase, that I get my ass over to his office as soon as I could. "And take a cab," he said. "We'll go see the cops immediately afterward."

"All right," he said, after he ushered me in, "tell me everything. I'm on the job now."

I was taken aback by his assumption I'd already hired him. As I sat and sipped coffee his assistant brought, I took a good look at him. My first thought was that Loren hadn't done me any favors, and maybe I should have found a lawyer on my own. He looked sloppy, for one thing. He was in his mid to late thirties, and was one of those guys who'd been athletic when young, but was going to seed as he got older. He was fleshy and his face was red—but he was good-looking in that former jock kind of way. He was losing his dirty blond hair, but to give him credit, he wasn't trying to hide it with a comb-over. He was wearing a canary yellow dress shirt with a dove-gray suit, and his tie was bright red with yellow stripes the exact shade of his shirt. He had intelligent-looking eyes above thick cheeks, and as I told him my story—beginning with being hired to trace the e-mails, he sat and listened, occasionally jotting notes on a legal pad he balanced on his lap. When I finished, he stroked his chin, and I noticed a patch of hair he'd missed when shaving that morning. "So," I asked, "what do I do now?"

"Let me think about this for a minute," he replied, and finished his coffee.

I sat there, waiting for him to speak. The silence stretched uncomfortably. I was just about to say something when he finally spoke. "Well, one thing is for sure. We do need to go talk to the police—immediately. And you need to tell them everything you know."

I was a little irritated. I needed to pay a lawyer to tell me something I already knew?

"Don't tell them anything besides the absolute fact," he went on. "Nothing extraneous, like your impressions or what you think—there's no need for that. Just the facts—they hired you to trace these e-mails, you think you saw Freddy coming out of Glynis Parrish's house, they want you to work on the case, and that the e-mails came from Glynis's computer. Other than that, you don't say a word."

Well, duh.

"You're in a hell of a mess, but that's why I'm here." He beamed at me. "I'll be with you when you talk to them—I'm pretty sure I know the detectives assigned to the case." He barked out a short laugh. "They're not exactly fond of me, but they're honest and they can be trusted, and they know I won't jerk them around." He stared at me. "You're pissed at me, aren't you? You're thinking, *Who is this asshole telling me what to do?* I'm the asshole who's going to protect you, that's who I am. I'm the person who is not going to let anyone chew you up and spit you out." He put the legal pad back into his briefcase. "If I say don't answer a question, you don't answer it. You do not talk to the media. You do not talk to either the police or the district attorney's office without me present; in fact, all meetings and talks with them must come through me. They are not to contact you without going through me."

"Two of my best friends are cops, and my best friend is a reporter," I replied. "So, until this is all cleared up, I shouldn't talk to them?"

He narrowed his eyes. "Sure you can. Just not about this case—this is off limits. You can't discuss this case with anyone but me from this moment on, am I clear?" He leaned forward. "I know that probably seems nuts to you, but *I am a lot more familiar with the law than you are.*" He waved me off as I started to talk and went on, "Yes, I know you have a degree in criminology. I know you were a cop for two years and you've been a private eye ever since." He shrugged. "I had my secretary dig up some information on you after Loren called me last night. I wanted to know what I was getting myself into. And, Chanse, I will do everything I possibly can to protect you and look out for your interests. *I'm on your side, and no one else's.* All I ask is that you do as I tell you and never lie to me about anything. I can't help you if you lie to me. And the most important thing you have to do is stay as far away from this case as you possibly can."

"But—"

He cut me off, and gave me another hard look before shaking his head. "I can't decide if you're naïve or just plain stupid," he said.

That was it. I was done with him. But before I could tell him, he went on, "I understand that you want to investigate—I get it, really, I do. But that's just insane—" He paused, implying, at the very least, that I was going to wind up losing my license. "Do you really want to start a whole new career at this stage of your life?"

"Well, no." I crossed my arms. He was getting me slightly worked up, despite the fact that I really can't imagine what you'd have to do to lose a PI license in Louisiana.

He sighed. "It's bad enough that you took their money. That's going to weaken your credibility as a witness."

"But my testimony is damaging to Freddy Bliss. I'm the only person who can place him at the crime scene."

"You said yourself that you were certain it was Freddy until you talked to them." Storm shook his head. "Now, you're not so sure." He cleared his throat. "Mr. MacLeod, when you saw the man walking out of Glynis Parrish's home, were you certain it was Freddy Bliss? And remember, you are under oath."

"At the time, I was," I answered, and immediately saw the trap. My heart began pounding in my ears.

"But now you're not so certain?" He put a twist on his voice that clearly implied, *I don't believe a word you're saying.*

"I'm relatively certain," I replied. "But—"

He cut me off. "And just how much money did Freddy Bliss pay you for your services?"

"He and his wife paid me twenty thousand dollars . . ."

"And what is your going rate? And remember, Mr. MacLeod, you are under oath."

"Okay, okay, I get it, all right?" I sighed. "But there's no way they could have known when they paid me . . ." I stopped.

Storm folded his arms and looked at me. His eyebrows were raised. "You see now how it sounds? The one witness who saw Freddy Bliss come out of Glynis's house just happens to have a twenty thousand dollar check from Freddy's lawyer. It smells to high heaven like a payoff."

"But there's no way in hell they could have known I'd *see* him coming out of Glynis Parrish's house around the time of the murder. There's no way they could have known I'd be there on Ursulines at the right time. No one could have known where I'd park the car. Only my friend Paige even knew I'd be in the Quarter last night."

Storm stared at me long and hard before answering. "You still don't get it, do you? *It doesn't matter whether or not they could have known any of that beforehand.* The district attorney's job is to convict Freddy Bliss—if it comes to that— and he is going to make sure of two things: That when you saw whoever it was, you *thought* it was Freddy. And then, after you talked to Freddy, you changed your mind and became unsure of who you saw. And their lawyer wrote you a check for ten thousand dollars, Chanse. *There is no time stamp on that check.* Even the date doesn't matter; anyone can write whatever date they want on a check—you know that as well as I do."

I was starting to agree with him. I *was* stupid.

"Please tell me you deposited the check yesterday afternoon, *before* the murder."

I bit my lip. "Um, no. I haven't been to the bank yet."

"So now the district attorney could make it seem as though they bribed you last night to change your story." He sighed. "Chanse, when you go in to talk to the police, you cannot tell them you were positive it was Freddy you saw and then changed your mind. You can't. You saw someone coming out of the house you thought *resembled* Freddy, is all. You didn't see his whole face, did you?"

"Well, no. Like I said, he was wearing a hoodie sweatshirt with the hood pulled down low over his face. All I really saw was from about the nose down. He did look a lot like Freddy."

"And if Freddy's arrested, the district attorney isn't the only person you're going to have to worry about, my friend." He laughed. "You don't think Freddy Bliss isn't going to have the best team of criminal attorneys money can buy? He makes twenty million dollars for every movie he's in. He has more money than he knows what to do with . . . and *his* lawyers are going to move heaven and earth to convince the jury you aren't reputable. And it won't be that hard. Freddy and Jillian aren't just anyone. They're fucking world famous movie stars, Chanse. The jury, no matter how much they try to be objective, won't be—they've seen their movies, they know what they're doing here in New Orleans, they've been all over the television news and the newspapers and magazines. People feel like they *know* them, like they're friends or distant relatives. And with no offense intended, who are you?" He gave me a nasty smile. "Have you ever killed some-one, Mr. MacLeod?"

I licked my lips. "Yes. In self-defense."

"More than once?"

I squirmed a bit in my chair. "Twice."

"Were you ever charged for these killings, Mr. MacLeod?"

"No, as I said, they were in self-defense."

"You were a police officer, weren't you, Mr. MacLeod?"

"Yes, for two years."

"Are you acquainted with the investigating officers in this case, Venus Casanova and Blaine Tujague?"

I stared at him. "Venus and Blaine are assigned to the case? Yes, I know them both quite well."

"Were they by any chance the officers who investigated the two killings you committed?" Again, he used that accusatory tone that made me want to punch him in the face.

"Yes, they were."

"Okay, let's stop there for a minute," Storm replied. "You see where I'm going with this, don't you?" He shook his head. "O. J.'s lawyers were able to convince a jury that despite all the overwhelming evidence against him, the entire Los Angeles police department had entered into a conspiracy to frame him, and may have even murdered Nicole Simpson and Ron Goldman themselves to bring O. J. down. How hard would it be to convince a jury that Venus and Blaine conspired with you to frame Freddy Bliss? Not hard at all.

"The two men you killed were murderers. You saved the city—and the police department—a lot of hassle and the cost of a trial by killing them, you know that?"

"That isn't what happened!" My mind was starting to spin out of control. "Glenn Austin was trying to kill me—and Lenny Pousson was holding a gun on me and several other people . . ." I was having trouble breathing.

"Are you all right?" There was concern in his voice. "We can take a break, if you need to collect yourself."

"Let me get some water. There's a fountain in the hall, right?" It was the beginning of an anxiety attack. I got up, black dots dancing in front of my eyes. *Focus on your breathing, you're on a warm beach with white sands.* I staggered out into the hall and drank, taking small sips, trying to keep my breathing steady. When I was back under control, I walked back into Storm's office. "I'm sorry," I said. "Since the flood, I occasionally have anxiety attacks. I can control them—but sometimes . . ."

"I totally get it. No need to explain to me," he replied in a gentle tone. "Did you stay, or did you evacuate?"

"I evacuated."

"We stayed," Storm replied, a weird look coming over his face. "I sometimes think those of us who stayed behind had it easier—I mean, those of us whose houses didn't go under. Well, mine did—I lived near Broadmoor—but my grandparents have a house in the Garden District and we went there, my wife and I, and the rest of the family."

"Where are you living now?" I took another sip of the water.

"Still with my grandparents." He shrugged. "What can you do?"

"I'm sorry." We all had stories. In the months after the flood, as everyone came back with their own horror stories, we sometimes got tired of talking about it. But, as I told Paige, we couldn't cut people off and not let *them* talk about it. Talking was helping people heal, even though it reopened our wounds. There was a long time when it seemed like none of us would ever be able to move on, because just when we established some semblance of normality, of control, we'd run into someone else who'd just come back. They'd have to tell their story, and you'd have to tell yours, tearing the scab off the wound.

He waved his hand. "Well, we're rebuilding. It's just taking forever. You have no idea how bad I want to get back into my own house. Can't really complain—I'm living in the height of luxury in a mansion instead of a FEMA trailer—but it's not home." He shrugged. "You ready to continue?"

I nodded. "Let's go."

"Why were you hired by the defendant, Freddy Bliss?"

"I was hired to find out who was sending him threatening e-mails."

"And did you find out?"

"Yes, they were sent from a laptop computer registered to Glynis Parrish . . ." I stopped. "Oh my God."

"Exactly. *You* were hired to find out who sent the e-mails. *You* found out it was Glynis Parrish. *You* were on the street, the very block, she lived on around the time she was killed. *You* have killed two people before, in 'self-defense.'" He made air quotes with his fingers as he said "self-defense." "Loren, or whoever Freddy's attorney is, should it get that far, is going to need to create a reasonable doubt in the jurors' minds. Ask yourself, Chanse—if you were on that jury, trying to decide if Freddy Bliss, a movie star you feel like you know, someone you are familiar with, killed his ex-wife—or was it this shady private investigator, deeply connected to the investigating officers, who has already killed two people and gotten away with it—possibly with the assistance of the police?" He finished his coffee and set it down on the table. "And the police are going to be looking long and hard at you too. The police are never really thrilled with coincidences— at least that's been my experience. And now . . ."

"Uh . . . Storm . . . there's one other little coincidence you should know about."

"Oh, Lord. I don't think I like that tone."

"There's a good chance my fingerprints are on the murder weapon." I told him about handling the Emmy.

And now, sitting in the very same interrogation room I'd been taken to after I'd killed Lenny Pousson, a psycho who'd been responsible for the deaths of at least thirty people, I could feel my mind starting to go down the dark path of terror. *But Venus knows me, she's my friend, she knows the circumstances in which I've killed before. She's not going to believe for a minute that I killed Glynis Parrish. Deep breaths, Chanse, you can't have an anxiety attack in here.*

I'd considered taking a Xanax, but Storm had vetoed that. He felt it was better for me to have an anxiety attack in front of Venus rather than have my mind addled by drugs.

"So, you have information about the killing of Glynis Parrish?" Venus's face was impassive. "Why does that not surprise me?" She shook her head. "You always seem to have your nose stuck into places it shouldn't be."

"Yes," I replied, ignoring everything else she'd said. It was a technique I recognized, trying to goad me into saying something I shouldn't.

"Start at the beginning." She pulled a digital recorder out of her jacket pocket. "Any objections to having this interview taped?"

"None whatsoever, Detective," Storm replied.

She gave him a look that was part irritated, part affectionate. "Thank you, counselor. How's the family? I haven't run into that annoying brother of yours lately."

"He's doing quite well." He returned her look with a broad smile.

She clicked the recorder on. "Good. Shall we start?"

I glanced over at Storm, who gave me a slight nod. "Yesterday afternoon, I was hired by Loren McKeithen to conduct an investigation on behalf of clients of his. The clients were Freddy Bliss and Jillian Long."

The only change in her facial expression was the slight lift of her right eyebrow. "And what, pray tell, did they hire you to find out?"

"Don't answer that," Storm interrupted. "I am instructing my client not to answer any questions regarding the investigation he was hired to conduct." He opened his briefcase and handed her a copy of the confidentiality agreement.

Venus pulled out a pair of reading glasses and read it over. A vein was throbbing on her right forehead—a sign she was getting irritated. "All right then. But I have to ask, in that case, what are you doing here then, Chanse?"

"Last night, I was meeting Paige for dinner at Port of Call." I went through the entire thing, from the moment I found a parking spot till I rounded the corner of Ursulines and saw someone walking out of the house. "At the time, Venus, I would have sworn it was Freddy Bliss . . . but now I'm not so sure."

Her eyes narrowed. "You were sure, and now you aren't? May I ask why?"

I swallowed. "Well, it was from a distance of forty yards and it was dark outside. The person I saw was about the same height as Freddy, and he had the same kind of build. So I automatically assumed it was Freddy. Now I'm not so sure." I cleared my throat.

"Have you spoken to your clients since then?"

"Yes. When I was leaving Port of Call I received an unexpected call on my cell phone from Loren McKeithen, who asked me to come to their house. This was around seven-thirty, eight o'clock; I'm not entirely sure of the time. I went over there, and once I arrived, they told me that Glynis

Parrish had been murdered, and they asked me to stop investigating what I was working on, and to start looking into Glynis's death. That was when I told them I'd seen Freddy coming out of a house on Ursulines just before six o'clock. They told me I was mistaken, that Freddy and Jillian had been together since they left Loren's office and our meeting."

"And that's when you began to question your identification." Venus held up a hand. "Chanse, since you're not sure—" her voice took on a sarcastic edge, "—who you saw coming out of the crime scene, you need to give me a description. If you would be so kind."

"Well, he looked to be about five-five, maybe a hundred and forty pounds?" I closed my eyes and thought. "He was wearing an LSU hooded sweatshirt, the hood pulled down low over his face. The upper part of the face was either covered or shadowed. When he got under the streetlight, I got a pretty good look at the exposed part of his face, and that's why I thought it was Freddy Bliss. This person had the same kind of jaw structure as Freddy, but I couldn't really get a good look at the nose. He was wearing an old pair of ratty-looking low-rise jeans, and I didn't get a look at his shoes.

"He stopped under the streetlight, lit a cigarette, and started walking in the direction of the river, very quickly. I thought about calling out to him—thinking it was Freddy—but when he got to the corner at Dauphine Street, he started running, and then disappeared in the fog." I shrugged. "I just went on to meet Paige."

Venus gave me a ghost of a smile. "Did you mention any of this to Paige?"

"Um, no."

"She's going to kill you, you know." The smile broadened. "She's been bitching about having to get an interview with

Freddy and Jillian for a couple of days now—and you have, or had, access to them?"

I gave her a sickly smile back. "She mentioned it at dinner, actually. But I'd signed a confidentiality agreement . . ."

"Like she'll care?" Venus's smile grew wider. "Off the record, I wouldn't want to be you. She's going to skin you alive."

"Are we finished here?" Storm asked, glancing at his watch.

Venus gave him a look that would have killed a lesser person. "For now, yes. But I will most likely have some more questions for your client." She turned back to me as she said *your client.* "For your sake, Chanse, I'd advise you not to speak to either Freddy Bliss or Jillian Long, and of course, don't leave town. For any reason."

I bit my lip. "Do you have an exact time of death yet?"

Venus sighed. "We've already released this information to the press, so it won't hurt anything for me to tell you. Her assistant, Rosemary Martin, left her alone in the house around four. Glynis Parrish asked her to leave as she was expecting someone, and she wanted to meet with the person privately. She told Ms. Martin not to come back until after six. Martin returned around six-thirty, and found the body." Her eyes glinted. "And I am sure you already know that the first people Ms. Martin called were your clients, rather than the police."

"So, basically, she was killed between four and six-thirty?"

"Yes."

"Fingerprints on the murder weapon? I'm asking because I touched it."

"You *what?*"

"In the course of my investigation for Freddy and Jillian, I interviewed Glynis Parrish. She invited me to pick up her

Emmy." I was wincing inwardly, knowing how lame it sounded. But Storm had advised me to mention it upfront.

Venus repeated what I said, her voice displaying a dangerous edge. "She invited you to pick up her Emmy."

I shrugged. "She said everyone wanted to."

"Uh-huh." She stared at me, perfectly conveying that she realized I was either crazy or a liar.

I kept silent, not wanting to blink first.

"We're running the prints now." She waved tiredly. She turned the recorder off. "Thank you for coming in, Chanse. We'll be in touch."

Storm handed her a business card. "I want you to know that my client is available whenever you need him, but the arrangements need to be made through me. No one from the police department or the district attorney's office is to speak to him or make any arrangements to talk to him other than through me."

Venus sighed. "Understood."

Once we were outside the station, Storm clapped me on the back. "That wasn't too bad, was it? Can I drop you at home?"

"No," I replied, giving him a weak smile. "Thanks, though. I think I'm going to go have lunch somewhere."

"Well, you have my cell if you need me." He leaned closer to me. "Stay away from Frillian—I think that's the wisest thing you could do right now."

"Thanks." I walked down Royal Street. The sun was shining, and it was in the low seventies. I pulled my cell phone out of my pocket and turned it on. It beeped to let me know I had a message.

I dialed into the voice-mail, and winced.

"Chanse, you miserable lying sack of shit!" It was Paige. *"I cannot fucking believe you sat there and listened to me*

*bitch all that time about how impossible it would be to get an
interview with Freddy and Jillian, and the whole time you
could have gotten me in there! This is how you pay me back
for all the goddamned favors I've done for you over the
years? You are DEAD to me, you hear? DEAD. TO. ME. I am
so pissed off at you right now—oh, wait a minute. They made
you sign a confidentiality agreement, didn't they? They all
do that. But damn it, Chanse! How could you not even HINT
at this? Call me when you get this—I promise I won't rip off
your head and shit down your neck the way you so richly
deserve . . . Jesus Christ on the cross, Chanse. Do you have
any idea what you've gotten yourself into? You'd better not
be giving interviews to anyone besides me, do you hear me?
If you do, I will skin you alive, I will boil you in oil . . . if you
don't give me an exclusive, I swear I'll—"* BEEP.

I couldn't help it, I grinned. I hit the call back button, and
she answered on the first ring. "Where the *hell* have you
been?"

"You free for lunch?" I asked, keeping my voice as calm
as I could. "I *might* be persuaded to give my oldest friend in
the world an exclusive interview."

There was a pause. "Chanse," she said, her voice low,
"you are a *witness?*"

"How did you—"

"They have the television on here in the office. It just went
out over CNN. You saw the murderer leaving Glynis's house?"

*Someone in the police department had already called the
press. My God, I just told Venus, and already it's on the news.*

"Meet me at El Gato Negro, and I'll tell you everything," I
replied, closing the phone.

I took some deep, therapeutic breaths, and started walking through the Quarter.

CHAPTER EIGHT

"Wow. That really sucks," Paige said when I'd finished my tale. She shook her head and took a sip of her iced tea. "*Do* you think Freddy killed her?"

I glanced around. We were the only people in El Gato Negro other than the staff. Our waiter was wiping down a table on the far side of the room. We were seated in the corner furthest from the front door. I shrugged. "I don't know what to think, to tell you the truth. I'm pretty sure it was him I saw coming out of the house. And obviously he's never going to admit being there. So it's my word against his."

"I guess I can kiss any access to Frillian goodbye then." She rapped me lightly on the knuckles. "You couldn't have gotten me in to see them before you accused him of being at a crime scene?" She sighed. "They're not going to be talking to any reporters anytime soon—and when they do, it's going to be Larry King or someone like that." She gave me a dirty look. "The good news, though, is Coralie has assigned the murder to me."

"Well, you're the paper's top reporter, so of course."

"Don't flatter me, you're not good at it." She gave me a smile anyway. "But that should keep me out of the office—and away from her—for a few days at least. Huzzah!" She tapped her pen on her notebook. She'd taken plenty of notes while I was talking. "But at least I have an exclusive with the one witness who can place Freddy at the murder scene." When I started to talk, she held up her hand. "Don't worry. I'm not going to say you saw Freddy—since you're not sure anymore." She consulted her notes. "I'll just print the description you gave me and let the readers draw their own conclusions. Although—"

"What?"

"You know, it's entirely possible Freddy was there, but didn't kill her." Paige shrugged. "Try this on. Suppose, after Loren told them that Glynis sent the e-mails, he went over there to confront her, and found the body. Knowing how bad that would look, he got out of there and is denying ever being there." Her eyebrows came together in a frown. "He went back home, told Jillian, and they decided to alibi each other because they didn't know he'd been seen—and now they're stuck with the lie."

"How did he get into her house without being let in?"

"The killer maybe left the door open?" she suggested. "Freddy got there, found the door open, got concerned, and went inside?"

"I suppose it could have happened that way." I thought for a moment. "And of course, now he can't change his story without making himself look guilty as hell."

"Yeah." She shook her head. "I guess it depends on whether his fingerprints are on the Emmy. In addition to yours, of course." She shook her head. "How did Venus react when you told her about handling the Emmy?"

"Not well, and thanks for reminding me." I pushed my plate away. I had about half of my burrito left, but I'd lost my appetite. "Did you interview Jillian's mother yet?"

"I'm heading over there when I leave here." Paige

glanced at her cell phone. "Do you think she might know something?"

"I don't know." It was frustrating. "She and Jillian have been estranged for years—since before Jillian hooked up with Freddy. It stands to reason that whatever those e-mails were alluding to, she wouldn't know. How would she?"

"Yeah, yeah, I know." Paige flipped back a few pages in her notebook. "That makes sense. I kind of got the impression when I talked to her on the phone that she really doesn't know much about them—she's just looking to get some attention from the media. And you know me, always happy to oblige a has-been." She made a sour face. "But you never know—she might know something pertinent. No stone left unturned, that's my motto—and when I'm done with her I'm meeting with Sandy Carter, see how this might affect Project Rebuild, if at all. And she might know something, you never know. She probably knows Frillian better than anyone else in town, and maybe, just maybe, she can get me in to see them—now that you've blown it. And I have a breakfast meeting with Jim Corliss in the morning. He's the director of Glynis's movie." She raised an eyebrow. "He might know who Glynis was seeing. I hear that movie sets are hotbeds of gossip. I'll talk to some of the crew while I'm there."

"What's the deal with the movie anyway? I mean, now that the star's dead . . ."

"When I talked with Jim he told me they were going to recast. They'd only shot a few scenes, and if they can get someone to take the part over quickly, there won't even be much of a delay—although he seemed to think it might not be easy getting someone to replace Glynis, given the circumstances." She sighed.

I played with the straw in my drink. My head was starting to ache. My cell phone vibrated in my pocket. I pulled it out and looked at the caller ID. ROSEMARY MARTIN. I held up a finger to shush Paige, and answered it. "MacLeod."

"Chanse?" The girlish voice sounded slightly out of breath. "This is Rosemary Martin, Glynis's assistant? We met yesterday?"

"Yes, Rosemary, I remember you." Paige started to say something but I waved my hand and shook my head. She nodded and winked back at me.

"I was wondering if you could meet with me?" She let out a half-sob. "I just don't know what to do. I spent most of the night being treated like a criminal by the police and I just thought maybe you could, I don't know, maybe give me some advice?" She started breathing harder. "I don't really have any friends here in New Orleans, and you were so nice to me yesterday, would you mind? I don't want to impose . . . if you're busy I can understand. I just need someone to talk to."

Interesting, I thought. I didn't recall being anything more than polite to her. "I'm finishing a meeting right now, but I'm in the Quarter. I could meet you in, say, about half an hour?"

She let out her breath in a rush. "Oh, thank you, that would be wonderful! How about Café Envie? Do you know where that is?"

"Yes. I'll see you there in half an hour." I clicked my phone shut. "Apparently, I've made a friend."

"Was that the assistant?"

"Uh huh." I scratched my head. "She wants me to meet her. She doesn't have any friends in town and needs someone to talk to."

"See? I told you it always pays to be nice to people. Maybe now you'll listen to me." Paige signaled our waiter for the check. "You get what you can out of her—and see if you can track down the other people on Glynis's staff. I'll handle the stuff I've already arranged. I should be back at my place around six. You want to meet up and compare notes?" She handed the waiter her credit card. She smiled at me. "This is my treat. Well, actually the paper's." She shoved her notebook back into her bag. "I'll type up your interview before then—I'll let you read it before I turn it in, make sure I've got it right." She took the slip from the waiter and signed it. "You're lucky you're my friend, you know? No other reporter is going to be so accommodating."

"Thanks." She was right. Now that my name was out there, the thought of what was being said about me on the news and on-line was a bit unnerving. "I do appreciate it."

"Well, I have my own selfish reasons. You're going to be a great source, and I'm the only one with access—so make sure it stays that way. Any other reporter asks you anything, you'd better say 'no comment' or I'll make you sorry you were born." She stood up. "And no need for that bitch Coralie to know who my source is. Everyone else covering this story is just going to be recording gossip and trying to get leaks from the police department—which is already happening. I still can't believe your name was leaked before you even left the building. Venus must be ready to kill someone." She ran a hand through her already messy hair. "But unlike those other incompetent boobs, I still know how to be an investigative journalist." She picked up her bag, and gave me a grin. "Talk to you later, okay? And remember—NO COMMENT."

I walked out with her and gave her a hug before she headed for her car. I took a deep breath and walked around the corner. Café Envie was only about a block from El Gato Negro, on the uptown corner of Barracks and Decatur. It was my favorite place in the Quarter to get coffee. They also served liquor—and somehow managed to evade the city's new non-smoking ban. As a result, all the caffeine addicts who smoked crowded in there all day long. Café Envie also allowed pets—something unique among the city's coffee shops. As a result, it was always hard to find a table, as everyone out walking their dogs would stop in for a snack or a cup. The outdoor tables were full as I walked across Decatur, and there were about three people waiting in line when I walked in, one with a dog I knew. I reached down to pet Rambla, the friendly tri-color spaniel who was pretty much the neighborhood mascot, barely remembering to say hi to her owner. I stood back up as the young guy being served took his big mug of coffee and walked over to the condiment bar at the far side of the shop. *Nice ass,* I thought, shaking my head and feeling like a pedophile. He looked like he was a teenager. He was wearing baggy, gray fleece sweatpants, black Converse high tops, and a white ribbed tank T-shirt. His hair was trimmed down in a buzz cut, his waist very narrow, and his exposed shoulders bony. He was wiry and lean—one of those kids who had high metabolisms and couldn't gain weight. He took an empty table in the far corner of the shop. He had a pleasant enough face, with a pierced eyebrow and tattoos on his upper arms. He caught me looking at him, and flashed me a friendly smile.

I smiled back and turned my attention back to the line. *He looks familiar,* I thought, and then dismissed the thought. Everyone in the Quarter looks familiar. New Orleans is a very small town, no matter what anyone thinks, and you see the same people all the time. I ordered a large regular coffee and walked over to the condiment bar. I added sweetener, half-and-half, and some vanilla powder. I walked outside and grabbed a table that a couple of kids who looked like gutter punks had just vacated. I sat down and sipped my coffee.

I was about halfway through the coffee when Rosemary Martin came walking up Decatur Street from the direction of

Esplanade. She waved at me and smiled. She was wearing a cloth jacket over a University of Kansas sweatshirt and jeans, and a baseball cap that she'd tucked her hair into. She darted across Barracks Street. "Hi," she said, sitting down breathlessly. "Thanks for meeting me." She wasn't wearing makeup, and there were dark smudges under her eyes. She looked as if she hadn't slept.

"Not a problem. Do you want some coffee?"

She shook her head. "No, I've had plenty today. Any more and I wouldn't be able to sleep for a week." She yawned, covering her mouth with her hand. "Sorry. I was with the police till really late last night, and then I was too upset to sleep. Every time I started to drift off, I had nightmares." Her eyes got watery again, and she closed them, biting both lips. "I'm still in shock, I guess."

"It had to be a terrible experience for you," I said, injecting sympathy into my voice.

"Oh, it was so awful!" Her voice trembled, her eyes widening. "She was just lying there, in a puddle of blood . . ." her voice trailed off, and a tear slid out of her right eye. She wiped at it. "Sorry."

"It's all right." I reached over and placed a hand on top of one of hers.

"If I'd only known I wouldn't have left her alone in the house!" she cried out, and her entire body trembled. "I would have never left her, you have to believe me, Chanse!"

"So, do you mind telling me exactly what happened yesterday afternoon?"

She got control of herself again. "Well, she was in quite a state after you left—I mean, she was already in a bad mood—I think you could tell that, couldn't you?" She sighed. "After I let you out, I went back and insisted again that I hadn't been on her computer. But she didn't seem to care. I asked her if she wanted me to call everyone and ask them about it—you know, Darlene and Brett and Charity"—I recognized the names from the list she'd given me—"and she said to forget about it, she didn't care. She was in a really bad mood—it was more than just a migraine. She told me to fire Darlene and Charity—and replace them."

"She didn't want to fire Brett?"

"Oh, no." She gave me a sly smile. "She'd never fire Brett. Then, she got a call on her cell phone. She sent me out of the room . . . and then she called me back in about half an hour. She was in a much better mood then. She told me she was expecting someone to come by around five, and she gave me the rest of the day off, told me to go on home, she wouldn't need me again until morning." She blew out her breath. "I hadn't been back to my own place in days, so I was pretty happy about it. I decided to treat myself to dinner at Angeli, and so just before five I left the house."

"She didn't tell you who was coming over?" I asked. "Was it the guy she was seeing?"

Rosemary rolled her eyes. "Oh, she told you about that? No, it wasn't Brett—she wouldn't have made me leave if it was just him."

"She was dating her trainer?"

"I wouldn't call it *dating*." Rosemary made a face. "They never went anywhere—he just came over to the house. It wasn't anything serious, you know. Brett was just for fun." She leaned across the table and lowered her voice. "I got the impression it was Freddy Bliss who was coming over." She looked around to see if anyone was within earshot. "I mean, she didn't say it in so many words, but she kind of hinted at it. It wasn't the first time she'd sent me out of the house because she wanted privacy." She gave me a knowing look. "She never did that when Brett was coming by. She didn't care that I knew about *him*. I pretty much knew everything that was going on in her life, but these secret visits . . . there weren't a lot of them, you know. Just every once in a while—and she always sent me home."

"You never asked?"

"Of course not!" She looked shocked. "It wasn't any of my business . . . although now I wish I had." She sighed. "She wouldn't have told me anyway, I guess. She would have just gotten mad. She had quite a temper . . . especially if it was one of her bad days."

"Why did you assume it was Freddy Bliss who was coming over?"

"Who else would it have been?" She shrugged. She leaned forward and lowered her voice again. "Besides, one time when she told me to leave, the next morning I found a cell phone in the living room. It wasn't hers." She blushed. "I checked the stored numbers . . . and called one stored as MAIN HOUSE. Jillian Long answered it herself." She gave me a sly look. "I just said I'd found the phone on the street, and she thanked me and asked me to put it through their mail slot." She gave me a triumphant smile. "Jillian had no idea what was going on, but I *knew*. Freddy and Glynis were seeing each other behind Jillian's back."

I didn't respond. My head was spinning. If Freddy and Glynis were seeing each other, not only did Freddy have a stronger motive—it also gave Jillian one. "Did you tell the police all of this?"

"Of course I did. Why wouldn't I?" She made a face. "I didn't work for them."

I nodded. "So, why did you go back to the house?"

"I forgot my car keys." She sighed. "I keep the keys for Glynis's house on a separate ring. I don't like having lots of keys, and after I ate dinner, I got to my car and realized I didn't have MY keys. So I went back to get them." She gave a shudder. "I mean, I knew Glynis would be mad at me for coming back, but I figured I could slip in and out without her knowing I'd been there. I always put my own keys on the table in the front room, and I was in such a hurry to leave that I just walked right out without them." Her eyes filled again. "But when I got there, and put my key in the front door, I *locked* it. Then I knew something was wrong. Glynis was a stickler about locking the house—she would have never let someone in and left it unlocked.

"She kept her own keys in the lock on the inside of the front door. So I unlocked the door and went in—and her keys were there on the inside, hanging from the lock, where they should be. The house was, you know, really quiet." She took a couple of deep breaths. "I picked up my keys, and went down the hall to the living room—I just figured, you know, I would check and see if she was all right. I wouldn't go back to the bedroom, in case Freddy was still there . . ." Her voice trailed off for a moment, and her eyes filled with tears. This time she let them flow. "The living room door was open, and from the hall I could see her. She was just lying there . . . her head in a puddle . . . and I started screaming." She wrapped her arms around herself. "It was so awful . . ."

"Why did you call Freddy and Jillian before you called 911?"

"I did?" She shook her head. "Yes, yes, I guess I did." Her lower lip continued to tremble. "I wasn't really thinking, I guess."

"How did you know their number?"

"I—" She thought for a moment. "Yes, my cell phone wasn't charged, I remember now. I got my phone out and it was dead. Glynis's phone was there on the table, so I picked it up and I must have hit redial when I turned it on. Yes, I remember now. I spoke to Freddy, I told him what had happened and asked what I should do. He told me to call 911." She gave me a funny look. "How did you know I did that? The police didn't ask me about that. I'd completely forgotten about it."

"Freddy told me," I replied. I watched her face. "The police will ask you about it. They'll check her phone for incoming and outgoing calls."

"Oh." She shrugged. "It's not a big deal, really. Is it?"

"It looks funny," I answered, "that you would call Freddy and Jillian before you called the police."

"Well, I didn't do it on purpose. Like I said, I must have hit redial when I turned her phone on." She narrowed her eyes a bit. "Chanse, you have to understand. I was in so much shock, I wasn't really thinking, you know? It was a horrible thing. Horrible." She shuddered. "It brought back so many horrible memories . . . I found a suicide once."

"I beg pardon?"

"My parents died when I was really young." Her voice got very small. "I was in foster care. When I was a teenager, I was placed with this family who took in about twelve foster kids on a farm. One of the boys killed himself. I found him." She began to shudder again. "And when I walked in and saw Glynis . . . it was like reliving that whole horrible time again." She started crying in earnest now, her small body shaking.

"I'm so sorry. I didn't know." I took both of her hands in mine and squeezed them. "That must have been difficult."

"Being in foster care was no picnic." She struggled to get hold of herself. "Would you mind getting me a water?"

I stood up and walked back inside just as the kid with the gray sweatpants was walking out. He smiled at me, and I saw the row of braces across his lower teeth. I smiled back and went to the counter. There was no line, and as I ordered the bottled water, I looked out the front windows and saw the kid talking to Rosemary. *That's weird,* I thought, paying for the water and walking back out. The kid was gone. I saw him about halfway up the block walking toward Esplanade. I handed her the water as I sat down. "Who was that kid? He looks familiar."

She opened the water and took a big slug. "Joey?" She gave me a weak smile. "He's just one of the neighborhood kids. He's really sweet. I met him one morning when I was outside smoking on the stoop—Glynis wouldn't let me smoke in the house. He bummed a cigarette from me, and we started talking. He's a good kid, really. He's had it rough— not foster care, like me, but his parents threw him out." She shrugged. "I pay him to run errands for me every once in a while. You know, just to help him out."

"I'd swear I'd seen him somewhere before."

She gave me a sly look. "Ever go to a place called the Brass Rail? He dances there on weekends."

Thinking maybe she'd brought up a gay bar to test the waters, I replied cautiously, "I've been there, but not in months." I didn't like the place. One of the more disreputable gay bars in the Quarter, it was not in the St. Ann axis. It was on Burgundy, further uptown in the Quarter. Its primary draw was the kids dancing on the bar in their underwear—and it attracted an older crowd. The Brass Rail only hired dancers who looked like they weren't legal—and rumor had it they were also for sale. On the rare occasions when I went there, I always felt kind of sleazy. The dancers were very forward—as opposed to the ones in the Fruit Loop. That made me uncomfortable—I'm not opposed to strippers, as long as they don't try to get money out of me. If I wound up there, it was only after I'd been drinking and someone else made the suggestion. I never stayed for long.

"Anyway, I need to get going." I made a show of checking my watch. "Oh, do you know if Brett trains at a particular gym? I haven't had much luck getting him to return my calls."

"He trains at Bodytech, Uptown. I think it's on Magazine Street." She shrugged. "When Glynis was looking for a trainer, I saw his ad in *Gambit* and called him."

Bodytech was my gym, but I didn't know any of the trainers there. I wondered which one he was. "And how about Darlene? She hasn't called me back, either."

She frowned. "Why do you need to talk to them?"

I smiled back. "Just tying up some loose ends, is all."

She shrugged. "Darlene's a little strange, to tell you the truth. Something about her always bothered me, but I could never quite put my finger on what it was. I'll call her and tell her to call you."

"Thanks." I stood up, and she rose as well. She startled me by coming around the table and hugging me.

"Thanks." She wiped at her eyes. "I don't really have any friends here."

"Well, you can call me anytime," I replied. "What are you going to do now? For work?"

"Go back to the agency I worked for and hope they can find something for me," she replied.

"What agency?"

"Girl Friday." She wiped at her face. "Maybe the person I worked with before I took the job with Glynis will take me back." She shook her head. "I wouldn't blame her if she didn't, though. Mrs. Clifford was really good to me—she didn't deserve my leaving her the way I did." She sighed. "It was wrong of me, but I really wanted to work for Glynis."

"Not Sophia Clifford?" New Orleans was truly a small town. I'd done some work for Girl Friday when the agency first opened, doing background checks on prospective temp workers. I also knew Sophia Clifford slightly. A widow, she'd moved to New Orleans after her husband died with a lot of money to burn, and had gotten involved in the arts scene as a patroness. Originally from Greece, she had a thick accent and was prone to always wearing incredibly elaborate hats and gloves. The first time I'd run into her after the hurricane she'd rushed up to me and exclaimed, "Chanse darling! My house was looted by drag queens! All they took were my gloves and my hats!"

"You know her?" Rosemary was peering at me. "Maybe you could put in a good word with her for me?"

"Sure." I smiled at her. "I'd be glad to. And call me any-time."

"Thanks." She wiped at her face again. "It means a lot." She smiled.

I watched her walk up Barracks Street. I sat back down and got my little notebook out of my back pocket. I wrote down some of what she had told me, and then wrote the name *Joey* and circled it.

What she'd told me was interesting, but none of it was verifiable. If Freddy had been having an affair with Glynis, he certainly wouldn't admit to it now. And she had no proof; it was all just conclusions she'd drawn from what she'd ob-served. It also didn't make a lot of sense—why would Glynis be sending Freddy those threatening e-mails if they'd rekin-dled their romance? Unless, of course, she was using her knowledge of Freddy's past to blackmail him back into her bed. That didn't make sense, either. There was no need for Glynis to send him threats if she were seeing him in person. And if Freddy knew Glynis was the threat, he wouldn't have hired me—and he certainly wouldn't have told Jillian about it. She would be the last person he'd want to know about the e-mails.

Talking to Rosemary had just made the mess even messier. She only *suspected* that Glynis was involved with Freddy again—and the only evidence she had was a cell phone she'd found in the house one morning. It could, actually, have been *Jillian's* phone rather than Freddy's.

If Jillian knew Freddy and Glynis were reconciling, that would give her a motive—but then, that didn't wash with me either. Freddy was Jillian's fourth or fifth husband. It's not like she was a stranger to failed marriages. I doubted very seriously she would be so enraged she'd kill Glynis. She'd just get a lawyer and divorce him.

I glanced at my watch. It was now after three. I flipped open my phone and dialed Bodytech. Allen would most likely be gone.

After the hurricane, I'd started seeing Allen Johnson, who owned Bodytech. I'd known Allen for years. He and his long-time partner had separated after the flood. We were both lonely, and I hadn't been surprised when Allen and his partner had gotten back together again. Things between us had been uncomfortable for a while, but they were getting better. Still, these days I chose to work out in the evenings when I knew he wouldn't be there.

My therapist called it *avoidance*. I called it working out in peace.

"Bodytech Fitness," Mallory answered, the nice young woman who worked the afternoon and evening shift at the front desk. I liked her a lot.

"Hi, Mallory, this is Chanse MacLeod. I was wondering if I could make an appointment with Brett for training?"

"Seriously?" She laughed. "I'm sorry—you caught me off-guard. You want a training session?"

"Well, I feel like my workouts are getting a little stale,

and I thought maybe a few sessions with a trainer would motivate me," I lied. "And Brett was recommended to me."

"Let me check the book." There was a clunk as she set the phone down. "Okay, he has an opening tomorrow morning at ten. Does that work for you?"

"Nothing tonight?"

"Sorry, no, he's booked solid. Should I put you down for ten tomorrow morning?" Her voice became businesslike as she went into her spiel. "There's no charge for the first session, but after that it's fifty dollars a session, in advance, unless you buy a package, and that's $200 for five, or $375 for ten—both of which are deeply discounted on paying one at a time. Ten, of course, is the best deal. It works out to $37.50 per session."

"Thanks, Mallory, put me down for tomorrow morning."

CHAPTER NINE

I CALLED A CAB from Café Envie to go home.

The day was beautiful. The sun was out and there was a nice breeze blowing in from the river. I crossed the street to wait for my cab. I leaned against the black wrought-iron fence in front of the old U.S. Mint building. There were a surprising number of pedestrians out—and from the looks of them, mostly tourists. My lungs ached for a cigarette. I thought about walking over to a little shop I knew about midway down the block that sold cigarettes, but fought off the urge. Quitting had been an incredibly terrible experience. Now that I was off them for good, I wasn't going to put myself through that again. I felt better now that I wasn't smoking. I didn't get out of breath as quickly as I used to; when I was doing my cardio at the gym, my lungs felt better, and I seemed to have more energy than I did when I smoked. Besides, the price kept going up, and it was ridiculous to spend that kind of money on something intangible that gave such little pleasure. I wondered if the desire to have a butt would ever go away once and for all.

Somehow, I doubted it. An addiction is an addiction. From what I heard, alcoholics never stopped wanting a drink, so why would nicotine be any different?

I just wanted to get home and be by myself, smoke some pot, open a bottle of wine, and decompress. I'd already had a couple of close calls with anxiety attacks, and I was in no mood to tempt fate. There's nothing more horrible than those things, and I'd had enough of them to know that I was dangerously close to having one that no amount of calming exercises would head off. I'd much prefer to be in my house if it happened—and my Xanax stash was in the medicine cabinet. My heart rate had been getting steadily faster since I set foot in the precinct building, and the exercises my therapist had taught me to ward off the attacks were losing their effectiveness. I just stood there, leaning against the Mint's fence, my eyes narrowed to slits, and tried to regulate my breathing. In and out, nice and slow and steady—I knew that as long as I had my breathing under control, my heart rate would gradually slow down and I'd be safe. The cab pulled up and honked, and I climbed into the back, giving the cabbie my address. As soon as I settled into the backseat and the cab pulled back out onto Decatur Street, I closed my eyes and imagined a quiet beach, with palm trees and white sand, gentle green waves lapping at the shore. I pulled out my phone. I'd turned the ringer off before meeting with Rosemary.

The little digital window informed me that I had two new voice-mail messages.

I checked the messages as we crossed Canal Street. The first one was from Paige. *"Hey Chanse, Paige here. You are so not going to believe what happened during my interview with Shirley Harris! I still don't believe it myself. I did get some rather interesting dirt on both Freddy and Jillian before we were interrupted—and therein lies a tale like you wouldn't believe . . . Sandy Carter had to postpone—I'm meeting her for breakfast in the morning. So, call me when-*

*ever you get home so we can get together and compare
notes. Why don't you just come over to my place and we can
order in? I am dying to hear what the assistant wanted to
talk to you about, and if you got anything out of her. Love
ya!"*

I punched the seven key to delete it. I smiled to myself. I
was definitely curious to hear her opinion of the Rosemary
conversation. The Shirley Harris thing sounded good too—
Paige's voice had been in her high-pitched "I don't know if I
can keep from laughing" mode.

*"Chanse MacLeod? Hello, how are you, this is Veronica
Vance, from CNN Headline News. I would love the opportunity to interview you tonight on my show. It airs at seven
o'clock eastern, and I can guarantee you I'll be the most fair
journalist you could speak to. Please give me a call back at
415-555-0909, so we can make arrangements for the satel-
lite feed from either your office or your home, or from a local
affiliate's studio; whichever is the most convenient for you. If
you're familiar with my show, you KNOW that I am the only
journalist who would give you a fair shake to tell your side
of the story. Thanks in advance, and I look forward to talking
to you further."*

I couldn't delete that one fast enough.

Oh yes, I was familiar with Veronica Vance, all right. Before the flood, I'd found her shrill and obviously affected
Southern accent offensive—as offensive as her regular
claims to be fair and unbiased. She was one of those horrible
"journalists" who never allowed her guests a chance to finish anything they were saying, cutting them off rudely, and
while she claimed to be giving them an opportunity to tell
their side of whatever story she was reporting on, she usually came across as a cross between an avenging harpy and
a banshee. Every once in a while, I'd watched her show

when I was bored and nothing else was on. But after the levees failed, when all the news networks were reporting on New Orleans 24/7—I'd grown to hate her with the burning intensity of the sun. The lies and inaccuracies that had flown out of her mouth, while she sat in her high and dry studio in Atlanta, wrapped in her usual cloak of sanctimonious superiority, made me burn with rage. She placed blame everywhere but where it belonged—with the Army Corps of Engineers and the White House. She blamed the mayor, the governor, the people who hadn't evacuated—you name it, she blamed them.

To me, she was the epitome of everything that was wrong with the news media.

I wondered how she'd gotten my cell number. Undoubtedly, she had sources everywhere. I sighed and took no small pleasure in deleting the message. There was no way in hell I was going to call her back—let alone agree to an interview.

The car swung around the corner of Euterpe onto Camp Street and came to a dead stop. The traffic on Camp Street was intense—which was rare. I craned my neck forward to see what was going on, and my jaw dropped. I felt all the blood draining from my face.

The street in front of my house was clogged with news vans.

The sidewalk in front of my house was filled with photographers and cameramen.

Oh my God, oh my God oh my God.

"Stop here and wait a minute," I said to the cab driver, my voice shaking.

How am I going to get into the house through that mob? I thought.

My heart was beating so loud I could hear it in my ears.

My breath was coming fast.

A panic attack. No, please God, no, I can't melt down in front of the media.

Somehow, I managed to croak out Paige's address to the driver. He pulled around the vans along the curb and headed up Camp Street.

I tried to measure my breathing as I scrolled through my stored numbers.

I found Paige's number and hit call.

"Tourneur."

"Paige, it's Chanse." I was beginning to hyperventilate. I tucked my head down and tried to control my breathing. "Please . . . I need . . . help."

"Are you okay?" Her voice was alarmed. "Where are you?"

"There's a—there's a crowd of reporters in front of my house." I forced myself to take long, slow, deep breaths. I was getting faint. There was a roaring in my ears, and my heart was pumping so hard it felt like it was going to jump out of my chest. *Breathe, just breathe, focus on your breathing, everything is going to be okay.*

"Don't answer the door, make sure the curtains are closed, and don't answer the door whatever you do." She instructed. "Those fucking vultures."

"I'm . . . not . . . in . . . the . . . house . . ." I started gasping for air. *Think about your happy place, think about the beach, get a hold of yourself, you can do it, Chanse, you can stay calm and focused.* "I . . . am . . . in . . . a . . . cab . . ."

"Oh God, where are you right now?"

"On . . . my . . . way . . . to . . . your . . . house."

"You're having an anxiety attack, aren't you? Shit, fuck, SHIT! Hang on, how close are you?"

"Corner . . . of . . . Melpomene . . . and Camp . . ." I swallowed. "I . . . think . . . I . . . can . . . make . . . it . . ."

"Buddy, are you all right?" the cabdriver asked as he turned up Melpomene.

"Hang in there, Chanse! I'll be out front waiting for you." Her voice was panicked. She hung up.

"I'm . . . fine . . ." I said to the cabdriver. "Just . . . drive . . ." I put my head down between my knees.

Breathe, just breathe, you're on a beach, close your eyes and imagine you're on a beach, with the sun shining and the waves coming ashore and . . .

It wasn't working.

My mind raced on. Horrible thoughts filled my mind, one after another, each one worse than the one before.

I hadn't had an anxiety attack in months.

They're terrifying, absolutely terrifying. There's nothing worse than having your mind race out of control. What makes it even worse is there's a flicker of awareness, of your normal mind working, and it KNOWS you are acting crazy, that your mind is racing out of control and there's not a god-damned thing you can do about it. You can't stop yourself, no matter how you try, and while it's going on you want to die, you pray to die, anything would be better than letting it go on.

I'd thought they were a part of the past.

After I'd returned from the evacuation, they'd happened almost daily. They would come on suddenly, without warning. One moment, I'd be perfectly fine. The next moment, I'd be on the floor in a fetal position, my mind racing out of control, my breathing so fast I was close to hyperventilating, my heart beating so fast I thought it would explode. My doctor had prescribed Xanax for me to handle the anxiety attacks, and Lexapro to handle the depression. It didn't take long before I was addicted to both.

But I'd kicked them both, and now the last of the Xanax

sat in my medicine cabinet collecting dust for those increasingly rare anxiety attacks. I'd been proud of myself, and my therapist had given me some control exercises—breathing, creative visualizations, all that psychoanalytical mumbo jumbo I'd always dismissed as stupid in my past life. But much as I hated to admit it, they did work most of the time.

But they weren't working as I waited for the cab to get to Paige's house. Time seemed to have slowed to a complete standstill. Nothing was working. All I knew was that I was helpless, melting into a puddle in the backseat of the cab. I tried imagining myself on the beach again, tried imagining myself in any number of happier places, tried to remember times when I enjoyed myself and was happy . . . and nothing would come to replace the panic overwhelming me. Tears began streaming out of my eyes as I fought for my sanity, to keep my grip on reality, to stay out of that dark pit where I'd spent so many horrible hours.

I wanted to die. I wanted someone to just shoot me to make it stop.

Maybe I could just crawl out into the street in front of a car . . .

The cab pulled up in front of Paige's. She dashed over to the cab, shoved a pill into my mouth, and gave me a bottle of water to wash it down with. "Come on, baby, you're going to be all right, come on, just get out of the car and we'll go back to my house, okay, you're going to be just fine . . ."

"I'm sorry, I'm so sorry," I blathered and babbled as she somehow helped me out of the cab, and I leaned on her. I was vaguely aware of her tossing a bill and talking to the cabdriver. I couldn't understand what she was saying to him. My entire body was shaking. "Breathe, Chanse, focus on your breathing," she shouted as she walked me through her front gate. I just kept my eyes closed, waiting for the Xanax she'd given me to take effect.

Then, I was walking along the side of the house to Paige's apartment in the back. I had just stepped onto the small set of stairs to her door when suddenly the terror stopped and as she fumbled with her keys, a curtain of calm came down over me.

I collapsed onto her couch, and Nicky, her thirty-pound Maine Coon cat jumped into my lap, purring and rubbing his head against my chest. "Thanks, Paige." I took a deep breath. "Sorry about that."

She lit a cigarette as she poured herself a glass of red wine at the small bar she had set up in the corner of the living room just beneath the curving staircase to the second floor. "No problem." She handed me a glass. "I take it you weren't expecting the media circus to be waiting for you at the front door, huh?"

I took a swallow of the wine. "No. No, I wasn't." I ran my other hand through my hair. It was damp with sweat. "It was coming on before then, though. I knew when I was at the precinct this morning that it was coming."

"You should have gone home and taken a pill then. You know better."

"I know," I replied. "When I see the signs, I should just write off the rest of the day and take one." I took another deep breath and exhaled. "I just wasn't expecting the media waiting to ambush me."

"Yeah, well, you should have been. I warned you they already had your name." She plopped down in the reclining chair. "All the damned news networks are all Frillian, all the time." She shook her head. "It's fucking insane, and they're all talking about you."

"About me?" I tried to stand, but my legs were still weak. I sat back down. "What are they saying?"

"Trust me, you don't want to know what they're saying. It'll just bring on another attack. Let the Xanax work its magic, and then we'll turn on the television and you can hear it for yourself."

"Okay. So, tell me what Shirley Harris had to say." I was starting to feel a lot calmer, if a little bit foggy, from the drug.

"That was something." Paige started to laugh "It was kind of sad, actually. I really felt sorry for the old woman. She was, shall we say, definitely in her cups when I got there. She looks *terrible,* poor thing. And she was so pathetically grateful to see me. She offered me a drink—I declined—and then poured herself a huge tumbler of vodka."

"You said she had all kinds of dirt on them?"

"Oh, yeah." Paige sat down on the couch and crossed her legs. "Did you know that Jillian, Miss Adopt-every-Third-World Orphan in the world, had an abortion when she was sixteen? And then had her tubes tied when she was twenty because she was afraid of what having a baby would do to her figure?"

I shrugged. "I don't really see how that's relevant." I paused, then added, "That's just embarrassing stuff—nothing for them to get worked up over."

"It isn't—but it is good dirt, and stuff I doubt very much that Jillian would want to be public knowledge." Paige replied with a sigh. "And it's certainly nothing I would ever use in a story without confirmation of some kind."

"Did she have anything on Freddy?"

"Get this." Paige leaned forward. "When they started seeing each other, Shirley hired a private investigator to check him out. Apparently, Shirley did that with every guy her daughter got involved with. And there was something unsavory in his past. When Shirley brought this report from the detective to Jillian, *that* was when they had their big blow-up." She shook her head. "Shirley started crying at this point, about how her daughter had turned on her, how all she wanted was what was best for her, on and on and on." She made a face. Paige's mother was a drunk, so she had little patience with them. "It was sickening."

"She didn't tell you what the unsavory thing was?"

"This is where it gets good." Paige leaned forward. "I was just about to ask her to get specific—and she was just soused enough I think to spill the big secret, when the door bursts open, and guess who is there? None other than Jillian herself! And some of her hulking bodyguards. She ordered me out—and when I said I was Shirley's guest—well, Shirley was no help whatsoever. She was so glad to see Jillian—if Jillian told her to jump out of the window she would have. The thugs escorted me, not only to the elevator, but all the way out of the hotel." Paige laughed. "Talk about a bum's rush! I'd always wondered what that was like. Now I know."

"It's weird that they showed up like that in the nick of time." I struggled to keep my mind focused. It wasn't easy. Nicky started kneading my chest with his front paws. He was purring, and he started head butting my chin. I scratched him under his chin, and his purring got even louder. Such a sweet cat . . . I smiled at him.

"Well, if I had to hazard a guess . . . I think Shirley let Jillian know she'd be talking to a reporter." Paige shrugged. "From everything Shirley said, she's been trying to reconcile with her since the blowup." She shrugged. "I guess threatening to spill the big secret to a reporter finally did the trick. Now, what did Rosemary have to say for herself?"

"Apparently, she was the last person to see Glynis alive, other than her killer—and she found the body," I replied.

"I'm not sure if I believe her or not, to be honest. She said that Glynis wanted her out of the house, gave her the night off. She left around five, and went to have dinner at Angeli. She forgot her own keys and went back and found the body shortly after six." I frowned. "I'm not sure I buy the forgotten key story."

Paige reached into her purse and pulled out her notebook. "And you saw Freddy leaving Glynis's just before six? Right before you met me at Port of Call, right?"

"Rosemary thinks Glynis and Freddy were meeting secretly—because there was someone coming to see her that Glynis didn't want Rosemary to know about. She doesn't know for a fact it was Freddy, but she knew about the trainer Glynis was sleeping with. I booked a training session with him tomorrow." Nicky jumped down to the floor and sat down, staring at me. "Now, I'm not so sure it was Freddy I saw." I shrugged. "I go back and forth. At the time, I would have sworn it was Freddy—but now? The guy I saw was built like Freddy, but I didn't see his whole face. It could have been someone who looked like him."

"Well, what Rosemary said goes with your identification. And come on, Chanse. I mean, how many guys are there that look like Freddy Bliss? It's not like they're a dime a dozen, unfortunately." She sighed. "And after the way I was thrown out of the Ritz-Carlton today by Jillian's thugs, I don't know if I'm convinced they're so innocent in all of this." She lit another cigarette. "They definitely have something to hide."

"We need to figure out how to find out whatever it was he did they don't want us—or anyone—to know," I said slowly. My mind was clouded by the Xanax. I was having a hard time focusing.

"Are you hungry? Let's order some food." She closed her

notebook and shoved it back into her purse. "Enough of this for now . . . we can eat and get back to work. I'm starved." She grinned. "Getting thrown out of places seems to make me hungry. What are you in the mood for? Bar burgers from the corner?"

"Yeah, that's fine." Pretty much anything sounded good at that point. I didn't care one way or the other.

She placed the order and hung up the phone. "Are you up for some television?" She picked up the remote. She looked at me. "See what they're saying? You're going to have to hear it at some point—might as well get it over with."

I nodded. She clicked the television on, and switched to a twenty-four hour news network. I groaned. It was Veronica Vance's show.

"Can you believe it?" she shrilled in her overdone drawl. "The witness—who claims to have seen FREDDY BLISS coming out of Glynis Parrish's house the night of the murder, is a MURDERER himself!" She shook her head dramatically. A picture of me flashed onto a split screen. It was so ridiculous I almost laughed. It was my picture from the LSU football program my senior year. Across the bottom of the picture ran a graphic: CHANSE MACLEOD, WITNESS IN PARRISH MURDER, HAS KILLED TWICE.

I was vaguely aware that Veronica was droning on in an outraged voice. The entire thing didn't seem real. She was talking about *me*, and she was making me sound like a dangerous maniac. She wasn't really lying—that was the thing. I had killed two men. But she didn't mention the first one I killed was trying to kill me. She didn't say the second one was holding a gun on a room full of people. My picture disappeared, and on the split screen another woman's face appeared. She was standing just off the curb on Ursulines, and in the background I could see Glynis's house. The crime scene tape hung across the front door. Flowers were piled on the sidewalk, along with candles and what looked like pictures of Glynis propped up against the railing. The sidewalks were full of people. The woman on Ursulines—her name appeared as a caption below her face: KATE JUDSON, NEW ORLEANS—was talking to Veronica.

"MacLeod is a former New Orleans police officer, Veronica, and left the force to go into business for himself as a private eye. According to a source very close to the investigation, MacLeod has a very close relationship with the two detectives assigned to the Parrish murder, Venus Casanova and Blaine Tujague."

Oh, shit, I thought.

"Is this another example of that old time Louisiana justice, Kate?" Veronica went on. "A good ole boy network closing ranks to protect one of their own—even if he's not on the force anymore?"

"Is she out of her mind?" Paige's face was turning red.

"No one is saying that, Veronica."

"Well, you have to admit it's an awfully big coincidence. And one thing I learned as a prosecutor—coincidences in a murder case are few and far between. I can't tell you how many times in one of my cases what looked like a coincidence turned out to be nothing of the sort. And now we're going to take a break. When we come back, we'll have more breaking news from New Orleans on the Glynis Parrish murder. I'm Veronica Vance."

A toothpaste commercial started hawking the plaque fighting power of a new, improved version of an old brand.

Paige muted the television. "Are you okay?" Her face was still red, and she was shaking.

"Yeah," I replied. I was fine. It was probably the Xanax.

"I'm not." Her voice shook with controlled rage. "I knew it would be bad—but I didn't think it would be *that* bad. It never occurred to me that she'd drag Venus and Blaine into the mud, too." She lit a cigarette. "That lousy bitch! And those so-called sources aren't in the police department."

"It doesn't matter," I replied. "It doesn't matter where it's coming from."

"It's coming from Frillian, is where it's coming from." Paige puffed on the cigarette so hard I thought she might snap it in two. "*You* saw Freddy—so they're trying to discredit you, divert attention away from them by making it look like you're guilty—and Venus and Blaine are covering up for you." She got up and started pacing. "The police don't think you're a suspect because there was no reason for you to kill her, not because you're friends with the investigating officers." She walked into the little alcove and fired up her computer. "I know exactly what my next article is going to be about." She gave me a wicked smile.

"Paige—don't do something crazy. Think about it and calm down before you write anything you might regret later."

"Don't worry." She waved her hand unconcernedly. "I know what I'm doing."

I felt warm. I took another swallow of the wine. My palms were damp. I felt a bit nauseous. I stood up. "I'm going to go pick up the food." I stretched. "I think I need some air."

"You sure you're okay?" Paige slid into her desk chair. The cigarette dangled from her mouth. When I nodded, she said, "The spare keys are on the nail by the door."

I took the keys and locked the door behind as I stepped out. It had gotten dark while I was there. The temperature had dropped about twenty degrees, and the air felt damp and cold. I shivered, and wished I'd brought a jacket with me. I walked alongside the house and unlocked the front gate. I stepped out onto the sidewalk and pulled the gate shut behind me. Once I was out in the open, I caught the full blast of the cold wind. I shivered. *You can make it to the corner, it's not that cold,* I told myself.

What I really wanted was a cigarette.

I can buy a pack at the bar, I thought, and started walking towards St. Charles. I walked fast, my shoes making scrunchy noises on the wet pavement. The bar was just on the corner—just a short walk. I shivered again as a blast of cold wind pierced through my shirt and my jeans. Ahead of me, a practically empty streetcar went by. There was very little traffic on St. Charles. Behind me, I heard a car door shut. I stuck my hands in my pockets to keep them warm. The mist had come back. The windows of the cars on Polymnia Street were covered in condensation. The lights on St. Charles were haloed with yellow and blue light. I walked past the house next door to Paige's and was almost past the vacant lot when I heard running footsteps behind me.

I turned around to look just in time to take a blow right across my face.

My head jerked back hard and I was suddenly looking at the cloudy sky. My weight was driven backwards and my feet rolled back. And then I was falling. It seemed to be happening in slow motion. My thoughts slowed down and I could hear, over the spreading pain from the blow to my face, someone breathing really heavy. My shoulders hit the hard sidewalk first, and all of my weight jolted onto my upper spine. My head fell back. It hit the sidewalk with a loud cracking sound that echoed through my mind. Then all I felt was a sudden dull pain in the back of my head. My eyes crossed and I couldn't see anything else. All I was aware of was pain and darkness.

Then all the breath was knocked out of me as a foot drove into my side with enough force to roll me over. I tumbled over and over again until coming to a stop on my back.

I wasn't on the sidewalk any longer. My back was on soft, wet mud. My legs were in a shallow puddle.

My clothes started to soak through.

I tried to get to my hands and knees. I started coughing, deep racking coughs that felt like a lung was going to come up. My entire body was tingling from shock. My breath was ragged, harsh, not doing me any good. My head was clouding, my scalp tingling. My eyes couldn't focus. *I have—to get—away,* I thought somehow through the grayness engulfing my consciousness.

Then I was being kicked again. I didn't know if there was more than one of them, and I didn't want to see. There was nothing I could do except curl up into a fetal position for safety. It was pure instinct, training from a long-ago self-defense class at the police academy. The blows kept coming, one after the other. I didn't have time to register pain before the next one came. I started shivering. I wanted to scream, to beg them to stop, but I couldn't catch my breath. And still the blows came.

One after another without a break, without any kind of respite.

I was conscious of nothing other than hurting.

This can't be happening. I can't be kicked to death only fifty yards from the door to a bar.

It went on.

I don't know if I just lay there or if I rolled to try to get away.

More kicks. In the back. On my head, my arms, my stomach, my legs.

Pain screamed from every part of my body.

I raised my hands to protect my face and head.

I thought, *My God, they're going to kill me. Somebody please stop them.*

And finally, mercifully, my mind went into overload and I blacked out.

CHAPTER TEN

I DON'T KNOW HOW LONG I was unconscious.

I came back to reality cold, wet, and aching. My ears were ringing.

Even my hair hurt.

I rolled over onto my back and winced. I moved my arms and legs. They hurt, but they still moved. I used my hands to push myself into a seated position. I felt dizzy for a moment, but willed myself to get to my knees and stand up. My head spun again when I got to my feet, and I staggered over to a chain link fence in time to keep from falling down again. I leaned against it while I ran my hands carefully over my ribs. They ached, but I was able to breathe without a lot of pain. The knuckles of my left hand were swollen, and I winced again as I pulled up my shirt to wipe the mud out of my eyes.

Whoever had attacked me was long gone.

I staggered around to the sidewalk. My head was throbbing, and I felt along the back of my head until I found a nice-sized lump where my skull had connected with the sidewalk. I ran my tongue along the inside of my teeth—they were all still there. I licked my lips, tasting dirt and blood.

They were swollen and cut, but overall, I seemed to be relatively okay.

I gritted my teeth and staggered along the sidewalk until I got to Paige's gate. I slid the key into the gate and slammed it shut behind me. Despite the throbbing pain coming from various points of my body, as I walked, my mind became clearer and the staggering seemed to be under control. My legs were sore and aching. I climbed the short staircase to her door and went in.

Paige looked up from her computer and gave a slight scream. She sprang to her feet, knocking her chair over. "Oh my God! Are you all right?"

"I didn't get the food," I said. The ringing was getting quieter. Now it was more like a dull buzzing sound.

Paige's face was pale, her eyes wide. "What happened?"

"I got jumped." I walked through her kitchen to the laundry room and turned on the hot water spigot in the sink. I looked at myself in the mirror and could understand why she screamed. I looked like something that had been dredged up from a swamp. I had a black eye and an ugly, swollen bruise across my right cheek. My lips were cut and swollen. I reached for a washcloth, splashed hot water on my face, and started patting the mud and dried blood off my skin.

"You need to go to the hospital," Paige said from the doorway. "Come on, let's go."

"I'm fine," I growled back at her and looked again in the mirror. "Does Ryan have any clothes here that would fit me?" I stood back to my full height.

"You need to get checked out."

"I'm not going to any fucking hospital," I snapped. "Clothes! Now!"

Without a word she walked away. I heard her going up the stairs to the second floor. I pulled my shirt up over my head. "Ow, ow, ow." The shirt was ruined, so I tossed it in the garbage pail. I started soaping up my arms and got a good look at my chest in the mirror. There were ugly bruises all over my chest and abdomen. I washed the mud off my arms. I undid my pants and eased them down. My legs were bruised as well.

"Here." Paige placed a pair of sweatpants and a sweatshirt on the washing machine behind me. "Chanse, are you sure about going to the emergency room? You look horrible, really."

"I'm just bruised up is all." I knelt down with a moan and put my head under the rushing hot water. I massaged soap into my hair, carefully rubbing around the lump. I rinsed the soap out and wrapped a towel around my head. I took off my filthy, muddy underwear and pulled the sweatpants on. She handed me two Tylenols after I gingerly pulled the sweatshirt over my head. I felt somewhat better. And with the mud and blood washed away, I just looked like I'd been in a fight. A bad one, granted, that I hadn't won, but at least I wouldn't scare small children anymore. I walked into her living room and popped the Tylenol. I sat down on the couch.

"Maybe we should call Venus and Blaine—"

"I didn't see who it was, Paige." I eased back against the back cushions. "I heard someone running up behind me, and when I turned around I took a nasty punch to the face. I got knocked down, and the son of a bitch kept kicking me until I passed out."

Now that the shock had passed, I was starting to get mad.

"This wasn't a mugging," I went on. "This was a warning. From Frillian."

"You don't know that—"

"Jay Robinette did this." I shushed her. "I'm not that easy to take down. Whoever hit me was strong enough to knock me off my feet—and he was at least as tall as I am, if not taller." I pointed to the bruise on my right cheek. "Look at this! No one shorter than me could have hit me so hard here. Or bruised me like this." I placed my own fist up against the bruise. "See the angle? It was a straight-on punch, not from below." I was getting angrier. "It was Jay Robinette, all right." I clenched my teeth. "I may not be able to prove it, but Frillian sent me a message tonight. Obviously, they don't want me to find out what Freddy did."

"Movie stars don't—"

I interrupted her, pointing at my face. "Whatever Freddy did in his past, it was bad. Bad enough that they don't want anyone to ever find out about it. Well, this time, they fucked with the wrong private eye." I gave her a grim smile. "I'm bringing those Hollywood assholes down."

"Chanse—" But then, she closed her mouth and suppressed a giggle. "You sound kind of Hollywood yourself, John Wayne." After a moment, she went on, "Okay, count me in. But promise me you're going to be more careful."

"Trust me, I don't want to go through this again." I smiled at her. I stood up, wincing. "All right, I'm going to walk home."

"Walk? Are you insane?" She walked into the kitchen and grabbed her purse. "After what just happened? I'll drive you."

"No, I want to walk." I grimaced. "It'll be okay, Paige. Robinette isn't out there anymore. His job is done. If he'd wanted to kill me, he could have. That wasn't part of the plan."

"If you aren't going to the hospital to get checked, you should stay here," she insisted. "What if something's wrong—like you have a concussion and you don't know it?"

I gave a half-laugh. "Paige, I'm fine. Really. Besides—" I waved at her couch. It wasn't a full-sized couch—more of a longer loveseat, really. There was no way I could stretch out on it. "As sore and battered as I am, sleeping on your couch isn't going to help. I need my own bed tonight."

She surrendered and put her purse down on the coffee table. "Okay, fine, you stubborn asshole."

She walked me out to the gate, her lips pursed in disapproval as I hobbled along. The more I walked, though, the easier it got. But she kept her mouth shut until she'd shut the gate behind me. "Call me and let me know you're home safe, okay?"

"I will."

The street was deserted, and there was no traffic on Prytania Street as I crossed it. I wasn't sure if the media circus had been disbanded, but I didn't care, either. Frillian wanted war, did they? Well, I'd be more than happy to fire some shots back.

When I reached Coliseum Square, I looked across to my house. The vans were gone. The sidewalk was clear. But a car I didn't recognize was parked in front of my house—it didn't belong to any of my neighbors. My heart started beating a little faster—*You idiot, Paige was right, what if whoever beat you is waiting to finish the job?*—but I took some deep breaths and started walking across the park.

As I drew closer to Camp Street, I could see two people sitting in the car. A cigarette lighter flared, and with no small relief I realized that the passenger was a woman.

I crossed the street and headed for the gate. I had just started to open it when I heard car doors shut.

Get inside the house! My mind screamed at me.

"Chanse MacLeod?" a woman's voice said from behind me.

I turned, and a bright light blinded me. When my eyes adjusted, I realized it was the light from a video camera.

The woman approached me. The man with her was holding the camera and was aiming it at me. She smiled. She was in her late forties, with graying dark hair. She was holding a digital recorder in her hand. "I'm Debra Norris, with *The Veronica Vance Show*. I was wondering if I could ask you a few questions about the Glynis Parrish murder?"

"I'm sorry, but I can't comment on the case," I replied.

"What happened to your face?"

I shrugged. "This is what happens when you tell the truth about movie stars." I turned my back and walked up my steps. I laughed grimly to myself. *Chew on THAT when it airs, Frillian!* Once I was inside my apartment, I called Paige to let her know I'd gotten home okay. She sounded relieved, and I promised to call her again when I got up. I walked over to my desk. I got out my cell phone and dialed Jephtha.

"Hello?"

I took a deep breath. "Jephtha, I need you to do something for me." I closed my eyes. I bit my lower lip. I'd never specifically asked him to do anything illegal before—and it didn't sit well with me. He'd probably done some illegal things over the years, but we operated on a *don't ask, don't tell* policy. This was the first time I'd asked him to break the law and risk his freedom.

But it was the only way I could think of to get the information.

"Sure."

"How hard would it be for you to break into a university's database?"

He didn't answer at first. I was about to tell him to forget it when he replied, "Not hard, really. It depends on their security system. Their main concern is student hackers trying to change grades." I heard him inhale. "Sure, it's not exactly legal to break in. But I think I can do it without leaving a record."

"I just want you to retrieve records on a student from about twelve years ago." I swallowed. "But I don't want you to do anything risky."

He laughed. "Well, it shouldn't be difficult at all. No one ever wants to access old records—they usually don't protect that stuff much. It just depends on if they converted the old paper files to digital, or when they started keeping records on the computer. But twelve years ago—I'd imagine most colleges had started using computers by then."

I grabbed the case file I'd started. I gave him the name of the university and the dates attended. "The student's name was Frederick Bliss."

"Freddy Bliss?" He whistled. "Okay, boss, I'll get right on it."

"Thanks, Jephtha—but be careful, okay?" I hung up the phone.

I sat down at my computer and checked my e-mail.

The in-box was full; all of the messages from addresses I didn't recognize. Some of the subject lines were insulting, to put it mildly. I marked them all as spam, and went to bed. I set the alarm for eight. That would give me plenty of time to shower and wake up before meeting Brett. My body still ached a bit, but the Tylenol was working. I closed my eyes. I was exhausted.

I didn't dream, and slept like a stone.

I woke up in the morning feeling sore and tired. I took a long, hot bath while the coffee brewed, letting the hot water work its magic on my muscles and joints. I got out of the tub feeling much better. I was still stiff in places, but for the most part, I was functional. I took some more Tylenol. I still looked awful, but that couldn't be helped. The lump on the back of my head seemed to have gone down a bit as well. With a full cup of coffee, I sat down at my computer and logged on.

The first headline on the welcome page screamed at me: *Witness In Parrish Murder Beaten.* There was also a photo of my battered face. I clicked on the link, and it brought up one of those video links. I clicked on the play button—and there I was, on the sidewalk in front of my house. I closed my eyes as I heard myself saying, *This is what happens when you tell the truth about movie stars.*

I glanced at the Web site header line. It was a gossip site. My heart sinking, I started reading the accompanying article.

"Chanse MacLeod, a New Orleans private investigator who claims to have seen Freddy Bliss leaving Glynis Parrish's home the night she was murdered, apparently was attacked and beaten—and from his comments to a reporter from 'The Veronica Vance Show,' caught on tape, seems to think Frillian was behind it!

MacLeod, an openly gay man, has been involved in several homicides over the years in New Orleans. Sources tell us here at tarnishedtinsel.com that he has actually killed twice—his first victim a gay prostitute named Glenn Austin. He also was involved with soft-core gay wrestling video star Cody Dallas, whose real name was Paul Maxwell. Several years ago, Maxwell was kidnapped and murdered by a deranged fan."

I swallowed. There was a picture of Paul wearing a skimpy bright yellow bikini, with a come-hither look on his face. The caption read, *Murdered soft-core porn star Cody Dallas.*

Christ, I thought. I knew I should stop reading, close the page, and forget about it. But somehow I couldn't. I had to pick at the scab.

"*MacLeod, who was a New Orleans police officer and still has strong ties to the department, is himself a suspect in the murder of television star Glynis Parrish—but one the New Orleans police don't seem to be taking very seriously. Their investigation seems to be targeting on super-sexy star Freddy Bliss—primarily based on what MacLeod claims to have seen the night of the murder! But the gay private dick was in Glynis Parrish's home the day she was murdered, and sources tell us that his fingerprints were found on the murder weapon—the Emmy Glynis won for her long-running television series,* Sportsdesk. *Another source tells us that MacLeod was actually on Frillian's payroll, and was fired the day after the murder. MacLeod was questioned by the New Orleans police department, but let go after an interrogation that didn't last longer than an hour. It doesn't hurt to have connections, apparently—looks like corruption is alive and well in the Big Easy!*

"*MacLeod, who runs his own private investigation business, has thus far refused to talk to the press. No police report was filed on the altercation that bruised his face. What does the gay private dick have to hide?*

"*Two murders in New Orleans can already be chalked up to Chanse MacLeod. Is it really that much of a stretch to think he might have something to do with Glynis Parrish's murder? Not according to the NOPD! The NOPD refused to answer questions about the investigation, or why they weren't taking MacLeod, a two-time killer, seriously as a suspect. All we know is once a killer, always a killer—unless you live in New Orleans and have friends at the cop shop.*"

I set my coffee cup back down on the desk. *Deep breaths*, I told myself. *It's just a gossip website, and no one could possibly take it seriously. It's not like it's a reputable news agency. And it's going to get a hell of a lot worse. So ignore it, forget about it. There's nothing you can do about it, anyway.* I stared at the picture of Paul, and started to get angry all over again.

There was absolutely no need to drag Paul into this. I hoped Fee and the rest of his family didn't see this garbage.

At the bottom of the article was a place to post comments. My jaw dropped. There were over 36,000 comments already.

I clicked on the link to the comments page.

The first post started, *That faggot got what he deserved— whoever beat him up shouldn't have stopped there, they should have killed him for the lies he's spreading about Freddy Bliss . . .*

No need to read this crap, I thought, switching over to my e-mail in-box.

It was full again. I started marking the messages as spam and getting rid of them. The header lines included such charming statements as *Fucking faggot; Leave Frillian alone you fag; Someone should kill your gay ass;* and so forth.

I shook my head. Would it have killed me to say, "No comment"?

I got up from the desk and walked over to my front window, pulling the curtains aside. I walked back to my desk and sat down, reading the original article again. This time I remained calm. Now that the initial shock was over, all I felt was a dull spreading rage—and that wasn't a good thing. I needed to remain calm, let it roll off me, and stay focused. Sure, everything in the article was true—but it was the way it was written that made me sound like some kind of crazed monster. Undoubtedly, the reporter was also getting some payback for my not returning his or her calls.

I heard Jillian saying, "They'll print *anything,* with no re-gard for whether it's true or not . . . or they'll take what's true and make it sound as awful as they can."

"So this is what it's like to be a celebrity," I said out loud, finishing my coffee. "I think it *sucks.*"

No sense getting angry about it. I just hated the feeling of powerlessness. These people could write just about anything they wanted to, make any kind of innuendo, and there wasn't a damned thing I could do about it.

But it did make me wonder where they got their informa-tion from.

The only people who could benefit from my being dis-credited were Freddy and Jillian.

And why discredit me—*unless Freddy had killed Glynis?*

I was becoming more and more convinced. They certainly weren't acting like Freddy was innocent.

I scrolled down to the bottom of the page. I forced myself to read the comments. They were horrible, people sitting be-hind the anonymity of their computer screens passing judg-ments.

Chance McCloud—why didn't you mention that he's a faggot pervert? He's killed before, how do the police know that he didn't kill Glynis? He lives outside God's law, so the commandment against killing means nothing to him. He and all the other perverts in New Orleans should be rounded up and killed, it's what God com-mands . . . he and others like him are an abomination in the eyes of the Lord. Why else did God send the hurri-cane to destroy the modern Sodom? These are indeed sorry times for this country when perverts like that can subvert God's law and get away with it.

I wanted to put my fist through the computer screen. Fury filled my brain, and I clicked on the respond button on the page. Then I thought better of it and closed the window. *Don't get angry, just shrug it off. There's nothing you can do about it. And anything you could say would just inflame them more. Don't give them any attention; that's what they want. Just ignore them and don't descend to their level.*

In the five minutes since I'd emptied my in-box, it had filled up again. Most of the messages were interview requests, but the subject line of one was abusive: *You Should Burn in Hell.* The return address was a series of numbers and letters that made no sense;

Against my better judgment I opened it, and read:

You fucking faggot,

You can get away with your perversions in a disgusting city like New Orleans, but in the rest of the country we all live by God's law, and you are an abomination in His eyes. You obviously have some kind of agenda, some reason to try to destroy Freddy and Jillian, but it's not too late to recant not only your lies, or to make yourself right in the eyes of the Lord. You like taking it up the butt? Well, when you finish outraging good Christians, we have something to shove up your butt—a shotgun ready to blow you to Kingdom Come, and then when you face your maker, we'll see how defiant you are in your sin. You are an abomination, who has turned his back on the Lord. His judgment will way heavy on your soul. We'll be praying for you.

My hands shaking with anger, I forwarded it to Jephtha, asking him to trace the sender for me. I then saved it, moving on to continue emptying out my in-box. Sadly, that wasn't the only one of its type, and after reading for the fifth time how I was damned to eternal hell, I stopped.

I got another cup of coffee and sat down on the couch for a moment. I was breathing fine, and my heart rate seemed normal, which was great. I took a couple of cleansing breaths, and sighed. I called Paige, and she answered, screaming, "WHAT THE HELL DID YOU SAY THAT ON CAMERA FOR YOU BIG IDIOT!"

"Good morning to you too, did you sleep well?" I replied. "And yes, I'm fine, just a bit on the sore side."

"I'm counting to ten, give me a second."

"Okay, granted, it wasn't the smartest thing to do," I said. I could hear her counting. "But damn it, I couldn't just let it go. And I was hoping to stir up Frillian."

"Nine, ten." She blew out a long breath. "Good idea. If they sent someone to beat you up—which by the way we don't know for a fact—you're right. By all means, antagonize them some more. I could wring your neck."

"Jephtha's tracing some information for me from Freddy's college days," I said. With Paige, I've learned that it's sometimes best to ignore her and change the subject. "I'm going to stop by his place after I meet with Brett, the trainer, and see what he's found."

"Oh, and Shirley Harris is in rehab, by the way," Paige replied with a sad laugh. "It was on the news last night. Frillian hired a private plane and sent her to one of those celebrity places like Betty Ford—near Palm Springs. No one's going to be able to get anything out of her now. If you ask me, they sure are acting like they're guilty. We can write Shirley off as a source now." She sighed. "I'm having lunch with Venus later. I'm going to tell her about my interview with Shirley. Maybe she can get to Shirley, but who knows? I wish I'd been able to get the name of her private eye out of her."

"If her private eye was able to dig it up, we should be able to," I said confidently.

"What I don't understand," Paige said slowly, "is *why* it hasn't come up before. Someone out there has to know—and has to know it's worth a lot of money to either Freddy or the tabloids."

"Maybe they've been paying people off for years, Paige. We don't know." I closed my eyes. "And *someone* besides Shirley knows. Whoever sent the original e-mails. That's really what got this whole mess started. It couldn't have been Glynis. If she'd known, why would she wait until now to bring it all up?"

"Maybe she just now found out." Paige sighed. "Okay, I'm heading out now. Give me a call later, all right?"

"Yeah." I closed the phone and it rang almost immediately. "MacLeod."

"Hey, Chanse, Storm Bradley here. Just got off the phone with Casanova. Yeah, they found your prints on the murder weapon, all right—the Emmy. But the way your prints are on it, you couldn't have used it to strike the blow that killed Glynis Parrish. The forensics are all wrong."

"So I'm no longer a suspect?"

"Well . . . you could have used gloves for the murder, then planted the prints to throw the cops off, right?" He laughed; I didn't. "Maybe you're not quite off the hook, but it's a good sign."

"Oh. Well, thanks, Storm."

"No problem. If you need me, call me." He paused. "By the way, *nice* footage on CNN this morning. Did you intend to imply that Frillian had you beaten up?"

I didn't answer. "Yeah, well, it had just happened, and I was mad. I know I should have just said no comment, but I was pissed."

"Are you okay? Did you go to the hospital? Fill out a police report?"

"No, I didn't do either. I'm fine. Just a little sore and bruised."

"Well, if they have a problem with it I'll undoubtedly be hearing from Loren McKeithen. I'll let you know."

"Thanks." I hung up the phone. It was getting close to ten. I grabbed my wallet and keys and walked out the back door to the parking lot. From the sidewalk, people started shouting my name. I started the car and backed out of my spot, clicking the gate open with my remote. The reporters swarmed all over the driveway in front of my car, but I didn't roll the window down and kept moving forward slowly. I had to resist the urge to stomp down on the gas and take a few of them out. Cameras were clicking, questions were being screamed at me, but then the car was out onto Camp Street. In the rearview mirror I saw them running for the vans.

Christ.

The light at Melpomene was red. It was a one-way street going the other way, but I floored it and turned right. I swerved to avoid a white SUV that honked its horn at me. The woman behind the wheel flipped me the bird. I turned right on Magazine, and then took the next left at high speed. I took the next right, the next left, and finally wound up on Race heading towards Tchoupitoulas.

There was no one behind me when I checked my rearview mirror.

I smiled and headed uptown.

CHAPTER ELEVEN

BODYTECH WAS LOCATED on Magazine Street, just beyond Louisiana Avenue.

I pulled into the parking lot. Several other cars were there, but Allen's white Lexus wasn't one of them. I breathed a sigh of relief. I wasn't in the mood for small talk with my ex. I pulled into a spot and got out of the car. I checked for reporters, laughing grimly to myself. But I'd lost the ones who'd tried to follow me. Hopefully, none of them would figure out where I'd gone. The cars in the lot were empty, and no other cars pulled into the lot. I locked the car and walked into the gym.

A pumping dance remix of Fergie's "Big Girls Don't Cry" was blaring over the stereo system. Davina, a gorgeous young woman of Middle Eastern descent, was working at the front desk. She had her back to me, her long, thick, bluish-black hair hanging down her back in a braid. She was folding towels. I liked her—she'd been working at Bodytech since the flood. The gym she'd worked at in Mid-City had closed. I swiped my membership card, and said, "Good morning, Davina. I have an appointment with Brett." I glanced at the little tree with the trainer's business cards right next to the card-reader. His card was at the top: *Brett*

Colby, Personal Training. On the right side was a small black and white photograph of him in a white posing trunk. He looked vaguely familiar, but I'd probably just seen him around the gym. I took a card and slipped it into my pocket.

"Okay," she said. She turned around and gave a start when she got a good look at my face. Her eyes widened. She swallowed. "Um, good morning, Chanse. My God, what happened to you? Are you all right?"

"Haven't you been watching the news?" I gestured at my face and shrugged. "I got jumped last night." I gave a half-hearted laugh. "I know I look awful—but it looks better today than it did last night."

"Wow, they sure did a number on you." She shook her head and regained her professional composure. "It just took me by surprise." She stepped closer to the counter. "Are you okay?" She reached over and touched one of the bruises on my cheek. I flinched, and she pulled her hand back. "Sorry!"

"Ah, no problem." I smiled at her. "Yeah, I'm okay. I've been better. Is Brett here?"

She raised an eyebrow. "Yeah, he's in the trainer's office." She tilted her head to one side. "What are you doing making an appointment with a trainer after all these years?" She looked me up and down critically. She leaned on the counter with her elbows.

"I want to trim down some," I lied. "I've put on a lot of size these last few years, and I want to drop about twenty pounds." I winked. "That's my fighting weight. Besides, I've heard really good things about Brett."

"He's not the one I would choose, frankly." She rolled her eyes. "Not that he's not a good trainer. He's just . . . oh, never mind."

"What?" I leaned on the counter and lowered my voice. "Come on, Davina, spill."

"He's really arrogant." She pursed her lips. "Thinks he's God's gift, you know what I mean? He's never met a mirror he didn't like." She waved a hand. "But he's a good trainer. Just be prepared to know more about him than you want to." She picked up the phone. "Go on back. I'll let him know you're on your way." She pressed a button as I walked away.

The trainer's office was in the far back corner of the gym. The building housing Bodytech had once been a small sugar warehouse, so the workout area was one big room. The wall facing the parking lot was all windows, tinted to reduce the sun's glare. The front desk was on the right side, with the management office door to the left. The locker rooms were also on that side of the building. The opposite wall was all mirrors. The front area by the desk was where the cardio machines were, with a small aerobics room fitting into the front corner. I walked past the cardio machines, and glanced up at the huge TV screens hanging on the opposite wall. One was tuned into CNN, and I saw another view of myself standing on the front steps to my apartment, pointing at my face. Apparently, my little moment of fame was still in heavy rotation. Several people on treadmills with headphones on were staring at that television. I winced and started walking faster.

The trainer's office was all glass with a door. I could see someone seated at the desk in there, going over some papers. There was a file cabinet in the back corner, and a chair right next to the desk for a client to be seated. I crossed the weight area and knocked on the open door. "Brett? I have an appointment? I'm Chanse MacLeod."

"Hi." Brett closed the file on his desk and stood up. He reached his right hand toward me just as he got a good look at my face. His eyes widened in shock—a reaction I was getting used to.

I took his big hand and shook it. It was lined with cal-
luses. "Nice to meet you," I said. "And yes, my face takes
some getting used to."

"Sorry. Christ, man." He gripped my hand hard before
letting go. He stood a little taller than six feet, I estimated,
and had to weigh in excess of two hundred pounds. His
blond hair was buzzed down almost to the scalp. He had vibrant blue eyes. He was wearing a gray Bodytech T-shirt
with the sleeves cut off deeply so that it barely covered his
chest. The deep cut of the shirt exposed his thick lat muscles. His tan arms were lined with veins. His muscles were
thick and deeply defined. He sported a golden tan. He looked
to be in his early forties, I judged by the lines from his eyes
and mouth. When he smiled again, deep dimples sank into
his cheeks. "You know, when I saw your name in the appointment book I wondered if you were really the guy I saw
on television this morning."

"Well, the odds against there being two Chanse MacLeods
in New Orleans are pretty high." I replied. "Not exactly a
common name."

"No, it's not. Have a seat." He gestured toward the chair.
He sat down behind the desk again. "So, what can I do for
you?" He narrowed his eyes and scrutinized my body.
"You're pretty solid and in pretty good shape already. What
kind of changes are you thinking about making?" He thought
for a moment. "I'd recommend trimming down a bit—you're
a big guy. Maybe get a bit leaner? Or do you want to really
pack on some muscle size? The shape you're in, either
would be relatively easy to pull off with the right program
and diet."

"I don't need a trainer," I replied. Might as well put my
cards on the table, I figured. "I'm here about the Glynis Parrish murder." I watched his face.

He leaned back in his chair, folding his arms. His face was expressionless. "I kind of figured that's what this was." He set his jaw. "I told the police everything I know. And it's not cool to make an appointment under false pretenses. I'm pretty busy."

"That's smart," I said. "You should always cooperate with the cops." I pulled my wallet out and placed it on the desk. "I'm prepared to pay you for your time. I made an appointment for an hour with a trainer."

He laughed. "Fifty bucks? That buys you a workout for an hour. Not a conversation about one of my other clients." He leaned forward and smirked. "I got three tabloids willing to pay me ten grand to tell them everything I know about Glynis. Why should I tell you for fifty bucks?"

"Okay. Suit yourself." I put my wallet back in my pocket. "I guess I'll wait and read what you have to say in line at the grocery store." I stood up.

"Wait."

I turned and looked at him. He stared at my face. "What you said on TV—about why you got beat up—was that true?"

I nodded. "As far as I know, yeah."

"Do you think—" he swallowed. "I might be in danger?"

I managed not to smile in triumph. I sat back down. "That depends on what you know. You sure you don't want a tabloid payday?" I leaned back in my chair and waited.

I didn't have to wait long. He swallowed. "Just because I talk to you doesn't mean I still can't sell my story to them." He paused for a moment, thinking. "Well, I don't really know that much, to tell you the truth. About the murder, I mean." Beads of sweat appeared on his forehead. "I trained Glynis in the mornings, five days a week. On the days when she had an early call, I had to be there at five. The days she didn't have to be on set, I was there at seven. She always woke up

early. She said it was a holdover from the television show—
she had to always be up early and her body never adjusted."

"Were you there the day she died?"

He nodded. "Yeah." He swallowed again, his Adam's apple bobbing in his neck. "Yeah, I was there that morning."

"Did you notice anything unusual about her that day? Did
she seem different in any way?"

"No. She was the same as she always was. Wide awake
and ready to go. She was a great client that way—she never
complained, never cancelled, and was always ready to work
hard. She was into her workouts. I commented on it once
and she just said, 'I have to look great if I want to work.'" He
smiled. "We had that in common." He shifted in his chair,
and every muscle in his upper body flexed. "My body is my
best advertisement. If I don't look great, who's going to hire
me? She was the same way."

"Did she ever talk about anything personal with you?"
Allen had once told me that trainers were like therapists in a
way. You pay someone for their attention for an hour, and
you start telling them things you didn't even tell your closest
friends.

"Never." He shook his head. "When we worked out, it was
always about exercise, her diet, things like that. I was her
trainer, nothing more."

"But you were sleeping with her."

His eyes bugged out. "What?" His face turned red.
"Where on earth did you hear that?" He started laughing.
"Dude, I am not into women. I haven't slept with a woman
since high school." He whistled. "Not even the cops threw
that one at me. Seriously. Who told you that?"

"You're gay," I said. As the truth of the matter hit me, I
realized I knew why he looked familiar—he was one of the
dick dancers at the Pub. I'd seen him there, up on the bar,

shaking his ass for dollars. But Rosemary had been very definite that Brett and Glynis were sleeping together. I remembered the look of distaste on her face when she'd told me.

"Yes, I'm gay." He spread his arms apologetically—still managing to flex every muscle as he did so. I was beginning to see what Davina had meant.

"Rosemary said—"

"That one?" He interrupted me, making a face. "Please. You can't believe anything that crazy bitch says." He spat the words out.

"Why do you say that?"

"Well, she's a freak, man." He shrugged. "She was always coming in during our sessions, for one thing. It drove me crazy, her always interrupting like that." He laughed. "Even if I was straight, there was no way I could have been fucking Glynis during our sessions. Rosemary never left us alone long enough for that, you know what I mean? We would have had to do it in like five minutes or less." He grinned at me. "And I take longer than five minutes."

I resisted the urge to roll my eyes. Arrogant was putting it mildly.

He went on, "And she was overly friendly—even though I made it clear to her that I was gay from the very beginning. You know how some women never seem to get the message?"

"What do you mean by overly friendly?"

He sighed. "You know what I mean—I'm sure you get it too. You know, straight women who always talk about your muscles, how hot you are, wanting me to flex for her . . . I mean, at first it was flattering, I can't say that it's not. I kind of felt sorry for her—Glynis seemed to really keep her hopping. She told me she was relatively new in town, didn't know anyone, so I kind of always tried to be nice to her. But it was like she took my being nice the wrong way. She started buying me presents. At first, it was just kind of sweet, you know what I mean? Nothing inappropriate, just really nice stuff, like she always had the kind of protein bars I liked. She would have a protein shake ready for me when Glynis and I were finished. She would call me all the time—on the stupidest pretext, like always to verify my appointment times and stuff like that, which didn't make a lot of sense, because I always did that with Glynis every day before I left. I'm a professional, you know? But at first, it was kind of sweet. I figured she was just lonely and wanted someone to talk to. Then it started getting really weird." He hesitated. "She bought me underwear—which was weird enough—and then would say something like, 'would love to see you in it' . . . you know that kind of thing. Would I pose nude for her?" He shook his head. "It started really creeping me out. I let it go as long as I could. Finally this week I told her she had to stop buying me things and calling me all the time. And then she turned on me. She told Glynis I'd said some inappropriate things to her."

"Inappropriate how?"

"She claimed I was always, oh, I don't know, saying suggestive things to her? Commenting on her figure and so forth, and it was making her uncomfortable and nervous to be around me, the lying bitch. She was the one sexually harassing ME." He sighed. "I mean, I should be used to it by now—being sexually harassed, I mean. Just because I have this body doesn't mean its okay to hit on me, you know."

I bit my tongue. "Did you confront her about it?"

"No." He wrinkled his forehead. "Glynis told me about it that morning. Man, I was pissed."

"What did Glynis say about it?"

"Well, Glynis thought the whole thing was ridiculous. She

said she hired me specifically because I was gay—she'd had a bad experience with a straight trainer once, and said she would only hire gay ones from then on. She said she was telling me about it, not because she was mad, or anything, but she thought I should know. She said she would have a talk with Rosemary about it. She told me she would make sure from there on out that Rosemary wouldn't be there when I came by."

"How did Rosemary act toward you that morning?"

"She ignored me—the way she had ever since I asked her to stop." He rubbed his eyes. "She would open the front door and just walk away, not even acknowledge me, which you know, was fine with me, the crazy bitch. Chance, it was fucking freaky the way that woman acted. It may not seem weird to you, but she gave me the creeps. It's nothing I can put my hand on—but . . ."

I steered the conversation back where I wanted it to go. "Glynis never said anything about Freddy Bliss to you?"

"No. I told you, we never talked about her private life. I tried once to get her to open up about stuff—personal trainers are kind of like therapists. You get to know your clients and their business really well, if you know what I mean. So, I thought it was kind of odd that Glynis never really talked, you know? But she shut me down completely. In a way, it was kind of insulting—you know, made it very clear to me that I was staff, not a friend." He laughed. "In a way it was cool, though. I do get tired of listening to all that boring shit from clients. But you know, she was a star. She knew famous people. I wouldn't have minding getting gossip from her." He snapped his fingers. "I remember what it was. I asked her if Jared Heath"—one of her co-stars from *Sportsdesk*—"was as big of a tool as he seemed. She just gave me a look and said, 'I pay you to train me, not to gossip with.' I was like, 'Okay then, let's do crunches.'"

I took a business card out of my wallet and handed it over. "If you can think of anything else, give me a call."

"You sure you don't want a trainer?" he asked, smiling at me. Brett looked me up and down again. "We can turn you into a god in no time."

"I'll keep that in mind," I said, adding to myself, *You cocky, arrogant asshole.* I shrugged. "If I do, I'll give you a call."

I walked out of the gym, my mind racing ahead. Davina had been right—I couldn't remember the last time I'd met such an arrogant peacock. It was entirely possible Rosemary was just being friendly. He, of course, expected everyone he met to want to sleep with him, and would always misinterpret friendliness.

But why had she lied about him sleeping with Glynis? Revenge, because he'd asked her to stop buying him things?

That didn't make a lot of sense. Maybe she *had* thought he was sleeping with Glynis.

I was in the neighborhood, so I headed over to Jephtha's. It was early for him—since Abby worked late nights he kept the same hours. I parked in front of his house and knocked on the door. The dogs started barking. I was just starting to think I should have called first when I heard the deadbolt turn. The door swung open, and Jephtha grinned at me. "Dude, I'd hate to see the other guy." He yawned. His hair was standing up in every direction. He was wearing Saints sweats.

"He looks fine now, but that's because I didn't have a fair shot at him The next time, he's losing his teeth." I walked past him into the house. "Did I wake you?"

"Shhh, keep it down, Abby's still asleep." He yawned again. "You want some coffee?"

"No thanks." I shook my head. "Sorry to get you up."

"I haven't been to bed yet." He led me back into the computer room. He handed me a folder full of paper. "You know me, once I got started digging, I couldn't sleep until I got everything you wanted." He yawned and stretched again. "The bed's going to feel pretty good. Oh, yeah!" He rolled his eyes at me. "You know, it would have saved me a lot of time if you'd told me Freddy's real name."

"Huh?" I kicked myself. *Some investigator you are.*

"Freddy Bliss is his *professional* name. So, when I first, um, gained access to the Emporia State records, I couldn't find any record of him—because Freddy Bliss didn't exist back then." He grinned at me. "So, I had to do some more hunting. I found an interview he did where he talked about going to Emporia State, so then I had to find his birth name." He winked. "Frederick Bliss Osborne, of Newton, Kansas, enrolled at Emporia State thirteen years ago."

"Good work," I replied, still pissed at myself. Why hadn't it occurred to me that Freddy Bliss was a stage name?

But it hadn't been mentioned in any of the Internet research I'd done, which was kind of unusual. I opened the file and looked at his transcripts. "He wasn't much of a student, was he?" He'd barely scraped by—mostly C's. The few B's he'd earned were offset by an equal number of D's. Even in acting classes his grades had been average.

"Skip that shit—that's not the good stuff, trust me."

I turned a few pages. "What's this?" I scanned the page. I couldn't help myself, I smiled. *And here it is, Mr. Bliss. The big secret you don't want anyone to know about.*

"It's a disciplinary hearing." Jephtha grinned. "They erased it—afterwards. But nothing ever is truly erased from a computer hard drive unless you scrub it completely—and whoever deleted the file thought it was gone. It was still there, on the hard drive. It took me a few hours, but I was able to reconstruct it." He preened a little bit. "I kick ass, don't I?"

I started reading. Karen Zorn, a sophomore, had gone to the dean and accused Freddy Bliss of raping her at a party at Sigma Alpha Epsilon, where Freddy was a brother. She claimed that Freddy had gotten her drunk—feeding her tequila shots—and when she was so drunk she could barely stand, she'd asked if she could go lie down for a while. Freddy had taken her up to his room, and once they were inside, he locked the door and attacked her. She'd tried to scream but he'd put a sock in her mouth and raped her.

Freddy denied the rape, and two of his fraternity buddies—Bobby Wallace and Tim Dahlke—had sworn that Karen had been chasing Freddy for weeks. Freddy got drunk at the party and had slept with her, but it was consensual; it was *her* idea. In the morning, Freddy had buyer's remorse—and Karen threatened to accuse him of rape. And she had. Based on Bobby and Tim's testimony, the dean had dropped the whole thing.

I remembered my experiences at Beta Kappa. Would a fraternity brother lie to get another brother out of trouble?

Hell, yes. They wouldn't have had to be asked twice. The fraternity mentality was that all women were pieces of garbage to be used and abused—they weren't people.

They were just pieces of ass for the brothers to fuck and toss away.

Oh, yes, I could even understand why the dean would sweep it all under a rug. No university wants to deal with a campus rape trial.

It hadn't helped Karen much that the rape had occurred

at a Friday night party, and she'd done nothing about it until the following Monday. There'd been no rape kit, no trip to the emergency room, no police report.

Poor thing, I thought, getting a little angry. She should have gone to the police. I'd dealt with a few rape victims when I was on the police force, and I could understand her mentality. She was ashamed, she blamed herself, she didn't want anyone to know about it . . . and it had taken her a few days to get herself together and decide to do something about it.

And when she did, Freddy and his fraternity brothers had lied. The dean was more than willing to believe them.

I wondered what had happened to her.

"It gets even better," Jephtha went on. "I dug up the files on her and the other guys. The girl dropped out, and Freddy dropped out the next semester. Bobby and Tim went on to graduate—with honors. But get this—I was curious by now—so I tried to track them down." He flushed a bit. "I hope you don't mind. I know you didn't ask me to do that, so you don't have to pay me for that."

I flipped the page. The next page was the printout of a *Wichita Herald* newspaper clipping from seven years ago. Bobby Wallace was killed in a car crash when his brakes apparently failed. He'd been driving drunk, on his way home from a bar. He'd slammed into a tree and had been killed instantly. According to investigators, there'd been no brake fluid in his car—but he'd just had his car serviced. The lines hadn't been cut, but the fluid had drained out somehow. The mechanic swore he'd checked the brake fluid.

I felt a cold chill go down my spine.

"Go on," Jephtha urged.

The next page was another newspaper clipping. Six years ago, Tim Dahlke had been shot to death in his house. There were no signs of forced entry. Nothing had been stolen. There were no leads.

There was one more piece of paper in the folder. I looked at the last one. TWO KILLED IN MYSTERIOUS FIRE: *Victims were Emporia State Dean and his wife.*

"Holy shit." I looked at Jephtha.

He nodded, his eyes dancing. "I tried to find out what happened to Karen Zorn, but she disappeared after she dropped out. I couldn't find a trace of her anywhere."

Freddy was the only one left alive.

"Thanks, Jephtha. Send me a bill." I clapped him on the shoulder. "You should think about getting a private eye license. This is some really good work. I'll be in touch."

I walked outside and stood in the sunshine for a moment. I had to find Karen Zorn.

There was no way it was a coincidence that everyone involved in the cover-up of the rape had died under mysterious circumstances.

By the time the killings had started, Freddy was a movie star and not easily accessible. His stardom had, in a way, saved his life.

So far.

Outside, I stood for a moment. I dialed Loren. I got his cell phone.

"Hey, Loren, this is Chanse MacLeod. Tell Freddy and Jillian I want to meet with them." I took a deep breath. "Tell them I know about Karen Zorn."

I closed my phone and went home.

CHAPTER TWELVE

Maybe the reason Karen Zorn had disappeared was because no one had found her body.

The thought hit me as I was driving up Camp Street. It caught me so offguard I almost hit a parked car. But it made sense. Three of the men involved in the rape and cover-up were dead. She'd disappeared. Out of everyone involved, the only person still accounted for was Freddy Bliss—the one person who had the most to lose.

It made more sense that Karen had been killed than that she was the killer.

E-mails alluding to the rape had been sent from Glynis's computer, and she'd been murdered.

All roads led back to Freddy Bliss.

The hyena pack in front of my house wasn't as big as it had been when I left for the gym, but they still swarmed my car as I turned into the driveway. I turned up the stereo so I couldn't hear anything they were shouting at me. I parked in my spot and ran for the back stairs. The shouting died away once I was out of their sight.

I headed straight to my computer, and logged into the Internet. I opened the folder Jephtha had given me. Damn, he'd done a good job. I did a directory search for Zorns in

Olpe, Kansas. About ten listings came up. I started dialing. I struck oil on the sixth call.

"Karen?" a tired female voice asked in a flat Midwestern accent. "What has she done now?"

"I'm just trying to find her," I replied. "Do you know how I can get hold of her?"

"I haven't talked to her in years, and good riddance, thank you very much." She sighed.

"Mrs. Zorn—"

"What has she done now?" The voice was resigned. "I can't say as I'm surprised to hear she's done something else. Lord, what a trial that child has been to me, she's been nothing but *trouble* since the day I got pregnant." She gave a great heaving sigh. "Them pro-life people can carry all the signs they want to, and I know it's a sin and murder and all, but I should've had an abortion, is what I should have done. If I knew then what I know now . . ."

Whoa. "Mrs. Zorn—"

"You know, I got pregnant when I was in high school." She went on as though I hadn't said a word. I got the feeling she'd just been waiting for an audience to come along. Now that she had one, she was going to cut loose and let it all hang out. "Her daddy didn't want to marry me, of course, but his daddy and my daddy made him do the right thing by me. And back then I thought abortion was murder, the nuns said so and the nuns were supposed to know, so I had that damned baby. Talk about being punished for your sins for the rest of your life! The marriage was a mistake—he made it clear he thought I got pregnant just so he'd have to marry me. Wasn't that a nice thing to say to me? His wife? The mother of his child? And then he went and got himself killed in a car accident." She made it sound as if he'd done it deliberately, to punish her. "So, what has she done now? Something terrible, I'll bet. I was probably too easy on her. I should have beaten some sense into that girl. I don't care what Father Manion said, it says right there in the Bible you spare the rod you spoil the child."

Oh my God, what a horrible woman. I broke into her tirade. "I'm, um, actually just looking for some background information—"

"Well, what do you want to know? Speak up. You want to know what she was like? She was a horrible child, always causing trouble. She cried all night when she was a baby. I used to pray for guidance, for some relief, but no, she would just scream and scream and scream." She sounded aggrieved, like the baby had done it just to spite her. "And it didn't change as she got older, you know. She was always a handful. Always into everything, always getting in trouble— and if she didn't get her way, she would just scream and throw a tantrum, no matter how hard I spanked her. I could never believe a word that came out of her mouth. She lies as easily as she breathes. She *believes* her lies, even when you catch her at them, catch her red-handed, she'll look you right in the face and lie to you all over again. Like that time she claimed she was raped."

"I beg pardon?" My mind was reeling. This woman should have never been allowed to have a child. My sympathy for Karen was growing.

"I said, like the time she claimed she was raped." Irene went on, her tone making it clear she thought I was an idiot. "I broke my butt working two jobs to pay for her to go to the college over in Emporia. She wanted to go to college, of course—getting a job and working hard wasn't good enough for her, you know, even though she wasn't a good student— she never was much good at anything, to tell the truth, wouldn't even do her chores around the house, to help me out so I could come home from work and just relax, you know? I worked hard. And she could just drive there—even though the car I got her of course wasn't good enough for her—and live at home to save money, so of course I sent her to Emporia State." Her voice clearly showed she thought I was an idiot. "It's only about ten miles down the road. But that wasn't even good enough for the ungrateful little bitch." She let out a heavy sigh. "And then after she was caught in her lies there, she dropped out and went to work. Wasted all that money, and you think she offered to pay me back? Of course not, not Little Miss It's-All-About-Me."

I interrupted her, before she launched into another tirade. "You said she claimed she was raped?"

"Yes, I said it twice, I believe. Aren't you listening to me?" Her voice rose in agitation. "She went to some damn fool fraternity party. I told her and told her, those fraternity boys are nothing but trouble, everybody knows that. Find some nice Catholic boy, I told her, but oh, no! She couldn't be *bothered* with a nice boy. Probably had some damned fool idea one of them rich boys would marry her. Huh. There's only one thing rich boys want from girls like Karen, and it isn't to marry them, I can tell you that." She paused for a moment, and I could hear her breathing into the phone. I was about to ask another question when she started talking again.

"The Sigma Pis, I think it was. She came home early one morning and told me someone drugged her at a party and some boy raped her in his room while some other boys watched! How my heart broke for my poor baby! I was furious. So Monday morning, I marched right into that dean's office and filed a complaint. Had to take the day off from work, and for what? More of her lies. Turns out she'd been stalking the boy, telling people they were in love, and threw herself at him at the party. There were witnesses. And not just the

GREG HERREN

boys, either. Some of the girls at the party said so, too. Everything she'd said to me was a lie. That boy just didn't want her, and she wanted to make trouble for him. I have never been so embarrassed in my life. Turned out she was doing all these things for him—and *sleeping* with him, and she made up her mind that he loved her and was going to marry her—and it was all in her head." She snorted. "If only she hadn't been too old to spank!

"The dean threatened to expel her . . . I lost a day's work so I could go be humiliated. That was when I was done with her, you know. I told her to pack her stuff and get out of my house. And do you think she was even sorry? She wasn't." She sighed. "I'll carry that boy's name with me to the grave. It was Ricky—Ricky Osborne." She made another noise. "I think he was from Newton? Such a nice, handsome boy he was. Very respectful to me, and apologetic. And once he got those braces off his teeth, he'd be a real lady-killer. I suppose that's why Karen tried what she did."

"Thank you, Ms. Zorn, you've been very helpful. Do you have a picture of Karen you can fax or e-mail to me?" I crossed my fingers.

"I don't have a fax machine and I don't have a computer," she whined. "I guess I could have my brother do it. Where should I send it to?"

I gave her both my e-mail address and my fax number.

"If you see her you tell her to call her mother. I haven't talked to her in at least ten years, and my health isn't good," she whined. "I'm ready to let bygones be bygones."

"I'll do that. Thank you, Mrs. Zorn." I hung up the phone.

I went to a search engine for private eyes, and typed in KAREN ZORN, OLPE KANSAS, and the year of her birth. My phone rang as I waited for the results to come up. It was

Paige. I flipped it open. "Hey, Paige, you're not going to believe . . ."

"I just quit my job," she interrupted me. Her voice was shaking. "That fucking bitch Coralie . . ."

"What the hell happened?" I didn't know what to say. Paige loved her job.

"She killed my story, that's what. That has never happened to me once in all the years I have worked at that fucking newspaper. And when I asked her why, she told me that it wasn't in the quote paper's best interests to run a story so critical of Frillian unquote. I told her to shove Frillian up her ass, and then I quit." She sighed. "It was a matter of time, really, and better to quit now than keep being driven insane by her incompetence."

"What are you going to do?"

"*Crescent City* magazine offered me their editor-in-chief position earlier this week." She exhaled. "I told them I'd think about it—thank God I didn't just say no. Anyway, how did things go with the trainer?"

I filled her in on everything I'd uncovered thus far, and when I finished, she said grimly, "So our Freddy is a rapist? Can't wait for that bitch Coralie to find out about *that*."

"Accused rapist," I corrected her. "And possibly a murderer, to boot."

"Well, I didn't get anything of use out of either the maid or the massage therapist," she replied. "They liked Glynis, thought she was really nice, blah blah blah. They didn't much care for Rosemary, though. There was nothing specific, really, they just didn't like her. What's next?"

"Well, I'm waiting to see if Loren calls me back."

"Don't do anything stupid, Chanse," she warned. "You should give all of this to Venus and Blaine and let them handle it. Don't go meet with Frillian. They're dangerous, obviously."

"Okay," I said noncommittally. "What's next for you?"

"I'm going to go interview Rosemary, I think."

"Okay, well call me when you're finished. I'm curious to know what you think of her."

"All right, later." She hung up.

I turned back to my computer. The information on Karen Zorn had finished loading. She'd been listed at her mother's address until she got an apartment in Emporia—right around the time of the rape accusation. Well, that made sense—her mother had said she'd thrown her out. *Poor thing, bad enough she was raped and then wasn't believed, but to have your own mother throw you out over it.* But that apartment was the last listing for her, and she had only lived there for a year.

Karen Zorn had disappeared. A year later, the dean and his wife had died in a fire. The next year, Tim Dahlke had died. Another year went by and Bobby Wallace had also died.

All right around the time Freddy Bliss had been launched as a star in Hollywood.

My phone rang again. "MacLeod."

"Chanse, it's Loren McKeithen." He sounded perturbed. "Look, I got your message and I passed it along to Freddy and Jillian. They want you to come by their house. They want to talk." He paused for a moment. "Who the hell is Karen Zorn?"

"That's not for me to say," I replied. "Call them and tell them I'm on my way over." I hung up.

I made two photocopies of everything Jephtha had given me. I placed them into envelopes. I addressed one to Venus, care of the French Quarter precinct. The other I addressed to Paige. I stamped them. I walked back into my bedroom and got out my gun. I checked it to make sure it was loaded, and slipped on my shoulder harness. Once it was secured, I put on my black leather jacket and stood in front of the mirror. The jacket had been specially made for me to hide the shoulder holster. I smiled at myself. I would drop the envelopes in the mail on my way to the Quarter. So if by chance I disappeared, they wouldn't get away with it this time.

I got into my car and drove out of the parking lot, being swarmed again by hyenas. I smiled and waved at them, the stereo blasting. This time I didn't care if they followed me. There was going to be a much bigger pack of them in front of Frillian's gate, anyway. In fact, I hoped they did follow me. The main witness, visiting the prime suspect?

I was sure www.tarnishedtinsel.com would have a really good time with *that*.

I dropped by the post office on my way downtown and dropped the envelopes in one of the outside drop-boxes. I found a place to park on Touro Street, just inside the Marigny. I crossed Esplanade quickly. Some of the hyenas had followed me, but they were trying to find parking. For the first time in my life I was happy that parking in New Orleans was such a joke. And I'd been right—the pack in front of Frillian's brick fence was at least five times the size of the one in front of mine. I pushed my way through the crowd, ignoring the cameras and the questions being thrown at me. The gate opened just as I reached it, and I jumped inside. It slammed shut behind me.

"Jeez, someone sure did a number on your face," Jay Robinette said with a sly leer.

I resisted the urge to put my fist through his smug face. If there had been any doubt in my mind before about his guilt, it was gone now. "So, Jay, how long have you been doing their dirty work for them? It make you feel like a real man to attack someone from behind?"

His face flushed, and he clenched his fists. He stepped toward me. I didn't flinch or back up. I clenched my own fists. Adrenaline coursed through my entire body. I forgot about the soreness. I forgot about the bruises. *Come on, take a swing at me.*

The door to the carriage house opened and out of the corner of my eye I saw a young woman walk out with several young children. "Jay! What are you doing!" Jillian shouted.

He relaxed his fists. "They're waiting for you in the carriage house."

I laughed. "She's got you trained better than a pit bull." I sneered.

His eyes narrowed. "Count your blessings, faggot."

I walked past him. When I was a few yards past him, I turned back and said with as much contempt as I could, "This faggot is ready for you, fucker. Any time you think you can beat me in a fair fight, bring it on. And I will serve you your balls for dinner." I waved my hand at him. "Go on back to the kennel. She'll be whistling for you soon enough."

I didn't bother to knock. I just opened the door to the carriage house and walked in. Jillian was pacing in front of the bookcases, a cigarette in her hand. Freddy was sitting on the couch. "You smoke in front of the kids?" I asked. "Nice."

Jillian's head whipped around, her eyes slits. "You can't talk to me like that," she hissed.

"I'll talk to you any way I like," I replied, sitting down in an easy chair and crossing my legs. I smiled at her. "After all, he's a rapist and one or both of you is a murderer. Which one of you sent your thug after me last night?"

"What?" Freddy's face went white. "What are you talking about?"

"Drop the innocent act, Freddy." I shrugged. "Robinette did this to my face—and he doesn't do anything without orders from you two."

"I didn't—" Freddy started but Jillian cut him off. "Don't say anything, Freddy. I'll handle this." She crossed her arms. "How much do you want?"

"For what? Keeping his dirty little secret?" I leaned forward in my chair and looked Freddy right in the eyes. "How did it feel to rape Karen Zorn, Freddy? Did it make you feel like a stud, like a man?"

He swallowed. "I didn't rape her."

"Shut up, Freddy!"

"When exactly did Jillian cut off your balls, Freddy?" I went on. "Was it after Shirley Harris's private eye found out the truth? Is that when you two decided to start killing people to protect your precious career?"

"I DIDN'T RAPE THAT GIRL!" Freddy shouted. He turned to Jillian. "And don't you tell me to shut up. I didn't rape that girl and I didn't kill anyone."

"She disappeared, Freddy." I started ticking things off on my fingers. "Right around the time your career started to take off, Karen Zorn disappeared. Then it was the dean's turn—he *and* his wife, killed in a mysterious fire that burned down their house. Then your old fraternity buddy Bobby Wallace—shot and killed in his house by a burglar who didn't break in and didn't steal anything. And poor Tim Dahlke—the brake fluid in his car just disappeared two days after it was refilled. And Glynis. People who have access to your secrets have this really strange habit of dying under questionable circumstances." I shrugged. "Coincidences?"

"Bobby and Tim . . . are dead?" His jaw dropped. "I swear, I didn't have anything to do with any of that, Chanse, I swear."

"Well, they all died before you even met Jillian—so that pretty much lets her off the hook. How long has Robinette worked for you, Freddy?"

"Jay has worked for *me* for fifteen years." Jillian stubbed out her cigarette with a shaking hand and lit another. "All right, yes, I sent him after you last night. That was a mistake and I'm sorry."

"You did *what?*" Freddy stared at his wife in disbelief. "Jillian—"

"He was getting too close." She closed her eyes. "We've worked too long and too hard to let this get out now."

"I didn't rape that girl," Freddy said between clenched teeth. "Is that so hard to believe? Even you don't believe me, do you, Jillian?"

"It doesn't matter what I believe. What matters is what the tabloids will print—and what the public will believe."

"I guess I should be grateful you didn't order your pit bull to kill me." I glared at Jillian. "Is that what happened to Glynis?"

"I didn't have you beaten up." Her face reddened. "And no, I don't know what happened to Glynis."

"Save it for the jury." I turned back to Freddy. "Okay, I'm listening. Tell me what happened with Karen Zorn." I leaned back in the chair.

He took a deep breath. "Look, I wasn't the nicest guy, okay? I was pretty young. I'd always been really good-looking and used to getting my way with any girl I wanted—and if some chick didn't want me, I didn't need to rape her. There was always another one more than happy to hop into bed with me. I joined the fraternity. Karen Zorn came to our little sister rush. She was a nice enough looking girl, and she was nice. She got a crush on me." He shrugged.

"She used to bring me presents, buy me lunch and stuff

like that. I didn't have a lot of money, so yeah, I used her that way. She was always willing to buy beer or food or something. She was always around. It got to be a joke around the house—my little stalker. I wouldn't sleep with her. There was just something about her that didn't strike me as being quite right, you know what I mean? But at that party, I was just drunk enough. She came on to me pretty strong, and I was drunk enough to be okay with it. So I took her up to my room. I could barely stand. She undressed me. She got me into bed—she was on top because I was barely conscious. The next morning when I woke up she was there in bed with me." He swallowed.

"I was hungover and felt like shit. And she wouldn't shut up. She kept going on and on about how happy she was, and what a great future we were going to have together, and what we were going to name our kids. It freaked me out." He wiped sweat off his forehead.

"I told her I'd made a terrible mistake, that I didn't love her, and she needed to leave. She threw a fit—she started screaming at me about how I'd used her, how she did everything for me, she gave and gave and all I did was take and take, and she was going to make me pay for it." He winced at the memory. "She got so out of control Bobby and Tim had to come in and drag her out." He hung his head.

"It was a shitty thing to do. I should have never slept with her. There's no excuse for that. But she wasn't right in the head. And then on Monday she went to the dean and accused me of rape." He swallowed. "Her story didn't stand up. Bobby and Tim told the dean about how she'd stalked me, and how she'd threatened to get even with me that morning. The dean caught her in several lies . . . contradictions . . . and she finally broke down and admitted I hadn't done it." He took a deep breath. "And I never saw her again. I didn't rape her. Later that semester I asked the dean to expunge the disciplinary action from my record, and he did. I thought that was the end of it all." He looked at Jillian, his jaw clenched. "And all this time you knew about it?"

"That doesn't matter, dear. I was just trying to help—"

"By having Jay beat up Chanse? By having your mother locked up in rehab?" His hands were shaking. "And you never said a word about any of this to me. You never asked me about it—and you knew. Did you think I'd raped her, Jillian?"

"Of course not," she said in a soothing tone. "I just knew it was out there, and if it ever got out, it could do damage to you. So I tried to keep it a secret. I was just trying to help—"

"So, Freddy, when you first started getting the e-mails, it never occurred to you that they might be about Karen Zorn?" I interrupted Jillian. They could fight out their personal problems after I left.

He shook his head. "It crossed my mind, but I thought, you know, that it couldn't be. If Karen wanted to dredge all this up again, why wait until now? Why wait? She could have ruined me years ago with all of this—and really? It wouldn't have been a big deal. Celebrities get accused of this kind of thing all the time, and I didn't do anything wrong." He swallowed again. "I didn't really know what it was all about—and frankly, I wasn't that concerned. I get those kinds of e-mails all the time and they're usually just cranks. But Jillian was really worried . . . she was the one who insisted we get a private eye to check them out."

"You were sure the e-mails referred to Karen Zorn?" I turned my attention back to Jillian.

She sat down on the sofa next to Freddy—who moved several inches away from her. *Yes, there was definitely going to be a knock-down-drag-out once I left,* I thought, with no small degree of satisfaction. She fidgeted. "Yes. Because I got a call after they started coming. On my cell phone. From a woman whose voice I didn't recognize. All she said was, *Ask your precious husband about Karen Zorn.*"

"And you didn't tell me?" A muscle worked in Freddy's cheek. He was drumming his fingers on his knees.

"I was trying to protect—"

"I DON'T NEED TO BE PROTECTED!" He screamed at her. His face was bright red. He stood up. "Chanse, go ahead and make this all public. I don't care what it does to my career. I didn't do anything wrong." He shrugged. "If it kills my fucking career, I don't care. I have more money now than I know what to do with. I don't care. I don't want any of this hanging over my head." He walked over to me, and offered me his hand. "Thank you."

I stood up and shook his hand. I glanced over at Jillian. She was trembling. All hell was going to break loose any minute.

"And just for the record," Freddy added, "Jillian and I were together that afternoon. It wasn't me you saw coming out of Glynis's house."

I nodded and headed for the door. I put my hand on the doorknob and looked at the wall beside it. It was a "wall of fame"—framed photographs and magazine covers. There was one picture that didn't seem to belong—a headshot of a very young Freddy wearing a suit. He was smiling, but his mouth was closed. I stared at it.

I heard Mrs. Zorn saying, *When he got those braces off, he was going to be a real lady-killer.*

I looked back at Freddy. I stared at his lips. "You used to wear braces."

He nodded, a puzzled look on his face. "Until I was twenty-two."

The line of his lips was different than it was in the picture.

I put my hand on the glass and covered the top half of his face.

I closed my eyes and remembered.

It wasn't Freddy I saw.

The person I saw had braces on—his lips had that odd full look braces give people.

Another memory flashed.

The kid in Café Envie—the one Rosemary said was a neighborhood kid, who'd looked slightly familiar, who did errands for her every once in a while, who danced at the Brass Rail.

Joey.

He looked familiar because he was the man I saw coming out of Glynis's house that night.

CHAPTER THIRTEEN

Since the levee failure, granted, I hadn't gone out to the bars in the Quarter much—just on special occasions, like Halloween, Southern Decadence, Mardi Gras, New Year's, and so on. But I always stuck to the Fruit Loop—the bars ringing the area of St. Ann and Bourbon. There are five bars there, the loop stretching from Rawhide to Good Friends to Bourbon Pub and Oz to Café Lafitte in Exile. We call it the Fruit Loop because they're all so close together they're easy to walk between. One bar bores you—you grab your drink and head to another one. Though there are about ten more gay bars spread throughout the French Quarter, I never really went to any of the others with a great degree of frequency back when I used to go out pretty regularly.

The Brass Rail was one of those bars further up in the Quarter, on Burgundy Street near Canal. I'd been there a few times, but not since the levee failure. It was a small place on a corner, dimly lit on the inside, and its main attraction was the boys dancing on the bar. And when I say *boys,* I mean young men who look as though they're barely legal. Every time I'd been in there, I'd wanted to ask the dancers for ID.

It was frequented by older men, who would perch on bar

stools and give the dancers dollars in exchange for groping. I also suspected, that if the price was right, the boys would make their bodies available in private. They also sold lap dances, leading the patron to a darkened room with booths in the back of the bar. I always felt sorry for the young men, who often looked as if they were from small towns and working class backgrounds. It was different there from the other bars, where the dancers had thickly muscled bodies and seemed to be dancing out of choice. The boys at the Rail struck me as doing it because they didn't have many other options. It might be all in my head, but I sensed a sadness to them, and I found myself wondering what they would be like in five years—where they would be, what they would be doing when they got too old for the Rail patrons.

It also made me sad to know that these boys could make more money working there than they could anywhere else.

The dancers usually started their show around nine on Friday nights, and the highlight of the evening was a dance contest judged by three people in the audience who were selected by the drag queen hostess of the evening. The winner got $100.

Even that seemed sad to me—given what they had to do to win. The more skin they showed, the higher the likelihood of getting that hundred dollar bill. So they would pull their underwear down and reveal their butts. They always danced in underwear, which made me feel like I'd stumbled into a high school slumber party.

At eight-thirty, I found a parking place, and walked up Burgundy Street. The Quarter was fairly empty. The Mardi Gras tourists were long gone and the vast majority of New Orleanians were honoring Lent. It was a two-week season of rest for the city until the NBA All-Star game would bring more hordes of tourists and their money into town like the plague. I hadn't heard from Paige. I'd spent the rest of the day after getting home from the gym doing more on-line research on Karen Zorn, to no avail. There just wasn't much about her to find out. She'd vanished off the face of the earth. Her mother still hadn't e-mailed or faxed the photograph, either.

It probably didn't matter, anyway. Most likely, she was dead and her body would never be found.

I had also thought about calling Venus and telling her about Joey, but what could I really tell her? That I was now convinced he was the guy I'd seen coming out of Glynis's house? I'd also been pretty convinced it was Freddy Bliss, and without proof, my word meant nothing. I needed something a little more concrete than that to take to Venus and Blaine. And it did occur to me he might be more willing to tell what he knew to another gay man than to a police officer.

The cops probably weren't very welcome at the Brass Rail.

I paid my five-dollar cover to the big tattooed guy working the door, and walked into the bar. It consisted of two rooms—the big main room with the rectangular bar, and the seedy, dark, smaller back room where the dancers took their patrons. There were only about ten customers, all looking to be over fifty, seated on stools around the bar. Two young men with that scrawny underfed look the Rail patrons liked were walking around in boots and white underwear. As I watched, one of them stopped by one of the customers, who put a hand on his ass. The older man put his hand down the front of the dancer's underwear, and the dancer looked over to me with a bored expression on his face. Finally, the patron tired of groping him, handed him a five, and turned back to his drink. I took a seat at the bar and ordered a bottle of Bud Lite from the bartender. "What time does the show start?" I asked as I passed him a ten.

"Supposed to start around ten," he replied, sliding my change across the bar. He was in his early thirties, I judged, and a Cajun, with bluish black hair, blue eyes, and tattoos running up and down his bare arms. "But Floretta's not even here yet." He rolled his eyes. "Probably can't find her coke dealer. And you know no drag queen can go on without her nose full of candy."

I laughed and watched the young man who'd been groped jump up on the bar and start dancing. He was short, maybe about five-six on a good day, and had one of those silly looking hairstyles called a "faux hawk," where the hair is gelled to stand up in the middle of his head like a Mohawk. It was a look I hated, which also made me feel like I was a hundred years old—one step away from saying *Kids these days!* He had some acne scattered over his face, and despite the big smile plastered on his face as he moved his hands up and down his torso, he couldn't quite hide the sadness on his face. He was cute in a boyish kind of way, with thick red lips, a prominent nose, and big brown eyes.

He saw me looking at him and licked his lips, tilting his head down in what was probably supposed to be a seductive pose, pinched both of his dime-sized nipples, and then made his way over to where I was seated. He squatted down in front of me, his crotch about six inches from my face. I wondered if he had stuffed his crotch, but then realized if patrons put their hands down there, he couldn't. He leaned his head down to me, and said, "Hi. I'm Adonis." He touched his forehead to mine.

That was another thing I hated about the Rail. I don't like being touched unless I invite it. At the other bars, the strippers didn't touch you until you lured them in with a dollar bill in your hand—which was how I liked it. At the Rail, the dancers felt free to touch you at any time. But I needed information, so I was going to have to put up with it. And I was going to have to tip big. There might be some kind of dancer's code barring them from talking about each other. If that was the case, I'd have to find one with a grudge against Joey.

"Chanse," I replied as he brushed his lips against my cheek. Somehow, I doubted his parents had named him Adonis. He had a thick Mississippi accent, crooked teeth, and reeked of cigaretttes and vodka. He actually pronounced it Uh-DAWN-ees. But he was cute—if not the kind of looker a goddess from Mount Olympus would fall in love with. I doubted he even knew who the original Adonis was.

"Nice to meet you," he replied in what I assume was meant to be a coy voice. "You out looking for a good time, tonight? You want me to show you one?" He tilted his head down to one side. He was definitely trying for coy and shy. The effect was spoiled by his tired, sad eyes.

I shifted on my stool, pulling out my wallet and slipping out a twenty. "No, not really, although I'm sure you could definitely show me one."

His eyes lit up at the sight of the bill. "You want a lap dance, sexy?" He moved his hips a little bit.

"No, what I want is some information."

His eyes narrowed a bit. "You undercover vice?"

"No." I took the twenty and rubbed the edge of it over his right nipple. "No, I'm just looking for some information. I can get it from you—" I gestured to the other end of the bar, where a young Hispanic guy was dancing in red Unico briefs, "or I'll get it from him or one of the other guys. It's up to you. What do you say?" I felt a little nauseous about what I was doing. How much money did these kids make if a twenty got one of them so damned excited? And a lap dance for twenty dollars?

Maybe I was crazy, but that didn't seem like very much for what you got.

"What kind of information?" He licked his lips. "I know all kinds of things."

"I want to know about one of the other dancers. A guy named Joey." I brushed the twenty against his nipple again. "You know him?"

"Oh, *her.*" He hissed the words. "What do you want to know about that bitch?" He scooted closer to me. Now his crotch was so close to my face I could smell his sweat. "I'm a lot more fun than she is."

"Whatever you can tell me." I tried not to recoil from him. I hated when gay men referred to other gay men with feminine pronouns. But I'd hoped to find one with a grudge, and I'd hit pay dirt.

"She's a bitch." He shrugged. "Says she's from a Garden District family that threw her out when she came out. Bullshit is what that is. I might be just a small-town boy from Mississippi, but I know a yat accent when I hear one. She's from da parish. Acts like she's better than all of us. Thinks her shit don't stink." He smiled at me. "We call her Hollywood, because she always says she looks like a movie star, and she's going to go out there and be a big star." He spat the words out. "She ain't going to be no movie star. She ain't that pretty." He shrugged his thin shoulders. "I'm just as pretty as she is." He gave me another lewd smile.

"Does he do drugs?"

"Honey, we all do drugs." He reached into his sock and pulled out a crumpled cigarette. He lit it with a match from the bar. "That one—she'll do pretty much anything for money, I can guarantee you that. And she don't discriminate.

You name it, she'll do it. Me, I've got standards." He pinched one of his nostrils closed and made an exaggerated sniff. "If it goes up your nose, Joey will do it. Coke, crystal, K, she does it all."

I couldn't help myself, I had to ask, "You have standards?"

"I only do pot. And just because I let these dirty old men touch me for money doesn't mean I'm a whore." He gestured with his cigarette. "I ain't no whore, like Joey. I only do lap dances for guys I'm into. Like you." He leered at me. "You sure you don't want one? I can make you come in your pants."

How appealing. "Do you know where he lives?"

"She shares a shotgun in the Marigny over on Touro Street with some of the other guys." He shrugged. "They're about ready to throw her ass out. She owes them money."

"He working tonight?"

"She's in the dressing room right now." He made a face. "Joey don't ever miss a Friday night. She's won the contest three weeks in a row." He gave me a nasty smile. "It all goes up her nose, though."

"Thanks." I handed him the twenty. He smiled and put it in his sock, rising in one fluid movement. He moved away to a man about sixty a few stools down from me. I heard him introduce himself, and turned my head away as the older man slid his hands into the front of Adonis's underwear.

I wasn't really sure what my plan was when Joey popped up on the bar. I thought about going to the dressing room, seeing if I could get in there—but that might have the opposite effect from what I wanted.

I doubted very seriously that this kid had killed Glynis Parrish; it didn't make any kind of sense. Would anyone commit a high-profile murder like that and then show up for a shift as a dancer at the Brass Rail? But then, it didn't make any sense that a dancer from the Brass Rail was coming out of Glynis's house around the time of the murder, either.

Bizarre scenarios flew through my mind as I nursed the beer and watched two new dancers climb up on the bar. Maybe he was Glynis's drug connection—although that didn't make much sense, either. Nobody had ever said anything about her using drugs—but that could have been the "errands" Rosemary had referred to.

My curiosity was consuming me.

I ordered another beer and gave faint smiles to dancers as they tried to flirt with me, to coax a dollar bill into their underwear. The bar began to fill up, and Floretta Flynn finally showed up, grabbing a shot of something from the bartender and downing it. She was going for a country-western motif with a towering red wig and a green dress that looked as if it would have been the height of fashion at a prom in 1975. She gave me a brittle grin and walked back over to the sound system. Once she was there, she rubbed her hand across the bottom of her nose—the old make-sure-my-nose-is-still-there-because-it's-numb-from-the-coke-and-make-sure-there's-no-powder move. The three dancers on the bar jumped down and two more jumped up.

Bingo.

Joey looked good in black Calvin Klein underwear with a red waistband. It fit his body like a sheath. He was lean and muscular, his abs rippling as he undulated at the other end of the bar. His skin was completely smooth, no hair on his body anywhere except for a tantalizing glimpse of pubic fuzz. There was a tattoo of a cross on his right arm, which made me smile a little bit. *No kid from the Garden District would have that tattoo,* I mused to myself. I watched as he knelt down and let a heavy-set older man fondle his butt. He was good at his job. He clenched and tightened the muscles in his buttocks as the man slid his hands over them. Then, having earned his dollar, he got up and began moving his hips to the music. He danced over to another man, knelt down, and slid the front of his underwear down, giving the man a glimpse of his genitals. He was rewarded with a few more dollars, and he obviously was flirting with the man, whose hands reached up to pinch the small nipples on his muscled chest.

I had to give him credit. Out of all the dancers I'd seen, he was by far the best looking, and the best dancer. I wondered if Adonis's hatred was jealousy.

The other dancer, a pretty, young-looking blond, stopped in front of me, and got down on his knees, presenting me his crotch. He gave me a lazy smile, and then bent backwards. He straightened up and smiled at me. "Having fun?"

"You're very limber," I replied.

"I was a gymnast." He winked at me, and leaned in closer, whispering in my ear, "You have no idea how flexible I really am. Would you like to find out?"

"It's very tempting." I fished a dollar out of my pocket, and handed it to him.

"You can put it in my underwear." He gave me a dazzling smile.

"It's okay, really." I smiled back at him.

"It's your money." He took the dollar and moved away, and I turned my eyes back to Joey. He was making his way to my side of the bar. A remix of Stevie Nicks's "Stand Back" came on, and then he was in front of me. He knelt down and gave me a puzzled look. "You look familiar."

"I saw you at Café Envie the other day. With Rosemary Martin."

"Oh." He nodded, smiling. "And you came here to see me dance?

"You're very good."

He shrugged his shoulders and smiled at me. "Thanks." He traced his fingers down the side of my face. "You're very sexy. I love big men."

"Thank you." I put my hand on his boot. "You're very sexy, too."

"You know, I'd do you for free." He lowered his head shyly. "You are so my type. You want to go back for a lap dance? We don't have to do anything, if you'd rather not."

"I'd rather just talk, if that's okay with you." I stood up when he nodded. "Let's go."

He gave a delighted laugh and jumped down from the bar. He grabbed my hand and led me through the crowd. As we passed Adonis, who had some man's hands down the front of his underwear, he gave me a hateful look and turned his head away. Oddly, I felt bad, as though I should apologize to him. Joey pulled me into the back room, pushing me to a secluded booth in the very back. I sat down, and he sat next to me. He put his head on my shoulder. He placed his legs across mine. I stiffened at first, then relaxed. "Put your arm around me," he whispered. "If the boss sees us just sitting, he'll have my ass." After a slight hesitation, I put my arm around his shoulders. His skin was taut and cool. His entire body relaxed into mine. "I hate working here," he mumbled against my neck.

"Then why do it?" I asked. I was curious. With no offense intended to the other dancers, they weren't in the same league as Joey. With his looks and muscled body, he could as easily be dancing at the Pub—where he wouldn't have to do lap dances, where he wouldn't have to be groped by old men, where I would think he could make a lot more money. Maybe it had never occurred to him. "Can't you dance some-where else?"

"I'm not as big as they want in the other, *classier* bars."
He shifted, pulling a crumpled pack of cigarettes out of his
boot. He lit one and blew the smoke out. "What else am I going to do?" He shrugged. "I need money. I could be a waiter
or a bartender, I guess, but I only have to come to work here
two nights a week and I make enough money to live." He
sighed. "This isn't exactly what I had in mind when I moved
to New Orleans, but—" his voice trailed off. "What else can I
do? Deal drugs? No thank you. At least this kind of work—"
he hesitated. "You make people happy, you know? These
guys who come in here—they're lonely mostly, and they just
want to touch someone else. When they pay me to—you
know—most of the time they just want to hold me and talk.
A hundred bucks to let someone hold me for an hour and
talk at me is pretty damned good money. Can't make that
working at McDonalds."

"You know, I think I saw you the other night. Wednesday
night." I said, trying to keep my voice casual and conversa-
tional. "The night it was so foggy. I could swear it was you.
You were wearing jeans and an LSU sweatshirt. Was that
you?"

"Where did you see me?" he asked, delighted. He sat up
straighter, which drove his crotch harder into mine.

"Just talk," I said, pushing him gently away.

"You're really sexy, you know. Just the kind of guy I like,
big and strong and all muscle." He brushed his lips against
my ear. "I'd let you fuck me," he breathed into my ear. "I
don't let most guys, you know. I let the clients blow me sometimes, but I don't do penetration with anyone except men I
am attracted to. Like you. Do you want to fuck me?"

"I saw you over on Ursulines Street. You were coming
out of a house between Dauphine and Burgundy. Is that
where you live?"

"Hardly. That's Rosemary's house." He barked out a laugh. "I wish. That place is gorgeous. Someday I'm going to have a house like that, though. I'm going to be somebody." He sighed. "But for now, no, I live with three other guys in this dump in the Marigny." He started blowing smoke rings. "Half the time we don't even have hot water, and the roaches—" He shuddered. "They're everywhere. It's disgusting. It's living like an animal."

"How did you meet Rosemary?"

"I sat down on her stoop one day to have a smoke." He picked his head up and frowned. "She came out and started talking to me. She said I reminded her of someone she used to know. I was hungry, and didn't have any money. I asked for a couple of bucks. She said she was going to go run some errands, but if I carried some stuff for her, she'd buy me something to eat. I mean, it was a free meal, so why not, right?"

"Yeah." The statement was so incredibly sad, I didn't know what else to say.

"So we went to the Clover Grill after we did the errands, and she told me she'd pay me to do some errands for her from time to time . . . mostly it was picking up her dry cleaning every Wednesday." He laughed. "She sure went through some clothes every week! I'd pick up the clean stuff at the Quarter Laundrette, bring it by, and pick up the next week's load." He shrugged. "Sometimes she had other stuff for me to do."

"What about this last Wednesday night?"

"I went by there like usual." He shrugged. "It was really weird, but hey, you know, money's money, you know? And I was broke. So I showed up, like usual, and she let me in for just a second. She took the cleaning from me, but said she didn't have anything to go back out this time. That was a first. And usually she would make me a sandwich or some-thing to eat, and we'd hang in the kitchen for a while. This time, though, she didn't want to hang around. She looked out the curtains one time, and told me I had to go. She really rushed me out, you know. I was kind of pissed, to tell you the truth. I saw someone across the street when I came out—and I slammed the door to let her know I was pissed." He shrugged. "And that was you, right? And now you've found me." He sounded delighted.

"Don't you watch the news?" I asked. It was getting un-comfortably warm.

"Nah, I don't watch that shit. It's depressing." He shrugged.

"Did you hear about the actress who got killed?"

"Do I look like I'm deaf?" He dropped his cigarette on the floor. "Everybody's heard about that."

"She was killed in that house," I replied. "It wasn't Rose-mary's house, it was hers. Rosemary worked for her. That's whose dry cleaning you were picking up. And you were there, inside the house, the night Glynis Parrish was mur-dered."

"Dude," he whispered. "No way."

"You have to talk to the police, Joey. You have to tell them you were there."

"No, I am not talking to the police." He started to get up, but I grabbed his arm and pulled him back down. "Man, that *hurt*." He rubbed his arm. "I can't talk to the police. I got a warrant." His voice got whiny. "They'll put me in jail."

"I have friends in the department, Joey. I won't let that happen." I didn't know how much pull I had, but I'd do what I could. "You have to. If they find you on their own—and if I found you, the police can—it'll be much harder on you. With a warrant and all."

"Jesus." He got up. "I have to get back to work." He adjusted his underwear. He leaned down and brushed his lips against my cheek again. "I really do like you," he said softly. "That's not a part of my act, either. I really really like you. And you'll help me out? You aren't just saying that?"

I dug a twenty out of my wallet and handed it to him. "I'd like to spend some more time with you. Can I get your number? I'll take you out to lunch tomorrow if you'd like."

"You got your cell handy?"

I pulled my phone out of my pocket and programmed the number in as he gave it to me. "My last name's Rutledge. You didn't tell me yours."

"Chanse. Chanse MacLeod."

"Take a chance?" He giggled, and kissed my cheek again. "You better call me, man. Don't make me come looking for you."

"You won't blow me off?"

"I never turn down a free meal. And I want to get to know you better, too, big man. You're exactly what I look for in a man." He walked out of the back room and into the dressing room. The door shut behind him.

I slowly got up and pushed through the crowd. Three different boys were dancing on the bar. A Kylie Minogue song was playing. Adonis was one of the boys up on the bar, and when I passed him he stuck his tongue out at me. I had to get out of the bar.

I took a deep breath when I got outside, and leaned against the wall.

I felt sorry for him. His life was about to explode, but he wanted to be famous. He was about to get his chance. Maybe he could use the notoriety to improve his lot. The guy whose wife cut his dick off—Bobbitt? He'd made a couple of porn movies. Joey had the body for it. Maybe that would be his way out. Maybe he could make some money, get to make a fresh start somewhere.

I felt almost paternal towards him, and that was weird. He wasn't all that much younger than me. I started walking to my car.

I never pass up a free meal.

I shook my head and started walking faster until I reached my car. I got in and sat there for a moment, waiting for my heart to stop beating so fast.

Maybe I should wait for him to get off work, take him back to my place, make him something to eat . . .

. . . and what? Turn him over to Venus? I'd call her after I talked to him, have her meet us wherever we decided on for lunch.

Yeah. It was best to just drive home and call it a night. Go to bed by myself, and call him in the morning. It wasn't an act—there was no need for him to put on an act for me. He just thought I was some hot guy who was into him, who just happened to see him the night he'd made a hundred bucks for doing Rosemary a favor.

She was setting Freddy up.

The trick was going to be finding out *why* she was doing it.

I started the car, and pulled out onto Burgundy Street.

Paige was going to just fucking love this.

CHAPTER FOURTEEN

WHEN I GOT HOME, I couldn't get Joey Rutledge out of my head.

While sitting on my couch, listening to Amy Winehouse, I couldn't help but think, *There but for the grace of football, go I.* Had I not found football and used that to escape from Cottonwood Wells, I could have just as easily wound up a lost boy in the Quarter, dancing at the Brass Rail and whoring myself out to older men for dollar bills. How different would my life be had football not paid my way through LSU? It was the kind of thing I generally preferred not to think about—how one small thing can change the rest of your life. Had one of my coaches not been roommates in college with an assistant coach at LSU, it stands to reason I would never have been offered a scholarship there. LSU wasn't the only place that offered me one—SMU, Rice, and Ole Miss had also come knocking on my door—but I wanted out of Texas, and the proximity to New Orleans had been the true deciding factor in making my decision to go to school in Baton Rouge.

I didn't even want to think about what might have happened to me had football not provided me a way out of Cottonwood Wells. Would I have wound up stuck in that dreary little town, a gay man longing for the bright lights of the big city? Working in the oil fields with my father and hating every minute of every day of my life—or would I have managed to somehow escape? Joey had struck a chord in me. When I managed to go to bed finally, I wondered how much money he'd made tonight.

I never pass up a free meal.

He would be easy enough to find again.

I slept relatively well, which surprised me. I made coffee and while it brewed, checked through the blinds on the front door to see if the hyenas were back. I groaned. Apparently, there was no getting rid of them during the daylight hours. I turned the computer on and while it warmed up, got myself a cup of coffee. It was too early to call Joey. I called Paige instead, but got her voicemail. I asked her to call me with an update on Glynis's housekeeper and massage therapist.

I signed into my e-mail account and sighed with irritation. The mailbox was full again. A lot of people have way too much free time, apparently, and choose to fill it by sending nasty e-mails to people they don't know. I started cleaning it out, hoping that Mrs. Zorn hadn't tried to send Karen's picture and had it bounce back to her. I glanced over at my fax machine, but there was nothing there. I finished emptying the mailbox and leaned back in my chair.

I'd been pretty sure Freddy had killed Glynis. But now that I wasn't sure he was the one I'd seen coming out of her house, I wasn't so sure anymore.

I went to the *Times-Picayune*'s Web site. When it loaded, a headline screamed at me: *Another murder in the French Quarter!*

I clicked on the link.

Police responded to a report of gunfire in the 600 block of Esplanade Avenue at three in the morning. The responding officers found a gunshot victim in the neutral ground. He was identified as Joseph Rutledge, 23, originally of Lake Charles. Rutledge was pronounced dead at the scene. He had been shot twice in the chest. His discarded wallet was found next to the body.

Rutledge was a dancer at the Brass Rail, a bar in the French Quarter that caters to a gay clientele. Police theorize he was on his way home from work when he was mugged. A backpack he was wearing when he left the Brass Rail that contained his tips for the evening—estimated by coworkers to be around several hundred dollars—was missing, as well as his cell phone.

This is the thirty-fifth murder of the year—

I stopped reading. I felt numb.

Joey was dead.

There was no fucking way this was a random mugging.

I cursed myself for a fool. By talking to him last night, I'd put him in danger. I hadn't warned him, hadn't done a goddamned thing except promise to buy him lunch.

Nice move, Slick.

I was positive Rosemary had killed Glynis. But why?

I got up and started pacing around my living room.

She was the last person to see her alive. She found the body.

I'd been so distracted by Freddy and Jillian I'd forgotten a basic principle of murder investigations. Who had access?

Rosemary had access to Glynis's house any time she wanted. She had access to Glynis's computer. And she was the only person who knew about Joey Rutledge and his connection to the case.

But why? How did she know about Karen—

What if Rosemary Martin WAS Karen Zorn?

I picked up the file with the e-mails, and opened it to the first one.

You can fool the public, Freddy, but I know what you are.

My hands trembling, I went to a directory assistance Web site and typed in her name. Her address—down on Desire Street in the Bywater popped up. I went to an address search Web site. I filled in her name and current address, and clicked GO. A list of addresses came up. I cursed myself yet again. They only went back ten years. Beyond that, there was no record of her.

Just like Karen Zorn disappeared off the radar ten years ago.

The first address listed for Rosemary was in Wichita, Kansas.

I kept searching. Nothing—there was nothing on any sites online.

She hadn't existed before she got that apartment in Wichita.

I picked up my cell phone and dialed Venus. "Casanova."

"Venus, this is Chanse."

"Make it quick, I've got a lot on my plate right now," she replied.

"Venus, can you come by? Or can I meet you somewhere?" I gripped the phone tightly.

"To repeat what I just said, I'm kind of busy right now." She sounded exhausted. "We had another murder in the Quarter last night. And Mayor Do-nothing is putting a lot of pressure on us about the Parrish case, as I'm sure you know." She sighed. "The man is having hourly press conferences. He sure likes to see himself on television, doesn't he?"

"That's why I'm calling. It's about Joey Rutledge—*and* Glynis Parrish," I said. "The murders are connected."

That got her attention. "What?"

– 209 –

I cleared my throat. "Venus, he was a key witness in the Glynis Parrish murder."

There was a brief silence on the phone, and then she said in very quiet voice, "And why the hell I am just hearing about this now?"

"I'd rather not talk about this over the phone."

"Are you home?"

"Yes."

"I'll be right there. And this had better be good."

I shut my phone and started pacing again. *There was nothing you could have done,* I told myself. It may have had nothing to do with this case, it could have been a random act of violence—the violence that was ripping the city apart and making the streets run with blood. But no matter how much I tried to convince myself, I knew. There was no doubt in my mind now that Rosemary had killed him, the same way she'd killed Glynis Parrish. When I talked to him, and he'd told me why he was there the night of the murder, I'd sentenced him to death.

I could feel the anxiety coming back.

You are not the angel of death. It isn't your fault, there was nothing you could have done.

And that snide, horribly vicious voice in the back of my mind: *You could have waited for him to get off work, and brought him back here, kept him safe until he could tell his story to Venus and Blaine.*

I heard Joey say again, *I never pass up a free meal.*

Pull it together, Chanse, Venus is on her way and you need to get your act together. You have work to do.

And somehow, I managed to pull myself together.

My therapist would be proud.

Venus and her partner, Blaine Tujague, arrived about half an hour later. I heard the commotion outside. Reporters

were shouting things like, *Are you here to make an arrest?*
As I watched through the blinds, Venus and Blaine ignored
them completely—not even giving a "no comment." I opened
the door as they reached the top of the stairs and shut the
door behind them. "Sorry about that," I said.

Venus looked tired. "I'm getting kind of used to it. Fucking vultures. I hate the press."

"You and me both," I commiserated, sitting down in my
desk chair. "You two probably have it worse than I do."

Blaine shrugged. "It's a high-profile case." Blaine and I
had once been friends-with-benefits. We'd met originally
when I'd been on the force, and over the years had become
friends. He was a good-looking guy with a thickly muscled
body, curly black hair, and blue eyes. He looked as if he
hadn't shaved in a couple of days. He yawned. "Sorry—we
got called out on this kid's murder. I need to sleep for about
a week."

Venus flipped open her notepad. "Okay, you want to tell
me how this stripper kid was involved with Glynis Parrish?"
She gave me a look. "You sure you don't want your lawyer
present?"

I shook my head. "No, I don't need a lawyer." I took a
deep breath and started from the beginning. I handed over
the file with the e-mails. Venus and Blaine both scribbled
notes as I talked. I explained how I'd seen Joey for the first
time when I met Rosemary at Café Envie. I was explaining
the Karen Zorn connection when Venus interrupted me.

"You accessed the database at this college?" One of her
eyebrows went up, and she put her pad down. "I don't
think—" she glanced over at Blaine "—that we really need to
know any more about that. And I don't want to see anything
you might have downloaded or copied from their database."
She smiled. "We'll just call that an anonymous tip."

I went on, explaining how I'd seen Freddy's senior picture—complete with braces—and made the connection to Joey Rutledge. "I went to the Brass Rail last night and talked to him—" I ignored the knowing smirk on Blaine's face. "And he told me all about how he knew Rosemary Martin, and how he was there the night of the murder. And I planned on bringing him in today to tell you all this himself. My identification was all fucked up, so I knew we needed him to come forward."

She sighed and closed her notebook. "Yeah, I'm sure you would have. This just sucks, you know? You're absolutely positive he was the guy?"

"Every Wednesday afternoon, he picked up Glynis's dry cleaning and dropped it off at six. He ran errands for Rosemary sometimes. He thought it was her house." I cursed myself again. "I bought his innocent act, you know. I really thought he didn't know what he was involved in." I thought for a moment. "It's still possible he didn't know. But after I filled him in—he had Rosemary over a barrel. I'd be willing to bet he called Rosemary as soon as I left the bar." I groaned. "Maybe tried to get money out of her, I don't know. But his being there with her before she called anyone . . . her story was she came home and found Glynis right away was kind of blown."

"You know as well as I do none of this will hold up in court, Chanse—it's hearsay, and without the kid to back you up, no judge will allow it."

"And a defense attorney would have a field day with you, buddy." Blaine shook his head. "Your credibility is completely worthless, you know. Frillian paid you, first you were sure it was Freddy, now you're convinced it was this kid. And all Rosemary has to do is deny all of this. It's your word against hers. And you seeing the kid there—well, maybe he killed Glynis."

"I know, I know." I slammed my fist down on my knees. "I completely blew it. And now the kid's dead because I didn't think ahead. Why didn't it even occur to me he'd call Rosemary?"

"You want to know what I think?" Venus glanced over at Blaine, who shrugged. "I think Rosemary's our killer. Her story checks out, but barely, and it means nothing anyway. She could have just as easily killed Glynis, then left the house and run her errands, making sure everyone in every store and the waitress at Angeli remembered her—she made herself very conspicuous everywhere she went; making sure she talked to a clerk in every store about something strange—something they would be sure to remember later. And then she goes back to the house, meets Joey there, lets him in, keeps him there, and watches until someone comes along. Then she gets him to leave and he's seen . . ."

"And then he called her last night, and she killed him." I swallowed.

"Well, we were inclined to write it off as a mugging," Blaine replied. "He's a small guy, for one thing, and he was carrying a backpack filled with cash as well as his wallet. His fellow dancers warned him to take a cab rather than walk back to the Marigny—but all he said was, he wasn't going home. His phone was taken, his wallet was emptied, and the backpack, and he was shot twice in the chest. He was dead by the time help could reach him. Someone in the vicinity heard the gunshots and called it in."

Venus interrupted Blaine. "We're tracing his phone carrier to get a record of his calls. One of the other dancers, I forget his name, said that before he left he called someone and was talking very quietly on his phone. The other dancer just assumed he was setting up a trick or something. Apparently, Joey was very secretive."

I closed my eyes. "He called Rosemary, told her someone recognized him, was asking him questions about that night and what he was doing in the house?"

"And he asked her for more money."

"He played right into her hands. I wonder if she intended to kill him all along." I shrugged. "All she had to do was take his phone, his wallet, and his backpack, and presto! It looks like another random mugging, another murder in the Quarter."

"And we have no way of proving that she killed either of them." Venus sighed. She stood up and gave me a long, hard look. "Don't beat yourself up over this, Chanse. This wasn't your fault. You couldn't have known he was going to be killed—nor do you know for sure that it was because you talked to him."

"Thanks." I walked them to the door. It was nice to hear, but I didn't believe it for a minute.

"If you find out anything—not that I am encouraging you to keep investigating, mind you—next time let me know right away, all right?" She gave me a hug.

I closed the door behind them and ignored the sound of the reporters shouting questions at them. I lay down on the couch and covered my eyes. *Poor Joey. You never try to blackmail someone who's already killed. But then, he had no idea she'd been killing people for years.*

At least, if she truly is Karen Zorn.

My fax machine rang, startling me. I jumped up and walked over to it. It whirred, and a piece of paper started printing out. My heart started racing as I looked at the caller ID and recognized the Kansas area code.

When it finished printing, I grabbed it.

It was a reproduction of a senior class photo. Across the top of the printout, before the photograph, was written *This is Karen's senior picture. If you see her, tell her to call her mother.*

I stared at the picture.

She'd changed over the years, but there was no mistaking her.

Rosemary was Karen Zorn.

I remembered Brett saying, "*She told me she was relatively new in town, didn't know anyone, so I kind of always tried to be nice to her. But it was like she took my being nice the wrong way. She started buying me presents. At first, it was just kind of sweet, you know what I mean? Nothing inappropriate . . . , like she always had the kind of protein bars I liked . . . She would call me all the time—on the stupidest pretext. . . . I figured she was just lonely and wanted someone to talk to, you know? Then it started getting really weird. . . . I let it go as long as I could. Finally I told her she had to stop buying me things and calling me all the time. And then she turned on me. She told Glynis I'd said some inappropriate things to her.*"

And Freddy: *She used to bring me presents, buy me lunch and stuff like that . . . She was always willing to buy beer or food or something. She was always around. It got to be a joke around the house—my little stalker. I wouldn't sleep with her. There was just something about her that didn't strike me as being quite right, you know what I mean? But at that party, I was just drunk enough. . . . the next morning I was hungover and felt like shit. And she wouldn't shut up. She kept going on and on about how happy she was . . . it freaked me out. I told her I'd made a terrible mistake, that I didn't love her, and she needed to leave . . . and then on Monday she went to the dean and accused me of rape.*"

A definite pattern of behavior there.

I picked up my phone to call Venus just as it started ringing.

The caller ID said PAIGE. I flipped the phone open. "Hello?"

There was silence at the other end. "Hello? Paige, are you there?"

And then I heard Paige say, clearly, "Rosemary, you aren't going to get away with this, you know. You might as well put the gun away."

Goose bumps sprang out all over my body.

I heard Rosemary say, "It doesn't really matter at this point, does it? I don't really care about getting away with anything. You missed the entire point of this, didn't you? All of you?" She laughed, and it sent chills down my spine.

"You can't shoot me in your apartment and think—"

Her apartment. I had that address.

The phone went dead.

CHAPTER FIFTEEN

ROSEMARY'S HOUSE was in the Bywater, on Desire Street between Burgundy and Dauphine.

I tried calling Venus as I ran out of the house and got into my car, but only got her voicemail. My hands were shaking so hard I could barely hit the speed-dial number. I left her a very tense message, and then debated calling 911. I got the car started, pounding my hands on the steering wheel as I waited for the gate to open. *Come on, come on, come on!* I glanced at my gun, which I'd tossed into the passenger seat. Finally the gate finished opening, and I flew down the driveway and out onto Camp Street. I drove as quickly as I could, stopping for red lights only when I could see cars coming the other way. I didn't care if I got pulled over—although with the gun in the seat, it could be a very sticky situation. I made it through the CBD, and for the first time in my life, the lights were actually on my side. I flew around the curve where Rampart Street became St. Claude, and the traffic became heavier. I sped around cars, changing lanes and cutting people off, and the insane thought that I was living one of Jephtha's video games raced through my head. My palms were sweating and I was gripping the steering wheel so tightly veins were popping out on my forearms.

And my cell phone didn't ring.

It reminded me so much of the nightmarish drive out to Bay St. Louis, when I finally figured out the truth about Paul's disappearance. That drive too was little more than a flash of memory, my heart pounding the entire way as we drove about 100 miles per hour with the siren on Venus's police car screaming through the night. All those horrible memories were flashing through my head, and all I could think right now was that Paige, my Paige, was in the hands of a deranged killer. Nothing could happen to my Paige. Life just couldn't be that cruel. No matter how hard I tried I couldn't get those horrendous thoughts out of my head. *Paige can't die, that bitch can't kill Paige, nothing can ever happen to her, I don't even want to think about what my life would be like without her. Losing Paul was hard enough—that had been horrible. I don't think I could ever get over losing Paige.*

Memories flooded through my head, one image fading into another. The night we first met, in my room at the Beta Kappa house. My door had been unlocked and she'd let herself in to smoke a joint and listen to the Pink Floyd CD I had on, getting away from Little Sister rush. I'd walked in to find her standing in the middle of my room, the joint in her hand, grooving to Pink Floyd. And as soon as she opened her mouth, I knew I'd found someone special to be a part of my life, to make it richer and fuller. I was right. My life had been the better for knowing her. She was always there at my side, helping me by making me laugh, never bullshitting me, making me be reasonable when I wanted to be childish. She'd loved Paul too, but put her own pain aside when he'd died to help me work through mine. She seemed to people to be hard as nails, but I knew beneath that wise-cracking exterior was a soft and kind-hearted, loving woman whom I'd walk through fire for.

If that crazy bitch harmed so much as one hair on her head, I would make her sorry she'd ever been born.

I screeched around the corner and parked in front of a fire hydrant. The street was deserted, and I'd been right. The address was a double shotgun once painted a vibrant purple that been faded by years of exposure to the merciless New Orleans sun. There was no yard in front of it, no fence. It had all been paved over. I sat there for a moment. There was no sign of life from the house. I saw Paige's car parked farther up the block. I checked my gun, made sure the safety was off, that it was loaded. I picked up my phone and called Venus again. This time she answered, "Casanova."

"Didn't you get my message?" I tried to keep my voice calm.

"I'm sorry, Chanse, what's—"

"Right after you left, I got the fax. Karen Zorn is Rosemary Martin—and she's a killer. Paige called me." I cut her off. "She's at Rosemary's. I don't know how she managed to call, but Rosemary has a gun on her."

"Jesus fucking Christ!"

"I just pulled up outside the house. I'm going in."

"Stay in your car—Blaine is calling for backup and we're on our way—"

I hung up the phone. I wasn't about to wait for the police.

Paige was in danger, and every minute counted.

I'd learned that lesson the hard way when Paul died, and I wasn't about to make that same mistake again.

Gun in hand, I got out of the car and crossed the street. I crept up the stairs on Rosemary's side of the house. I peered in the window. The shutters were open, and no curtains or blinds impeded my view. The room was empty—no furniture, nothing. I couldn't see into the next room, and the house was raised about six feet off the ground. There would be no way I'd be able to see into the next room without going around to the side of the house, and I didn't want to take the risk of being seen. I turned the knob to the front door. The door swung open.

All the hair on the back of my neck stood up, and I stepped into the house, leaving the door open behind me. No sense in having to try to open it again if Paige and I had to make a quick escape. I slowly started making my way across the room, trying to be as silent as possible.

And then a board groaned under my feet.

"Is that you, Mr. MacLeod?" a voice called from the next room. "There's no need to try to sneak up on us, you know. You might as well come and join us."

"Paige, are you all right?" I called out.

"Do as she says, Chanse. She has a gun on me."

I walked through the door, and gasped.

The second room, like the first, was completely bare of furniture other than two rickety looking old kitchen chairs. Paige was tied to one of them. Her purse was open on the floor next to her. And Rosemary Martin was seated in the other chair right next to Paige. In her hand was a gun she had pressed to Paige's temple. Paige was very pale, and a dark purple bruise glared at me from her right cheek. In Rosemary's other hand she held Paige's iPhone. She smiled when she saw me, and tossed the phone back into Paige's purse.

"The police are on their way," I said. "You're never going to get away with this." I pointed my gun at her. "Karen."

"So, you figured it all out. But it looks like we have reached an impasse." Rosemary smiled at me. She looked terrible. Her reddish hair had frizzed and stood up in every direction, like she'd had an electrical shock. She was wearing a purple smock-type blouse over black sweatpants. "You shoot me and I pull the trigger. You might miss me, but I won't miss. And your friend here's brains will be splattered all over the wall."

"If you hurt her—" I hissed through gritted teeth. My head was roaring. In that instant, I hated Rosemary Martin more than I'd hated anyone in my entire life. I wanted her to suffer, I wanted her to die a long, slow, painful death. I wanted to pull out her fingernails one by one. I want to rip her frizzy hair out of her head, lock by lock, slowly, to make it as painful as possible.

"The two of you are smart," Rosemary went on. Her voice pierced through the haze in my head, shrill and not quite sane. There was a glint in her blue eyes that I had seen before. She wasn't sane, not by a long shot, and my heart sank even further. You can reason with a sane person. But she was crazy, had gone completely around the bend. "But not smart enough, you know. You figured out it was me—but you thought I was trying to get away with something." She laughed, and I'd never heard a more evil sound in my life. It was chilling. "I *don't care if I get away with it!*"

"I don't understand."

"I loved him," she went on. "I did everything for him in college. I loved him the first moment I saw him. I gave him presents, I wrote papers for him, I did everything I could to show him how much I loved him. *I did everything for him!*" she screamed, spittle flying from his lips. "But nothing was ever enough for him. It was always never good enough."

"So you accused him of raping you?"

"You spoke to my bitch of a mother." She snarled the words, and then smiled again. "Yes, I did. Maybe I did let him, maybe I did give myself to him willingly, but there are other kinds of rape, you know. He raped my soul. He raped my heart. And they let him get away with it, and he left . . . even though we were meant to be together. He went to Hollywood . . . and I knew it was because he wanted to be a star, to make a lot of money so he could make it all up to me, make up for telling me I was crazy, for acting like I wasn't good enough, and then he married that slut Glynis Parrish."

"So, you killed her."

"It was fate, you know? When I saw that he and that old whore he took up with were moving to New Orleans, I decided to come down here so I'd be here when he finally tired of that old bitch. And then Fate put Glynis into my hands, as though it were meant to be. I became her assistant, and I knew somehow I would be able to get through to him because of her." She sniffed. "What a horrible person she was! Every day when I would listen to her, I wondered what Freddy, my precious Freddy, could have seen in her. Why did he ever want that monster? She didn't deserve to live."

"But why frame Freddy?" *Keep her talking,* I told myself. *Venus and the police will be here soon, keep her talking, but don't agitate her. If that gun goes off Paige is a dead woman.* I strained my ears listening for sirens. But I heard nothing.

"He came by to see her." She pressed the gun tighter against Paige's head. "And he didn't know who I was. He didn't remember me. He looked right through me like I wasn't there." Her crazed eyes glistened with tears. "After everything I'd done for him, he didn't know who I was! And that's when I knew what I had to do. He had to be punished . . . and so did Glynis. She didn't deserve to live, anyway. But how? I wondered. How could I do it? And then I saw that boy one night sitting on the stoop smoking. I thought it was Freddy at first—but then I realized it was just someone who sort of resembled him. I went out and talked to him, became his friend. And then I knew. I could pay him to do errands—get him into the habit of showing up at the same time every week. It was fate, it was meant to be."

"So you killed Glynis, and poor Joey showed up right on time."

She smiled. "I realized, you know, that killing Freddy wasn't the best punishment for him. What meant more to Freddy was his damned career. It didn't matter if he actually did it or not. That was in Fate's hands. I didn't care if he was tried or convicted . . . just the suspicion would be enough to make him notorious instead of famous."

"And you killed Joey last night?"

"That was *your* fault." She shrugged. "He called me. Told me all about your little visit to the Rail, and how he now knew what the truth was. He wanted money. So I met him on the neutral ground and shot him. I wasn't ready to be betrayed just yet. And it was all a part of the plan, you see." Her eyes glinted at me. "You see, the just punishment for Freddy is really for me, the girl he didn't love, the one who wasn't good enough for him, to be even more famous than he is." She laughed. "And I will be. Our names will be forever linked from now on. No one will ever think about Freddy Bliss without remembering Rosemary Martin, the woman he scorned and betrayed, who killed his first wife. He'll never be written about, without my name being linked to his. We may not be married for real, but we will forever be married in notoriety."

"But you've already accomplished that. There's no need to kill Paige," I said, trying to keep my voice calm and soothing. "The police are on their way right now. Just put the gun down, and we can wait for them, and you can tell them your story. And Paige is a reporter, you know. She can write it for you."

She looked at me as though I were the one who was insane. "I'm not going to jail, Mr. MacLeod." She took the gun away from Paige's head. "And now, there's no need to kill your friend anymore. I know she's a reporter. She's heard the entire story now, there's no need for me to kill her. She's the only one who knows my story. It would be stupid of me to kill her." She shook her head. "No, that's not the plan." She smiled at me. "Tell Freddy I loved him."

She put the gun in her mouth and pulled the trigger.

EPILOGUE

It took about two weeks for my fifteen minutes of fame to come to an end.

I can't say I was sorry to see the pack of hyenas in front of my house gone for good. I don't know how celebrities deal with it on a daily basis.

I didn't talk to the press, other than Paige. When her first story for *Crescent City* magazine hit the newsstands, the magazine sold out the first day. It was, as she said, a great debut to make as editor in chief of the magazine. That bitch Coralie even called her to congratulate her—and Paige was gracious enough not to rub her face in it.

I, of course, would have. She's obviously a better person than I am.

Venus and Blaine got commendations from the city for their efforts in solving the case.

I never met with Freddy and Jillian again, but about five days after Rosemary Martin killed herself, I got another check from them in the mail. This time it was for ten thousand dollars. There was no note or anything, which was fine with me. All I cared about was whether the check would clear, and it did.

According to what I read in line at the grocery store, Freddy and Jillian's marriage is in trouble. I can't say that comes as a big surprise.

Interestingly enough, the gun Rosemary used to kill herself—and Joey—was a match for the gun used to kill Tim Dahkle. So, the Kansas cops were able to close an open homicide.

Paige is really happy working at *Crescent City.* The publisher has given her carte blanche to reshape the magazine the way she wants. She and Ryan haven't set a date yet, but there's no question in my mind it won't be long.

Joey's family refused to claim his body, so I did. It seemed like the least I could do. I'll never know what went through his mind that night. I'll never know if the Joey I'd talked to was just pulling an act, but I prefer to think he was just a nice kid caught up in something too big for him to really handle. I had his body cremated, and on a beautiful spring morning, I dumped his ashes into the river at Wollenberg Park.

I even allowed myself to shed a tear for him.

Jephtha and Abby are both taking a private eye course. I'm sponsoring them, and am even considering making them partners in my business.

Every once in a while, I catch a rerun of *Sportsdesk,* and I can't help but feel sorry for Glynis Parrish. She really was talented. Marrying Freddy had doomed her, but there was no way she could have known that at the time.

It really makes you stop and think, doesn't it?

ACKNOWLEDGMENTS

I AM, as always, in the debt of any number of individuals who assisted me either personally or professionally while this book was being written.

The biggest debt is to my editor, Julie Smith. Julie is not only an editor of deep insight and ability, but an enormously talented writer herself. She helped make this book a much better book than it was originally, but also understands the fragility of an author's ego and how to guide the writer into doing the best work that they are capable of—which is an extraordinary gift for an editor. Over the years, she has mentored me and given me career advice—which I have not always taken, and regretted every time. Perhaps someday I will learn.

I also want to thank Richard Fumosa and everyone at Alyson for making this book possible and making it possible for me to work with Julie.

I would be remiss in not mentioning my former Alyson editor, Joe Pittman, who resurrected this series and brought it back from the dead. He's moved on to other things, but I will always be in his debt.

I have the great good luck to have an amazing day job and incredible coworkers with the NO/AIDS Task Force.

From Noel Twilbeck to Jean Redmann down to the volunteers who answer the phones, everyone there is committed to doing good work. It's very inspiring.

The Community Awareness Project office of the agency is where I work usually; worthy of mention there are Josh Fegley, Mark Drake, Ked Dixon, Ryan McNeely, Jacob Rickoll, Jessica Gerson, D. J. Jackson, Allison Vertovec, and all the volunteers.

There are also my coworkers on the Surveillance project: Narquis Barak, Tia Tucker, and Diane Murray. Thanks, ladies!

In my personal life, I need to thank Bev and Butch Marshall, Becky Cochrane, Timothy J. Lambert, Marika Christian, Pat Brady, Mark Richards, Stephen Driscoll, Stuart Wamsley, Marc Scharphorn, Peggy Gentile, David Puterbaugh, Mark G. Harris, Rob Byrnes, Kathleen Bradean, and too many others to remember; forgive my faulty memory.

And of course, Paul J. Willis, who always makes me laugh and relax no matter how stressed out I might be.